The End of the World Is Rye

Brett Cottrell

rosariumpublishing.com

The End of the World Is Rye
by Brett Cottrell

ISBN: 978-0-9903191-0-8
LCCN: 2014939067

Rosarium Publishing
P.O. Box 544
Greenbelt, MD 20768-0544
www.rosariumpublishing.com

Cover art and design by Vincent Sammy

To Ellen

THE END OF THE WORLD IS

IS

RYE

It Begins in the Middle

A white Ford Mustang barreled across a desolate stretch of New Mexico highway, gripping the road tightly as darkness crept into the eastern sky. The eight-track played in nearly perfect time with the engine's forceful roar. Muscle cars and classic rock were made for each other, born of the same bell-bottomed enthusiasm. Had the driver looked in the rearview mirror, the sun would have blinded him as it set behind the Peloncillo Mountains. Had the passenger next to him not traded his ASU art scholarship for a free ride at Marijuana State, he might have said of this endless stretch of straight highway, surrounded on both sides by ruddy, undulating mountains, that it missed its chance to pose for Georgia O'Keefe.

"Hell yeah, turn it up bro', turn it up!" the driver shouted and stomped the rhythm into the gas pedal. The car jerked in unison with the music, occasionally lurching to a misplaced backbeat. "This is their best song!"

"You got the tickets?"

"Dude, don' worry. I told you back in 'Zona, I got 'em, right here in my pocket. They're keepin' my Mary J stash company," he patted his pocket for emphasis. It contained two tickets to the 1978 Texas Jam concert, some sand grains that had escaped the Grand Canyon, a lint ball that escaped his chest hair, and one rotund doobie that was about to meet its happy conflagration.

"This trip is goin' to kick ass, man! It's gonna rock! I've been waitin' for this show all year! All the bands are awesome! Every last one of 'em is out of sight!" He threw back his hair, revealing his bloodshot eyes. It's hard to use Visine when you're driving ninety miles per hour. "How far is Dallas, man? It seems like we've been driving forever."

"We've got a long way to go, bro', long way. Here, light this up, it'll help you relax 'n enjoy the ride!"

"Oh yeah, pass that doobie this way, come to daddy. Damn, I'm excited!" He put some flame to the spliff and choked a little on the pungent smoke as he held it in. The song abruptly changed mid-chorus, but it took the inebriated duo a moment to realize it. Their heads bobbed to a non-existent beat.

"I think this song is even better than the last one. Yeah, man! Yeah, crank it! Crank it!" The driver slapped the wheel between hits. Had either of them looked in the mirror at that moment, they'd have seen a stranger sitting silent but expectantly in the backseat. He wasn't there before the song changed.

"What gives? This stuff is really good 'cause I didn' even see you change the tape."

"Huh?"

"You heard me, man, this song ain't even on the same tape. When did you change it?"

"Bro', what the hell are you talking about? I didn' change nothin'."

"Well, somebody did, 'cause they ain't on the same goddamned album."

"You are so high right now, like the Voyager satellite! So high!"

The driver yelled, "Look, I don't even care that you changed it, but don't lie to me, man!"

"Hey, I didn' do shit!" His friend sat up and shouted.

The driver, overcome by a new, unwelcome and uncontrollable sensation, angrily twisted and stretched his neck. "This weed is makin' my brain itch, what the hell did you put in my stash?"

"What gives? You're paranoid! I didn' change the tape and I didn' put shit in your shit, man. What's wrong with you?"

As the sun finally sank behind the mountains and the glare disappeared from the rearview mirror, the driver looked up and noticed the nonchalant man in the middle of the back seat. The brain itch having grown into a nearly paralytic spasm, he looked in the mirror and asked flatly, "Who are you?"

"It's in the glove compartment," the interloper replied blankly.

Without warning, the driver hit the brakes as hard as he could. The car careened forward fifty yards before its inertia forced it halfway off the shoulder into the rocky New Mexico dirt.

"Dude! What has gotten into you?" The stoned passenger shouted as he looked behind him. "And who the hell is he? Where'd he come from?" He leapt from the car in confused terror. "Whoa, fuck this shit!"

"Okay, now will suffice," the backseat passenger spoke evenly, coolly maneuvering out of the car with an incongruous detachment. "I don't have all evening." The driver obeyed the man's unspoken instructions, leaned over to the glove compartment, calmly removed a revolver, took deliberate aim, and shot his best friend through the back of the head. A life of friendship destroyed in an instant.

"You know you changed it! Why couldn't you just admit you changed the goddamned tape?" He screamed, exasperated because his synapses were misfiring so badly; at this point consciousness was excruciating, but he couldn't think clearly enough to end it. A welcome epiphany, courtesy of the unknown man standing outside the car, gratefully showed him how to stop the throbbing anguish.

"What's your name, kid?"

"Scott ... and you?" he replied, tears searing his cheeks. His brain screamed with the confusion his mouth couldn't, such was the man's mental control over him.

"I am Insanity," he offered without a care, indifferent to the macabre scene before him. "Scott, can I have a cigarette?"

Scott took one from the pack in his sleeve and gave it to the inexplicable yet undeniably compelling man.

"Light?" Insanity asked.

"Yeah." Scott's hand convulsed wildly, and it took a Herculean effort just to cautiously light the cigarette.

Insanity softly inhaled. "Do you have a sandwich?"

"No."

"They never do, or seldom, at any rate. Sometimes I get lucky. Anyway, please get out of the car Scott. You look kind of heavy and I really don't want to have to clean up your mess. And the seats are nice, I'd hate for you to leave a stain," he told him as they switched places. "Is this a, what, a 1970 Ford Mustang Boss 302?" Scott nodded. Showing emotion for the first time, Insanity caressed the steering wheel, looked up at Scott, now standing in the middle of the road, and floored the pedal as he turned the car around and sped west.

There was just enough glow left from the sunset that had he looked back, Insanity could have seen Scott shoot himself in the middle of a deserted highway in a barren western New Mexico valley. But Insanity didn't look back. He never does.

The Good (Mostly)

A Meeting of the Minds

It was cold. Bone chilling and tree splitting. Even the icicles dripping from the streetlamps looked uncomfortable. A digital sign above an old gas station flashed "-40°." I didn't believe it was that warm, but really didn't consider it polite to question the instrument's veracity.

Februarys in Idaho's rugged mountains are always cold, and the town of McCall reveled in the part. Tonight would obliterate records. A stubborn snowstorm pummeled the valley mercilessly for three days, dumping four feet of new snow. Earlier this afternoon, however, the blizzard caught wind of a historically bitter cold front on its tail and had the good sense to leave.

McCall had always been a working-class logging town, but was now midway through a painful transformation into an upscale alpine tourist destination. The seasonally unemployed loggers dotting the taverns enjoyed this weather because it kept the flatlander yuppies in their place—far away from here.

We stood outside one of these bars, Foresters and Lager Heads, and should have been running in to sit at the fireplace. But we weren't. Instead, The Muse and I recklessly tempted frostbite, shivering our way through an amusing discussion about what appeared to be a large, frozen mariner. The Muse said it looked like a marble pirate. My sight was blurred by an angry breeze that bore the accumulated enmity of a thousand disappearing northern glaciers, but I did my best. "I don't think it's a pirate," I objected, "although to be fair I have no idea what an ice pirate might look like. Or what they would steal in a sea of ice and snow, for that matter."

She whacked me in the chest with an oversized, woolly mitten. "No, it's the way he's holding the telescope, with one leg propped on the bow, as if he's gazing beyond the lake and peering into the sky." She scanned the dark horizon. "There, the Milky Way, he's looking right at it. See it rising over the peaks? You never get such a great view near the cities." It was a moonless, frozen night high in the Rockies, the type of night when the enormity of the sky envelops you, falls over and around you, and fools you into believing that if you reached just a little further, you might grasp a star and hold it in your hands. Distance disappears.

I lost myself in the stellar sea and felt like I could dance on the fringes of Orion's Belt and witness the birth of a new star system. I felt infinite.

But part of what makes such a scene so precious is its transience. It may not be there tomorrow night, and certainly will be gone in the morning. As if to reinforce this ephemerality, my breath burned my lungs and brought me quickly back to the world at hand.

"What's he looking for, absolute zero?" I gestured toward the endless drifts that blanketed the city. "If he's an ice pirate, it's not like he needs to search the heavens. The telescope's unnecessary. Hypothermic myopia."

"I don't know," she replied. "Maybe he's searching for answers that elude him on his frosted treasure sea. Like, does he want more, or even know what to do with it, or why he has it for that matter? It's transcendental navigation!"

"Well, I don't have any answers, but I do have a question," I said. "How's he supposed to sail on a lake of ice? Are you sure it's even a sailor?" I doubted her pirate taxonomy, and squinted to get a better view across the street at the two-story snow sculpture overlooking Payette Lake to the north. My eyes rebelled against the acerbic wind by oozing tears that quickly froze to my ruddy cheeks—not an effective counter strategy—but I could see well enough to make out a problem with The Muse's theory. "Pirates didn't wear togas," I said, and stomped my feet into the snow to keep my blood flowing.

"I bet Greek ones did," she replied.

"Greek pirates?" Not particularly scary. I wondered if anybody had ever heard of such a thing, but she informed me that there have been pirates since there have been boats, the Hellenic world included. "Are you serious? Greek pirates?" I laughed and imagined feta-wielding Platonists. "Maybe you're right. Somebody had to steal clothes from the Spartans."

She thumped me again, "Then how about Romans? You know, like the ones who were executed for kidnapping Julius Caesar."

"They weren't Roman, they were Cilician or something like that," I told her. "Over by Turkey, if I remember correctly. Even if they did wear togas, nobody in the year 2000 is going to carve an ice sculpture of a Cilician pirate in a toga."

"Why not? It's just as plausible as any other pirate sculpture, isn't it?"

She made a good argument, but I didn't feel like giving in, so I just shrugged, "There's no fun in pre-rum pirates; everybody knows that."

A familiar and didactic voice broke the stalemate: "They didn't have telescopes back then," Genius deadpanned, stepping out of Foresters and Lager Heads. "And I don't think that's a boat," she continued undaunted. "It's a brick wall, not a ship's bow."

"Now that you mention it, I can't even say that it's a he," The Muse responded. I thought she might be right, but couldn't be sure. Tufts of driven snow clung to the sculpture, obscuring the details with a wispy opacity. "And something's amiss with the telescope, it's backwards don't you—"

"Androgynous ice pirates and teeth shattering cold notwithstanding, we should get inside," Genius cut her off. I considered my feet that I couldn't feel and decided Genius was right. As God's intellect, she often is. A blast of warm, boozy air welcomed us as we slipped inside the poorly lit dive. A fire roared across the room and cast our shadows on the darkly paneled walls—walls that smelled like dried beer and wet ashtrays, an enticing aroma for hard-luck drinking bars. I always liked it; I don't like to drink beer by the pitcher and shoot pool in a place that smells like cantaloupe and ginger.

"You're a few minutes early," Peter the bartending purveyor commented from behind a sticky wooden bar that, like himself, had lost all of its luster but none of its charm. The only other person there was a disheveled man with a scruffy gray beard and flannel shirt. He sat quietly on a vinyl-covered stool while Peter replaced his empty glass with a fresh pint.

"Take a table and I'll pour you a pitcher," Peter told us. "Michael and Uriel can't make it. The others will be here soon. Except Gabriel, he called and said he'd be a few minutes late. He had to tell somebody about something or other." This was a lie. The Archangel Gabriel didn't just tell anybody anything—he made pronouncements. All Angels, as God's limbs, have specific purposes: for example, Michael leads God's armies and Uriel is the keeper of the divine order. Gabriel is the vox dei—the voice—and his official announcements are angelically mesmerizing. When he's off the clock, though, he's whiny and shrill.

"How was the fishing this year?" I asked Peter as he handed me the beer, a neon sign on the wall illuminating his olive skin and keen brown eyes.

"Really good, actually. The trout practically jumped into my creel!" Despite his current occupation, Peter was a fisherman by trade and desire, and he beamed when talking about it. "I tell you, I don't know why I didn't move here earlier."

"Because the winters are miserable." I still couldn't feel my feet.

"Nah. That's bull. Sure it's cold, but it makes for great skiing and snowmobiling. And if you're not into winter outdoor sports, sit inside by a roaring fire with some hot spiced rum and cider." My expression let him know I didn't believe a word of it. "Besides, it's not usually this bad." He tapped the bar purposefully, "The gates to Heaven are where I

9

want them to be, and I choose here. Anyway, it's good to get away from all that fighting in the Middle East."

"Did you take up carving snow pirates?" The Muse asked him as she filled her glass from the plastic pitcher. "The sculpture across the street, is that yours? It's interesting, if a bit perplexing. The more I look at it the less I know what it is."

"That's the point," the burly man at the counter spoke up. Based solely upon his appearance, I expected him to sound as rough-hewn as he looked. But his voice was a friendly, if slightly intoxicated baritone. "If that's all you get from it, then you've got it all."

"That's Andrus's handiwork," Peter added, unnecessarily nodding in the direction of the hairy, immediately likeable man. "He enters one every year for the Winter Carnival." McCall had hosted a winter festival every year since at least 1965. Snowmobile races, a parade, and sleigh rides were popular, but a Snow Sculpture Competition attracted gawkers and participants from around the continent.

Andrus smiled and shrugged his shoulders, "Always come in last, too. Not really into the competition, though. It's just something to keep my mind busy during the winter. Staves off cabin fever."

"Is it a pirate?" asked The Muse.

"In a toga? Good God, no!" he laughed flirtatiously. "Pirates don't wear sheets!" The Muse rolled her eyes at me.

"Societies that wore togas didn't have telescopes, either," Genius said, "but that didn't stop you."

He took a gulp of beer and wiped the foam from his beard with his sleeve. "You're both on the right track, actually. Pirates don't wear togas and the telescope hadn't been invented when people still wore them."

"So it makes no sense," Genius concluded. "Glad we got that figured out." It made sense to me, I liked the incongruity. Genius made to walk away but quickly returned when she realized we weren't following her.

"Whatever he is, what's he looking at?" The Muse asked Andrus.

"Listen, Red, who said anything about it being a he?" Andrus addressed her by the hair color reflecting in his twinkling eyes. Curious as to how others perceive her physical appearance, I tried to imagine The Muse with red hair. She is personified beauty, and beauty remains in the eyes of the beholder; to see her is to see your ideal. To some, The Muse appears as a Venetian Siren with voluptuous hips and flowing, honey tresses; to others a proud and tall African King. People often see her as their earliest memories of their mother or father, even a doting grandparent. I once heard her described as Mother Theresa's doppelganger only moments after being taken for Brad Pitt. She's female to me, however, and her appearance often changes with my mood, but she usually looks like a young Donna Reed. And since she's fully aware of how others perceive her, every Christmas she calls me George Bailey and takes me to see *It's a Wonderful Life*.

The Muse grinned and was about to reply to Andrus, but was curtly interrupted by Leviticus and his younger brother, Deuteronomy, storming through the door, precisely on time, with habitual martial efficiency. "Are you talking about that frozen, androgynous, dress-wearing sodomite outside?" Leviticus demanded as they stomped the snow off their boots and maneuvered their hulking, seven-foot frames above a justifiably frightened Andrus. These two always mean business, and their business is always mean.

Deuteronomy removed his leather gloves and followed his brother's lead, threatening Andrus with a muscular finger. "Yeah, choose one, male or female! Get that? There's no role in-between, no space for gender-bending transvestites! It's not too difficult; we wrote it down for you—third and fifth books of the Old Testament! Is that too much for you to read? Hell, it's even in English, now!"

The Muse brushed the behemoths aside casually enough, yet with definite purpose. "Go have a seat at the table. We'll begin when everybody gets here."

"They're late?" Leviticus yelled, taking the topic-changing bait. "How difficult is it to get here on time?" Peter handed them each a beer and shut them up by directing them to our table near the fireplace, chatting them up about the latest biblical news.

"Are those jackasses friends of yours?" Andrus asked shyly.

"More family than friends, actually. But I suppose a little of both," I told him, as I considered my inability to give him a truthful answer he could understand. Leviticus and Deuteronomy, like myself, The Muse, Genius, Jesus, and Insanity, are God's personified thoughts; and God's thoughts have a life of their own. Although we exist as part of a coherent whole, do not confuse us, individually or collectively, with God. The Supreme Being is more than a sum of parts.

Genius picked back up our conversation. "Okay, so the sculpture isn't a pirate, and it is also neither male nor female. And it's looking to the heavens through the wrong end of a telescope. That's absurd!" She mumbled something about art not making any sense.

"And yet that's the smartest thing you've said about it! You just might be getting it!" His contagious smile beamed under a forest of whiskers. Ignoring Genius's derision, I asked him what the sculpture was supposed to represent.

"Sure, the telescope's backwards, but the person's not looking out—the person is trying to look in," Andrus, satisfied with himself, relaxed against the rail and waited. Not for long.

"Ah, I get it!" Genius spoke softly, like she had just solved a deceptively simple riddle. "It's not male or female, but entirely human, which makes sense as that's what it's meant to represent—humanity! By removing the gender, you intended to make it easier to see it as a symbol of both sexes, but instead confused us to its meaning because we're not used to seeing gender neutrality. It exemplifies the absurdity of our inability to see things for what they are." She looked at him with new appreciation. "That's pretty good, you know."

"I don't get it," I said, and I didn't.

"Well, take the telescope. Who looks internally toward their psyche with a telescope? What would you see?" Genius asked me.

"Stars, really tiny stars," I said. "Either that or small boats."

"Perhaps," she went on, ignoring my attempt at humor, "but either way the object of your sight wouldn't be that which you sought to find. People use telescopes to get a better view of, or discover that which they cannot see with their naked eyes. In this manner, they're very useful tools. But that which is great for determining one thing may not be good for determining another, and in fact may just be incredibly stupid. As a scientific tool for evaluating the physical world, telescopes are extremely beneficial. But as a method for evaluating something less corporeal, like our consciousness or our own existence, they're useless. Inane, in fact. It's like trying to hammer a nail with a power saw—sometimes you might get lucky and pound it in, but more often than not you'll just end up with a bloody mess."

"Or people laughing at you," Andrus said, looking at his watch. "Didn't you see the sculpted people below the wall pointing and laughing? There's a whole crowd of 'em. I guess they're snowed under now. I'd sweep it off if I thought anybody would get it."

"How do you look inward then?" The Muse asked Andrus the obvious follow-up question.

"Or more to the point," Genius spoke before he could answer, "how do you answer the unanswerable?"

"Like where we come from or why we're here?" He looked at her with a kind grin as he stood and encased himself in a poofy blue parka and fleece cap, the kind with a fuzzy ball dangling from the top. "Embrace our ignorance, I guess."

"That's not much of an answer, is it?" Genius replied.

"Well, it's a heap of a lot better than just making stuff up to mask the fact that we really don't know. Leastways I figure it's a lot more fun. The way I see it, our knowledge of our deficiencies drives us forward, motivates us to keep the journey alive, to enjoy it! It's a crazy big universe, and the fact that I'm sitting right here right now tells me I should bask in it, even if I'm not sure why. Never sniff a gift fish." I didn't think this a necessary instruction. I once smelled a jar of gefilte fish and immediately wished I hadn't. He polished off his beer and continued, "To deny this life in search of another is to seek death, and I'm far too alive for that—"

Genius interrupted him, "Then again, your analytical framework may not even be applicable. Or, as you may put it, your telescope of logic and faith might be facing the wrong way."

"Exactly!" he shouted a little too loudly.

"Hey, Andrus, you're not driving, are you?" Peter took a moment from his conversation with the brothers to make sure his friend wasn't drinking and driving.

"Nope, I'm walking over to Bethine's; it's just a couple blocks away. We're going to watch a movie, you know, the one that just came out on video with that funny guy." The Muse and I exchanged blank looks while Genius shook her head. He shook our hands warmly and trekked out into the cold, dark night.

Peter locked the door behind him, "He's an interesting fellow—perhaps the happiest person I've ever met, too." He may have said more, but just then the jukebox whirred to life, gears humming and compact discs shuffling. We turned, and the firelight flickered across a man striding out of the shadows with an air of disaffected relaxation. A dark, grating guitar accompanied him as he walked to the table and took a seat across from Leviticus. He wore black, square-toed boots and jeans, with an untucked white V-neck T-shirt under his worn, waist-length, black leather jacket.

"You're late," Leviticus sneered.

"Looks like it." Lucifer pushed his chair back and plopped his boots on the table, shaking it and nearly toppling Deuteronomy's beer.

"Hey, watch it!" he shouted.

"I was."

"If one drop of my brother's beer touches this table," Leviticus growled, nearly apoplectic with rage, "you'll find your knobby head outside on a spike." This wasn't an idle threat, and Lucifer couldn't stop him from carrying it out.

But Lucifer also couldn't be intimidated, and he stared down God's Anger with brusque belligerence. Lighting a cigar in his left hand with a flame he produced from his right thumb, he mocked, "In that case, I would be far less worried about finding my head than I'd be about finding my body." He blew an enormous smoke ring above his head that, eerily, didn't expand or drift away—its angry roiling was held in check by The Devil's supernatural wish that it be so.

Leviticus got up slowly, his angry expression restrained only by his leathery skin's lack of elasticity.

"Cut it out," Peter yelled, somehow convincing Leviticus to sit back down, but his glare continued to rain fire on The Devil. Lucifer just smiled broadly, and bade the smoke ring succumb to gravity just above his head like a sacrilegious halo. Leviticus had been flirting with the edge. This sent him well over it.

"That's it!" Leviticus shouted as he shot up and threw his chair across the room. "I'm going to kick your—"

"I call this meeting to order!" A booming, British accent suddenly echoed through the bar and interrupted The Devil's imminent ass-kicking with voluminous force. We all turned and faced Gabriel, who had materialized in the center of the room with the Archangel Raphael. To ignore an official pronouncement from Gabriel is impossible; its beauty is in its undeniable power. To respect it, however, is something entirely different.

"You're late!" Leviticus snarled as he snatched a chair from an adjacent table.

No longer making an official pronouncement, Gabriel responded with an indignant whine: "Well, be that as it may, it doesn't change anything. Uriel and Michael can't make it; they're still trying to convince Paul of the folly of misogyny." They'd been trying for years to right that wrong. "We can start the meeting now."

"No, we can't," Leviticus guzzled a pint while we all gathered around the table.

"Why not?"

"The Messiah's not here yet. Late as usual."

REMEMBER THE GOOD TIMES

I've known Jesus as long as I can remember and am extremely fond of him, but I didn't know why he called us here. None of us did. I rummaged through my memory for some clue as to his motivation, but couldn't come up with anything that would warrant an urgent executive meeting, and I'd seen Jesus a lot lately.

We had some fun with Insanity in a few Roman outposts—dust-blown hell-holes, salty lakes, and God-forsaken mountains where it's either too hot or too cold, often both before noon. And the whole place stunk. People didn't invent incense for its pleasant aroma, but rather because it glossed over a stunning Bronze Age olfactory violence.

While Jesus was wandering the desert, Insanity and I debated which was worse: the smell inside the mud-brick buildings or the smell in public roads and marketplaces. I put my money on the roads with their trash heaps and mounds of steaming oxen crap. Plus, they crucified people regularly just outside the city walls, and the smell from the festering corpses wafted back into the city with a vengeful stench—a hellish ass-hat far worse than the smell from any one abode.

And while the food, unlike the stench, didn't come from rotting corpses, it may have been partially born of crucifix effluvia. There's a reason Rome is known for its culinary delights while Bethlehem isn't on anybody's gastronomic map. We couldn't find a decent meal anywhere. These people needed to discover the joy of yeast! Nothing but tasteless flat crackers, salty fish, and rancid cheese. And sanitation? Forget about it.

"The Jungle, my ass," Insanity said, "good thing Upton Sinclair never came around here."

Insanity dared me to ask an innkeeper if I could spice up the balsa wood masquerading as bread with a slice of roast beef, some bacon, and cheddar cheese. Since the man was kosher and zealously obeyed Judaic dietary laws, this didn't go over too well. How was I supposed to know that he would consider my idea of a tasty sandwich a mortal sin? Insanity knew the reaction I'd get, though. He scarcely understands basic arithmetic but he knows crazy. The innkeeper slashed at me with his knife, but luckily it was too dull from hacking at bread-bricks all day to do anything more than give me a painful bruise. When he picked up a new, sharper knife, I ran. I made my way through the street hurdling camel dung and dodging clumps of horse manure, trying to ignore the smell below that was giving the putrid sky-gravy a run for its money.

Insanity fell to the road, laughing as the irate cracker hacker chased me. I'm not positive, but I even think he was rooting for him to catch me, probably because he was rolling in a fresh cowpie that turned his robes into an outlandish fecal Rorschach. Occasionally, the inability to be found is the better part of valor, so I hid behind an unfortunately flatulent camel.

I was in this pit because Jesus asked me to help with what he called preaching but I called mountain philosophizing. Apparently, Jesus had an enthusiastically receptive audience to his message of love, forgiveness, peace, and joy. Yet, despite his multiple mountainous musings, he couldn't completely sway the locals. "They long for it," he told me, "but just as they approach understanding, right when you see their eyes light up, they jump back. It's like they're hard-wired for pain. Contradiction," he called me by name, "they understand the message when it stands alone, they cry out for it, but are completely lost when they try to reconcile it with their existing belief systems. I need your help. Some things logic alone cannot cure."

Insanity jumped in. "They ask Jesus all sorts of crazy questions. You should see it! They're dumb, really. Well, I suppose all people are stupid when it comes down to it, but it's funny when they get up in Jesus's face! A Roman Centurion—you know, with the mohawk brush helmets—demanded: 'Why should I turn the other cheek after an affront when God makes condiments out of his enemies? Poor Lot's wife did nothing more than look back on her burning home, and God turned her into a pillar of salt! That's your God's mercy? And torturing Job and his family on a bet? I call that insecurity, not mercy.'"

Insanity exaggerated the local accents and mocked their mannerisms with a playful dance. "A pompous aristocrat—you've seen them with their bulbous noses and fat heads—anyway, he asked Jesus, 'Why should I turn the other cheek to a heretic who ate a vile pig? God declared these animals unclean, and would surely be insulted if I invited the sinner to smack me across the face! And you cannot seriously expect me to pronounce a woman who lays with another woman as unclean without judging, can you? I must acknowledge that she is unclean, as it is written; but to do so is to pass a judgment! God demands that I denounce her but you would have me love her as my neighbor!'"

I laughed, which only encouraged Insanity to continue. In small doses, Insanity is quite entertaining. "A smart woman wearing a funny shawl said, 'If God is omnibenevolent and omniscient, from whence comes evil? God created everything or didn't, Jesus. Even assuming that humans really did create evil, I cannot believe an all-knowing God was blindsided by this development! While I kind of like your message, I already have a God and master, and your God clearly isn't mine; and as you so often say, I cannot serve two masters!'"

This is where I came in, as those were the words I needed to hear— the inability to reconcile divergent thoughts, statements, or beliefs. I am Contradiction. My job, without which existence as you know it cannot function, is to resolve mental contradictions.

I give you the ability to say that both blue and purple are your favorite colors; that you sincerely love and hate your parents and often for the exact same reasons; that you abhor the cold but gleefully choose to live in northeastern Canada; that you have the heart of a champion but root for the woeful Chicago Cubs. You sense my presence when you see a lover knowingly jilted by infidelity steadfastly maintain that no such thing has occurred. On a deeper note, I provide you with the ability to simultaneously realize your universal insignificance and treasure the uniqueness that is your life. I reconcile the Holy Trinity and monotheism; without my cognitive dissonance, you'd see the irreconcilability of the two and be overcome by paralysis.

Sometimes, depending on the situation, I remove the contradiction entirely. Instead of making you deny the obvious, I adorn you with subjective shades through which you see an accommodating shade of gray. You know if good and evil exist that they must be epistemically immutable, just as surely as you realize that you cannot love John Wayne and Clint Eastwood movies. Adoration of the former's moral certainty should obviate veneration of the latter's post-modern subjective relativism—but I make it happen all the time.

Lucifer chides me by telling everybody that my job is to dumb people down and make sure they don't think too much. I believe it's the opposite, in that the "not thinking" I bestow is really a prioritizing contextual reference that serves as a prerequisite for any advanced cognition. Sometimes relationships, love, family, or self-preservation take precedence—logic be damned.

So I agreed to help Jesus and Insanity. We slept in barns and proselytized throughout the Middle East, paying our way with odd jobs, mostly carpentry—Christ has a knack for wood work and makes a great cedar likeness of Buddha. I finally left when it became apparent that great numbers of people could reconcile Jesus's version of God with that of the Old Testament. In retrospect, I don't know that either was a good idea. The reconciliation and leaving, that is.

An Agenda to Remember

Jesus materialized next to the fireplace and joined us at the table. "We have a problem," he said in a reserved voice. His frazzled beard expressed his dejection, and his rigid posture belied the exhaustion in his eyes. Across the table Lucifer's smoky halo drifted off to the rafters. I didn't have to look at Jesus twice to know that something within him had permanently changed. This man wasn't the Jesus I knew; this was Sisyphus condemned, Prometheus bound.

"I was in Imperial Rome, working with Insanity," Jesus paused and sighed with the manner of one who knows what he has to say but wishes he neither knew it nor had to say it. He and Insanity had been there alone together for quite some time. I don't know what happened after I left. I only know that Jesus said he still needed Insanity and was watching him, and that he also said he didn't need any help containing him.

Initially, I had concerns about Insanity working alone with The Christ for an extended time. As God's Love, Jesus can cure a great deal and manage most situations, but Insanity needs more than love, he needs Genius and inspiration, but most of all he needs control, a great deal of physical restraint. I regretted keeping my reservations to myself.

Christ continued, if somewhat reticent, "I've lost him." My confusion overrode any sense of comprehension—Insanity is not one to misplace. The first time he escaped he killed all the dinosaurs—we've never been able to figure out exactly how he pulled that off or why, for that matter. More recently, a few hundred years ago he slipped his chains and convinced the Aztec ruler Montezuma to greet the Conquistador Cortez as a Godlike apparition, instead of immediately killing him and his men, which is what any sane person would have done. Despite our best efforts, sometimes history is on Insanity's side.

"Shit, where the hell is he?" demanded Leviticus. Jesus held aloft Insanity's empty shackles. They dangled in front of the firelight, two perfect circles, perfectly empty, their supernatural glow accentuated by the flames. "How the hell did you lose him!"

Jesus looked too tired to respond with such determination. "Leviticus, this is not the time, he has to be found," he admonished.

"Jesus Christ! You're damn right he has to be found; you know what that crazy bastard is capable of when we're not around! Sodomites, adulterers, feminists, intellectuals!" Leviticus never missed an opportunity to rail against his enemies.

Although most of us disagreed with Leviticus's categorization of Insanity, we all fully realized the danger he presented without us. "Insanity without inspiration, God's love, or Genius is just insane," I said.

"Leviticus, calm down, you're not helping," snapped Genius as she looked first at Jesus, then the empty shackles, then back at Jesus. She was putting the story together about Jesus's dejection quicker than the rest of us.

"Go to Hell, Genius," Leviticus shouted her down, "I don't think—"

"That's obvious," she tersely cut him off.

The Muse chimed in pensively, "Insanity alone is like Puck without Oberon. We'll be lucky if we're only jackasses tomorrow."

"It's a great deal worse than that, Muse," squeaked Gabriel dismissively, "I should say that this is far worse than your literary foreboding." He obviously didn't know his Shakespeare.

The Devil eyed Jesus cautiously, leaning back so far in his chair that the fire's flames licked the varnish. "Look, we all understand that this won't end well. And since I know how it ends, I only want to know how it began. Just how did you lose him? Did you decide that the world isn't crazy enough already?" The sarcasm flicked off his tongue. Despite his flawless pronunciation, he sounded like a snake.

"That's not important right now," Jesus replied evenly.

"Oh, but it's the most fun part, let's not skip it!" The Devil grinned and then appeared to let it go. "It's not my problem; you find him."

Genius interrupted again, "He's already tried, and alone, haven't you?" She stared at him, astonished. We all know that nobody can conquer Insanity alone. It's not that Insanity can ultimately best Jesus, but rather he can throw so many obstacles in the way as to make recapture nearly impossible. He doesn't have to do anything crazy; he gets others to do his dirty work for him by infecting their minds.

I shuddered to think what The Christ went through in his quixotic attempts to get him back. Insanity's escapes are devastating on his captors, and getting him back is usually nothing short of apocalyptic. "What happened?" I asked Jesus, my concern for his mental state mitigated by my desire to discover Insanity's location. Everyone was now quiet, except for Leviticus, who was still agitated and had trouble controlling his angry fidgeting; were he flammable he may have spontaneously combusted. This has happened on more than one occasion, and although The Devil and I think it's funny, it really wasn't the time for the Bible Boy to turn himself into a kabob.

"I had been in Imperial Rome for some time with Insanity," began

Jesus, "Contradiction had been there with us for awhile."

"Why Contradiction?" asked Deuteronomy.

"Because people needed help reconciling God's love and God's hate," Jesus responded sensibly.

Leviticus followed his younger brother's lead and growled, "Why Insanity?"

"People need a little Insanity to help them to understand their place in the universe vis-à-vis God," Jesus said, not icily, but cold enough to get across the point that he didn't appreciate their tone.

I chimed in, more to stop the pointless pestering than for actual answers. "All true, but things seemed to be going fine when I left; what happened?"

Jesus pushed his long hair behind his ears and took a drink of wine from his golden chalice. He was delaying, not from any sense of embarrassment, but from a simple and understandable desire to forestall unwanted inevitability. As he swirled and smelled the wine, you could sense a hesitation that did little to belie his resignation, the calm smell before a tempest. A new austerity restrained Christ's dizzying emotions in very much the same way that his glass prevented the swirling wine from escaping its vessel. Life imitating libation.

He took a deep breath, "I put my trust in a good friend, a human, and he set Insanity free."

With that, Leviticus, God's Wrath in its purest form, bolted upright and took his anger out on the pool table, sending it crashing end over end into the bar with unbelievable ease. For a second that was the only noise to disturb the intermittent sighs of disbelief. Then the shouting, as one by one we started to scream and gesticulate wildly, blindly asking questions and demanding answers. Shocked silence had given way to clamorous bickering, except for The Muse and, interestingly, The Devil.

The Muse necessarily and instantly understands why people do what they do. The greatest motivators best understand individual motivation. She knows, while most do not, that why we think somebody should take any particular action is far less important than why they think they should. She hadn't a clue regarding the specifics, but she knew plain as day why Jesus trusted a human, and so remained calm, quietly empathetic. But The Devil's remarkably unremarkable reaction took me completely by surprise. He smirked and reclined with an easy relaxation, reveling in his cigar's spiciness as much as the belligerent ruckus.

As he smiled, The Muse knew what I did not: The Devil was excited to see somebody else take the blame. People unhesitatingly indict Lucifer for nearly anything that goes awry. It's true that he generally has the defensive personality to take it and the sarcasm to dish it back out, but deep down he's annoyed at constantly being a deflection for others' condemnable behavior. The Christ's responsible admission was refreshing, and he wanted to see where it would lead.

"Everybody shut up! We have to hear the story!" pronounced Gabriel, his powerful voice shoving the cacophonous melee into the rafters, leaving only an obedient silence in its wake. I usually hated it when he showed off, but appreciated his effectiveness in this instance.

"Thank you, Gabriel," Genius continued. "Jesus, we need to know the details. As many as possible. Don't leave out anything, no matter how small or seemingly insignificant."

"We don't need explanations. We just need to know where that little bastard is!" bellowed Leviticus.

Lucifer puffed on his cigar and plopped his feet back up on the table—he was enjoying this. "Why the rush? Sit back and savor this one a bit, it's going to be good. Peter, another pitcher!"

Leviticus snapped and pointed his huge finger at Jesus, "I don't even care what happened. I'll deal with you later! Damn you and your tolerance and faith in the goodness of people! We've got to get Insanity back right now." He stood again. "You all talk too much."

"Sit back down this instant," Genius commanded with startling authority. "You listen too little! You would happily gnaw your nose to spite your wretched face! We don't even know where Insanity is or what his plans are! On what can you act when you know so little?"

But Leviticus didn't sit down, and instead violently stalked his way toward Genius. His ample eye sockets barely contained his bulging eyes. Leviticus doesn't like to think or listen or plan or question—he only likes to smash and destroy—he is, along with his brother, Deuteronomy, God's Anger and Wrath. Piss the two of them off just a little and they will destroy your whole civilization. You've read their history in the books.

Without fully thinking it through, I stepped between Genius and Leviticus, cutting him off mid-stride. "Leviticus, sit down!" His rabid expression told me what he thought of my interposition, and he was ready to thrash me on his way to Genius. I had to think quickly to avoid having my head caved in. "We are going to need your help, and right now you can help us most by sitting down and listening. Insanity is on the loose, so you can rest assured there'll be plenty of smashing—probably even whole cultures to berate—but braining us won't help any."

"Please, Leviticus," The Muse added. "We appreciate your fervent zeal and valuable desire to set things right, and we'll do so, but right now we need your patience."

At this he stopped, nostrils still flaring, and sulked back to his chair next to Lucifer. The Muse has a way with Leviticus. I used to wonder how he saw her that she could always calm and soothe him. I asked him once, and he replied only, "The Muse looks like Moses on steroids." I always thought Leviticus had an unhealthy fetish for marshal regimentation, and his response proved my suspicions.

"Thank you, Leviticus," Jesus continued. "One day, not too long after Contradiction left, Insanity, Judas, and I were talking in the garden. This was a long assignment, and I had been there for years, at least a good half of an ordinary human life, at any rate. I acquired a group of trusted friends who helped me spread God's love throughout the region. A thoughtful friend named Judas asked if I knew God personally, and if there were others like me. I told him that I knew God well and explained Contradiction, Genius, and The Muse to him. Blinded by my message's focus on love and my decision to explain the good things about God first, his view of God became terribly one-sided.

"People like to compartmentalize and have a difficult time understanding God's complexity, as it doesn't generally lend itself to human understanding and simplistic classification. They agonize over the thought that the author of all that is good also authored all that is bad, or that the ultimate reason and the ultimate insanity are but limbs on the same tree. To define the good, you must necessarily define the bad, and for God, to define is to create. I told him that I, along with everything else, was a thought of God's. To be is to be thought by God. Like most, he did not understand. Contradiction's dissonant effect had waned on Judas, and I thought he needed a hard dose of reality. Even though I know Insanity infects people just by being near them, I thought the benefits of properly understanding God outweighed the risk of a brief but personally direct introduction. I was wrong.

"We were preparing for Passover, a traditional holy day, by having a large supper with my closest followers. I asked Judas to come early to introduce him to Insanity, whom I generally kept shackled in the backyard when I wasn't with him. 'Judas, as I am God's love, this is God's Insanity.' Insanity offered his hand, and Judas seemed surprised by Insanity's physical appearance—he probably thought he'd look like a demon or hydra, and didn't at all expect someone who looked so entirely human, so much like himself. I poured the wine as we sat in the cool shade below a pear tree."

BENEATH A PEAR TREE

We sat quietly while Jesus relayed the story of his disastrous liaison before the last supper.

Insanity wasted no time, "Jesus, you believe what you preach, do you not? I mean, you believe yourself, right?"

"Of course," Jesus laughed, "I would not waste my breath on words I don't believe."

"So, the Kingdom of Heaven shall belong to the poor in spirit then." Insanity somehow furrowed his brow while smiling. "That's a pretty empty statement, isn't it? I don't even know what a platitude is, really, but I'm pretty sure that is one."

Jesus replied with characteristic patience, "God's suffering is not eternal, and the poor in spirit shall therefore not suffer forever."

Insanity had already moved on. "And you also say that the meek shall inherit the earth. Well, how's that going to happen? Do they have some hidden powers? Meek lightening coming from their fingertips?"

Jesus smiled. "The meek are blessed, and for their suffering they shall receive the earth."

"Yeah, you say that a lot, but how shall they receive it, the earth, that is? Will they rise up?" Insanity stood and pretended to wildly swing a sword, making loud whooshing noises. "Okay, if the Meek, like this guy Judas and the rest of his pals, rise up and defeat the Romans, could we still call them meek? I mean, people who defeat the mightiest empire in the world aren't really meek, are they?"

"You mistake the lack of power for meekness." Jesus did not yet sense that Insanity was setting him up.

"How can I make a mistake when I don't even understand what you're getting at?" Insanity shrugged. "Look, however you define 'meek,' it seems apparent that they cannot inherit the earth in their lifetime. In fact, on the whole it sounds like they're screwed. Don't get me wrong, they get nice words, but not much else."

Judas interjected, "Do you mean to tell me, Jesus, that if we accept our oppression in this life that we'll be rewarded in the next for our patience?"

"No, Judas," Jesus told him. "People are only meek in response to injustice, and since justice and injustice must equal out in the long run, those without shall one day have."

Insanity gave Judas a sarcastic look. "Best translated as: shut up and take it; you'll get everything you want when you're dead and have no need for it! Platitude, I told you."

Judas blurted, "But if the meek use the gifts God gave them and choose to end the injustice themselves, they shall not receive a reward, but instead inherit nothing!"

"If they throw off their shackles and rule justly, then they shall inherit the earth." Jesus continued, still thinking he was having a rational discussion, easily falling into Insanity's trap. "To say inherit the earth is simply to say that the good shall be rewarded for their goodness—Augustus may forget, God does not."

Judas was coming under Insanity's thrall. "It sounds like you're telling me that I should prostrate myself before Augustus because someday, maybe, if I'm lucky, I will be rewarded in the afterlife?"

"That's not at all my point," Jesus said. "I would not have you prostrate your soul at anybody's feet. Obey the law of the land, but kneel only before God."

Insanity jumped in, "I don't really understand what you mean, Jesus, but for now I'll accept the position that the meek shall inherit the earth. It gives them hope, which is about all they have." He realized that he had some more work to do on Judas, and continued, "I'm meek too, right? Like this guy?" Insanity asked, holding up his shackled hands and looking as dainty and vulnerable as his goofy smile would allow. "Meek, reviled, and persecuted falsely. That's quite a trifecta. I don't even know how I did it!"

"How so?" Although Jesus knew Insanity was up to something, he unfortunately decided to find out. Jesus was about to break a cardinal rule for dealing with Insanity: when you think he's trying to get control of a situation, get out of that situation as quickly as possible.

"First," Judas practically yelled, "he is shackled, and has done nothing except that which God made him to do. He's damned from the beginning."

Jesus should have stopped, ended the discussion, gotten up, and left, but he didn't, "He isn't in shackles because he's meek, Judas, he's—"

But his Apostle would have none of it and spoke over him, "Since he cannot rise up and break his shackles, if he is to inherit the earth he must wait for you and your ilk to one day decide to set him free?"

Jesus raised his voice, "The things you're talking about don't apply to Insanity; he's not a person! He has no afterlife. Nothing to inherit."

Judas was cold in response, and stared down his Messiah. "True enough, but what's good for the goose is surely good for the gander."

Insanity smiled at the two men in the silence that followed.

Jesus regained his composure. "Not necessarily the other way around, Judas."

"Maybe ... maybe." Judas teetered between Insanity's control and Jesus's influence. At that moment he might have gone either way.

Insanity acted fast to topple him, "Well, setting aside geese and stuff—for the time being—am I reviled?" he asked Jesus.

"You're pissing me off right now," he replied completely out of character as he sat back down.

"And persecuted," Judas continued.

Jesus cocked his head, "Not falsely."

"What do you mean? How can it not be false persecution?" Judas stuck his finger in Jesus's face.

Jesus rose again and brushed off Judas's bony finger. "Christ, Judas, he infects people with varying degrees of insanity depending on his proximity. People kill each other and themselves, and cannot distinguish between reality and fantasy when he's around! He uses people by getting them to do crazy things. He's making you act this way right now!" Jesus looked at Insanity, who held up his arms and smiled innocently.

"But did you not bring him here to do just that?" Judas asked. "Did you not drag him here in chains to deliver insanity so that people could better understand their place in the world vis-à-vis God?"

"Yes, I did," Jesus replied. "Despite the dangers he presents, Insanity is necessary in the totality of the circumstances."

But Judas had stopped listening by that point. "What's more, does he mean to do any of those really bad things for which you revile and persecute him?"

Jesus was stunned. "Of course he means to! That's what he does! That's all he does! In fact, it's more appropriate to say it's not what he does but instead who he is."

"Really, Jesus?" Judas demanded as he began to angrily pace in circles around Insanity. "I actually don't think he has much of a choice, does he? Look, the least you could do is take off the shackles; he's not going to leave."

Jesus spoke sternly, his manner severe. "First, it's not punishment; second, he'll leave the first chance he gets; third, he stays in the chains."

"He's right, Judas," Insanity smiled, "I'd leave, the sandwiches are terrible. I haven't had a good one since we arrived, and believe me, I've searched everywhere. In Jerusalem I think it was, I got Contradiction—I don't know if you met him—to ask a kosher guy for a bacon sandwich with—"

"Look, Judas," Jesus ignored Insanity and tried to infuse his frustration with empathy, "I understand that you're not happy about this, but trust me, I'm not telling you to kiss Caesar's ass because you'll get yours in the afterlife. It's a parable; the point is less about punishment of the unjust than being just to humanity. Justice breeds justice! Love begets love! If you wish to see a just world, be just! And as long as I'm around, Insanity's not going anywhere! Yes, it's true that he has a role in the world, but not on his own. Obviously it takes more than God's Love to contain him—we keep him in shackles! Some people need love while others need restraints, and it's a wise person who knows the difference!

"I didn't bring you here to debate the value of his restraints, but to show you that God is more than love, that God is everything—good, evil, love, hate, reason, and insanity!" Jesus paused for a few seconds. Either Insanity had completely gotten to Judas or he simply didn't have enough cognitive dissonance to reconcile the problems of monotheism and evil and injustice and free will. "I'm sorry, I know this can be a little much to absorb, and you will, trust me. It'll take time, but right now, I don't want to talk about it anymore."

"I bet you don't," Judas said. Insanity smiled at his victory; Judas had fallen.

"Judas," Jesus shook his head, "this is a big night, please, get the breads and wine for supper." He left in a huff, and Jesus never saw him again.

Insanity Infects Judas

"So what happened then?" Genius asked, only interested in the bottom line.

"Judas betrayed me," Jesus remained outwardly stoic, but internally fraught. "My Apostle sold me out to some jealous local priests for a few shekels. They knew some Romans in high places who trumped up some charges against me. As soon as I was out of the way, Judas set Insanity free."

Genius then asked the question we all hoped none of us would have to ask. "And you tried to capture him on your own?"

"No. I know better than that; I didn't even have the chance if I had wanted to," Jesus replied. "Once free, Insanity devised a plan to keep me at bay."

Leviticus jumped in loudly, "Why didn't you come find us?" He was about to say more until he noticed The Muse signaling him to stop. He relaxed a little in his chair. Just a little.

"Insanity must have known that I'd get help and we'd get him back. He needed more than escape, he needed a head start. The Romans who held me prisoner were easy, unwitting accomplices," Jesus paused and looked at the fresh scars on his wrists. "He nailed down a plan to keep me out of the way. I would have come sooner, but they held me physically and waited some time before letting death release me."

Lucifer leaned back, looked up absently, and asked Jesus, "What'd Insanity do to Judas?"

"Hung himself," he said.

"He's good, you know, real good." The nature of The Devil's work gave him a great deal of access to Insanity—he knew better than we did how he'd operate. Chewing on the soggy end of his cigar, he said, "He could be anywhere."

"And any time," said The Muse. I thought about how time and space are wound together in a complex manner the likes of which only Genius really understands. It's her work. But for present purposes it's enough to know that time space isn't linear. We can move in and out of space and time at will, generally speaking, provided that we are not physically restrained in any particular space in time. This means Insanity could show up wherever and whenever. Like anything that exists in time or space, however, we leave a mark where we've been and ripples in the continuum that indicate where we're heading. It's not unlike a galaxy's red or blue shift; the closer to us you are in time and space, the easier it is to detect our movement.

While spacetime isn't linear, it's also not entirely malleable either. You cannot easily undo that which has been done. Going back and preventing Insanity's escape wouldn't change the fundamental fact that he had already escaped; it wouldn't change history, but instead just present another possible historical alternative. Like I said, I don't pretend to understand it, but we all know that in order to best see where he went, we needed to see where he was. The world is like that. If you wish to know where you'll go, look to where you've been. It's not always determinative, but there's always a connection.

Insanity could have easily had the Romans kill Jesus instantly. But he didn't need him dead so much as he needed an opportunity for his trail to dissipate. Judging by Jesus's demeanor, Insanity dreamed up some creative ways for the Romans to detain him.

"How long has it been since he escaped," Lucifer asked.

"Five days," Jesus said. That was a long time for Insanity to be on his own, and we all knew it.

The Muse twisted her curls, "Puts us behind the eight ball a little bit; I don't even know if we can pick up his trail after that long, but I'm not sure escape is his only motive. That's entirely too rational, right, Genius?"

"Insanity on its own doesn't mean much," she said. "He needs a frame of reference even to exist. If he hid somewhere alone in the universe, he'd kind of just disappear."

"What do you mean?" demanded Leviticus.

"In a very real way, Insanity exists only as a serious deviation from the norm," Genius replied didactically. "Remove the norm, and Insanity ceases to be."

"Plus it's his purpose to infect—he can neither stop it nor hide from it," The Muse chipped in. "I think he needs humans to define him, and he needs us because it's too rational for him to try to avoid us."

Lucifer grinned, "I don't figure he minds being found; he just doesn't want to be caught. Close enough to cause trouble and far enough away to avoid our shackles." He slicked his hair back with both hands and asked Jesus. "Did you try going back? I mean, it seems like you had so much fun the first time around."

"Yes," he answered, ignoring Satan's insult. "I went back a few days after I died to see if I could pick up his trail. I talked to some of the people I'd worked with who'd met him; nobody had seen him. Although there's a lot of residual crazy stuff going on there, he's long gone, the continuum is clean."

"Can I smash something now?" Leviticus asked with complete seriousness. "All this talk is useless."

"Not now, but trust me, Leviticus, to everything there is a season," responded The Muse comfortingly. "We'll need your energy, just not this way, not right now, at any rate." She knew we'd need him before this was all over. "Genius, can you find him?"

"No," she replied instantly, not missing a beat. "I've no more skills in that area than any of you. Lucifer, you don't have any idea? Muse? I mean, you both work with him so often."

"I know, but I cannot think of anything," The Muse answered, as she thought about how often Insanity accompanied her on inspirational journeys. He proved absolutely necessary for van Gogh, Virginia Woolf, and Edvard Munch, to name just a few.

Genius looked expectantly at The Devil, who responded by blowing a smoke ball in her face. She was furious but managed to hold it back. He paused for effect, "I've no clue. Follow the death count. It should be pretty high by now, wherever he is."

"This isn't going anywhere," I said. "We need to talk to God."

The Devil pointed his cigar at Jesus. "Wait, wait. Let's stop and smell the roses while the smell's still fresh! I want to savor the look on Wonderboy's face as he tries to talk his way out of this. I say we wait awhile and watch him seethe at our inaction."

"I'll go," I said while pushing my chair away from the table. "It shouldn't take too long."

Satan didn't want to let this drop. "Slow down, take it easy. Just a few minutes ago Leviticus was ready to crucify Jesus!" He stood and smacked Leviticus's massive arm. "And now you'd let him off the hook and deny Leviticus a good smashing?"

Genius rose to meet him and stuck her hand in his face. "Lucifer, Jesus has earned the benefit of compassion that you haven't."

The Devil downed his beer. "Give it a rest brainiac, compassion's not your strong suit. Since I'm going to take the blame anyway, let me enjoy this a bit more. I just want to cherish the intellectual honesty while I can. Listen up, I'll speak very slowly so there can be no mistaking this undeniable truth: people's inability to understand God unleashed Insanity on the world, not me."

"Enough of this damn yapping!" Leviticus yelled and put his fist through Satan's brain. His limp body sailed through air, raining blood before crumpling near the top of the back wall. It came to rest in an unrecognizable heap on the sticky floor. Oblivious to the horrified hush,

Leviticus walked back to his chair and muttered, "At least I got to smash something. He won't forget that one for awhile."

That had to hurt. The Devil would be okay, but it'd be at least a few hours before his face put itself back together. We don't die like most living things. Our hearts and lungs and brains can cease working from accidents or intentional pummeling, but unlike everything else, God grants us a pretty speedy resurrection.

"Do you want anyone to go with you to see God?" asked Genius, tactfully ignoring the bloody Jackson Pollack splatter projected through the room. "I could go with you. It's no problem."

I thought I could convey the problem well enough without any assistance. "I think I've got the gist of it enough that God will understand."

"I figure so," said The Christ. "That's not the issue—nobody should go to Detroit alone. Take Leviticus or Deuteronomy."

Inwardly I chuckled at his comment but met it outwardly with only a hint of a smile. I've always liked Detroit, not for any particular reason I can regularly articulate; but it is, like St. Louis or Chicago, a great mid-American city full of colorful history and spicy flavor, provided that you're looking for it by not looking for it. Just walk around aimlessly and you can't help but soak it up. "I don't need Leviticus on this one, it'll be okay," I replied.

The congealing goo that had been The Devil's face provided me an adequate reminder that God's Wrath didn't need to meet twentieth century Detroit. "Don't do anything until I get back," I said as I got up and started to walk out. I could spend days in Detroit and still come back to this meeting in mere seconds, which was of course my plan—I was morbidly curious to see the expression on Lucifer's face as it slowly reassembled. It was like maxillofacial plate tectonics!

LOSING HIS RELIGION

Insanity never thought again about the two stoners in New Mexico, but he did get hungry, so he stopped in the small town of Monticello, Utah. There weren't many places to eat, so he parked the Mustang in front of a giant chocolate-covered Twinkie. He wasn't going to eat the Twinkie. It was a taco shop that just looked like a Twinkie, a yellow, wooden A-frame building with dark brown trim. It probably served as somebody's home long before it served tacos. Actually, it didn't even serve tacos; it served sandwiches masquerading as tacos. Whatever people called them, they loved them. The food was eaten and prepared behind a glass door surrounded by windows that allowed you to consume your food in all the privacy of a well-lit fishbowl. The better to keep an eye out, Insanity thought as he entered. Although he hadn't seen any sign of his pursuers, he knew he was on borrowed time.

A friendly man stopped mixing a bucket of sauce and greeted his first customer of the day. "Hi there, you going to have one of our famous tacos this morning?" His ample belly hung over his splotched apron, and he had a bad, sandy blonde comb-over. Insanity thought a yarmulke would look better on his bald spot, less like a bacon slab. Gentiles have a lot to learn about making fashion out of male pattern baldness.

"Um, yeah, whatever. Maybe two, if they're any good." Insanity looked over his shoulder at the car. It usually didn't take them this long to catch up to him, but he hid his tracks well this time. That guy Judas was an easy mark. "What a chump!" he thought.

"Sure thing, would you like—"

"And a beer. Something crisp and hoppy." Insanity didn't let him finish his sentence.

"Little early in the morning, don't you think?" the man said. "Anyway, we don't sell beer or alcohol. I'm not sure any restaurant in town does either, leastways not before noon."

Insanity looked shocked and disgusted. Food without beer? What kind of people would do such a thing? And everyone thought he was insane. He'd heard of dry counties and religions that didn't drink, but had always maintained sense enough to avoid them. "What am I supposed to drink with your tacos? What do you drink with them?"

"Lemonade, mostly. Postum in the morning instead of coffee." He scratched his belly as he thought. "Maybe sometimes a caffeine-free iced tea—"

"That's stupid. Stop talking and call somebody and have them bring me a beer, and none of that watered down stuff, either. Good beer."

The proprietor was confused, but he lacked both the will to resist and the ability to consider that fact in any great detail. "Okay, I guess I can call someone and you can just pay them for it when they—"

"I'm not paying you for the taco, why would I pay them for the beer?"

For some reason this made perfect sense to the man, despite the fact that he didn't make nearly enough money to just give food away. He called his friend who owned and operated a regional liquor distributorship even though their religion forbade consuming alcohol. Vice ameliorated by profit and degrees of separation. Insanity only heard one half of the conversation as the man spoke into phone: "Yeah, I know that I don't have one ... yeah, I know ... yes it's early ... no ... no, I haven't ... I just ..." He covered the mouthpiece and addressed Insanity, "He says I don't have a license and he's not going to do it. Said I must be crazy or playing a joke on him."

"Gimme the phone." Insanity snatched it from his hands and chatted with the beer distributor for a few minutes while the man under the bad comb-over made the tacos. He returned the phone. "Seemed reasonable enough to me. He's on his way. I don't know why he told you no, maybe you need to work on your personal skills. Take a class on that or something." He tapped his hands on the counter and occasionally looked over his shoulder.

"Are you expecting somebody? Friends or something?" The man seasoned the slices of beef and stirred in some grilled onions.

"Yes. No. Maybe." He thought about the crucifixion—paragon of forgiveness or not—Jesus had to be angry. "I don't know, probably. Hey, is there some place I can lay low around here? Not actually here though, because it's kind of dreary and all the women wearing pioneer bonnets freak me out. It's hard to keep the centuries straight when they dress like that. They should drive wagons or mule trains, not cars. Anyway, some place with a view, maybe, so I can see the desert colors. I mean, if I wanted it to be difficult but not impossible for people to find me, where would I go?"

The man momentarily looked confused and rapped his greasy spatula against his forehead. Despite the fact that this request should have raised a thousand alarm bells and would ordinarily warrant an immediate call to the authorities, he found himself telling Insanity about the canyons around the confluence of the Colorado and Green Rivers south of Moab, a couple hundred miles to the north and west of Monticello. Difficult to access and harder to navigate, the area had provided a haven for outlaws since the Old West, and probably for the Anasazi, too. It was that remote. The financial strength of the U.S. Geologic Survey ultimately produced a definitive victory for the cartographers, but so what? We have maps of the moon, but that doesn't mean we can easily maneuver around on the lunar surface. Or that we would want to, for that matter.

"Hmm, that sounds good. I'm an outlaw now, I guess." Insanity pictured himself with Billy the Kid and Jesse James. He reminisced about them and their crazy adventures while the man handed him a platter of food that smelled wonderful.

Despite the aromatic ardor, Insanity was initially unmoved. "I ordered a taco. This is a sandwich."

"No it isn't, it's a taco. I know, at first it looks a bit like a—"

"Don't lie to me. Folding over sandwiches doesn't make them tacos." Insanity correctly observed. "I don't need Genius to tell me that and Cognitive Dissonance isn't here to help me ignore you."

"It's a marketing gimmick to bring in the tourists that pass through on their way to the National Parks and the ancient sites," the man explained earnestly, "but trust me, you'll like it." And Insanity did like it! He finished it off, and a second before the beer arrived. Throughout time and place, nothing matched this sandwich, the subtly of the sweet Vidalia onions grilled with turmeric and sweat cream butter, local grass-fed beef seasoned with salt and smoky Spanish paprika, chunks of fresh summer heirloom tomatoes, all served in a garlicky naan. And the homemade sauce from the bucket! Insanity couldn't peg the ingredients in a thousand years, but wouldn't choose to live another year without it. Wait until he told The Devil and Contradiction, they'd love it! But of course that'd have to wait until after they caught him. What was taking them so long?

"Crack open that beer. This calls for a celebration." He giddily gestured with the soggy remains of a sandwich toward the beer man, "Have you had one of these things? They're amazing, aren't they?" The man explained that he had them at least once a week, but Insanity wasn't paying attention. "Hey, another one, or a few. Just keep making them." The beer man sensibly left, and Insanity kept eating the sandwiches, if at a slightly slower pace.

"Okay," he said, "fat man, you need to come with me so you can make me these sandwiches. You'll be my sandwich guy. And lose that comb-over, it bothers me. It makes me want to hate you."

The man ignored the comment about his hair and thought about his family and community that he loved, that he would have to leave. He was a devoted husband and doting father and planned his whole life around his wives and children. How could he abandon them? Or his duties as a church member and vice chairman of the local chamber of commerce, for that matter? People counted on him. How could he leave all that to follow this stranger to the canyonlands? This made no sense, but he knew he couldn't refuse.

Panic. His pulse quickened and he labored to breathe; his head ached but didn't, he wanted to run but couldn't. The enormity of the reality swallowed him. What had been mostly odd had become frightening. Scary. He was trapped inside of himself, unable to flee. None of this made any sense, but resistance was no longer his to give. A lonely tear escaped and ran down his flushed cheek. "I have a family, can they come? I don't ... I think ... I don't want to leave them."

"Can they help you make these sandwiches?"

"The older ones, yes. They all started working a few shifts when they turned thirteen." Beads of sweat dripped from his forehead and the metal spatula clanked against the grill as his hands shook. "They ... I mean ... they won't be happy, and ... and neither will ... neither will ... the Prophet." He was scared from multiple angles.

"The Prophet? Huh? What the hell are you blabbering about? Oh, that's right, you're one of those Fundamentalist Latter Day Saints guys. I thought I remembered this area and the suspenders and pilgrim bonnets and the compounds teeming with babies. I've been here before. No wonder this place gives me the jeebies." Insanity pointed at him with a piece of bread. "You have a couple of wives, at least, I'm guessing. Probably three, right?" The man nodded. "Look, the Prophet isn't going to miss your older kids, not the boys, anyway. He doesn't want the competition. Sooner than you know it, he'll send them away to be, what are they, the Lost Boys?"

Insanity referred to the polygamist community habit of kicking out young boys—many underneath the age of seventeen—before they had the chance to compete with the adult men for wives. Young, uneducated, and homeless, thrown from their families and communities, many turned to drugs and crime. The man wept, he knew of the practice but had used his best cognitive dissonance to ignore it, telling himself that his boys would be different, that they wouldn't end up selling themselves on the streets of Phoenix. He loved his kids, and was close with them all. They wouldn't understand. Neither did he.

"The Prophet will be mighty ticked about your daughters though, that's for sure. If they're over thirteen and aren't married yet, you know he's got his eyes on them or promised them to a lackey. Probably one of his brothers or somebody like that. Don't lie to yourself anymore. But screw him, he's a jackass." This subjective opinion was an objective fact. Insanity was well acquainted with the Prophet—you don't get that kind of crazy without years of his help.

"I'm your Prophet now." Insanity beamed and thought about his time with Jesus and the Apostles. Why should Jesus be the only one to have a religion? It looked like it might be kind of fun without much work. He could get others to do all the boring stuff for him. It'd be an adventure. "Let's leave soon, maybe in a few hours," he commanded.

"We can't do that ... we ... I don't think ... I don't even have the supplies, there aren't any stores in the canyonlands. And I've got to ... I can't ... I've got to say goodbye to my wives and the younger children."

"No you don't. No time," Insanity told him as he looked again to make sure he wasn't being followed. "Call your suppliers, have them meet you here, and call the school and get your sandwich helpers here, too. Everybody we'll need."

"They won't come, they won't understand."

"Neither do you, dummy. I'm the Prophet now! Gimme the phone, I'll talk to them. Oh, and make a list, I want to make sure we don't forget anybody. I don't want to have to come back here; all you people are weird. You give me the creeps."

Over the next three hours they called dozens of local merchants, suppliers, family and friends and gathered them at the sandwich shop to meet their new Prophet. By mid afternoon they'd assembled about a third of the small town of Monticello, and caused quite a stir among everybody else.

News travels fast in a small town, gossip faster, and scandal fastest of all. The real Prophet, Wardell Jeffs, had gotten word of the usurper and was speeding in his BMW to get there and stop the convoy from heading out of town. What was happening to unravel his carefully constructed society in one afternoon? He didn't have a clue what he faced but was sure he could put an end to this nonsense and put his flock back in its pen.

Two of the sandwich man's wives weren't far behind, while the third stayed home to tend to their younger children. A teacher at the high school had called and told them that their husband and the Prophet just phoned the school, and then the principal took their kids and left. His wives thought there must be some emergency, like the time that Prophet Jeffs unexpectedly brought a busload of investors to the shop in the middle of the afternoon and there weren't enough people to serve them all. They could help, too, they thought. Their husband should have called them first before pulling the kids out of class. This was crazy and didn't sound like him at all.

Meanwhile, Insanity's helpless acolytes took boxes from the shop's shelves and stacked them neatly in the trucks assembled outside. Carpenters, beer men, sandwich makers, painters, drivers, staff, and all manner of necessary logistical support catered to their new leader's every whim, no matter how absurd. They were dejected as they painted Insanity's face on the trailers. Some wept, other sobbed, and all struggled to understand their motives. None succeeded in untangling their acquiescence.

"What in Satan's hell is the meaning of this heresy?" The original Prophet yelled as he barged through the door. He wore an ugly suit, and despite his homespun appearance, he seemed hypnotically slick. And now he was apoplectic. His pockmarked face barked at everyone to stop loading the trucks, but for the first time he could remember not one person heeded his word. Nobody had ever ignored him! He was accustomed to obedience, and his ire grew exponentially as Insanity smiled and told him that Satan most assuredly had nothing to do with it.

"Who do you think you are? What in the name of our Lord and Savior Jesus Christ are you telling these people?" He demanded of Insanity. "You are a charlatan! A false prophet! You are a liar! A fool who fears not the Lord and runs from the wisdom of the Holy Ghost. Your words spew from a tongue that is evil and forked! You are the Devil! The Antichrist! You don't offer salvation."

"Shut up and sit down," Insanity said, as the Prophet felt for the first time the horror of being powerless and speechless. He trembled, stopped talking, and sat down. "Of course I don't offer salvation. I don't even know what that is, really, and I know people who should know. But I'm going to try a little bit of it right here. Thank you very much for the opportunity. Hey, sandwich man, put down those cans of grease and come here for a second, I'm going to save you from Mr. Jeffs," Insanity said while everybody else continued to perform their duties in a trance. "How old is your oldest son, and what's his name?"

"Brigham, he's seventeen, almost eighteen."

"Is he a good kid? Does he do well in his classes and pay attention at Sunday school? Is he devout?"

The man smiled for the first time in hours, if sadly. "He gets top marks at school and is to be ordained to the next level of priesthood next year. He spends all his spare time studying scripture so the church will call him to serve the Lord through preaching the Gospel. He wants to be a missionary; it's all he thinks about."

"That's him over there, right? Beside the refrigerator?" Insanity signaled toward one of the young men loading the trucks. "Do you love him?"

His eyes sparkled as he nodded.

"Good. Now, ask your old Prophet and buddy Wardell Jeffs what the church really has in store for your son next year." He looked at the trembling man, "Come on! No sense having secrets between friends! Think of it as sanitation, a cleansing of the soul." He clapped his hands maniacally. "Ooh, this is fun!"

The Prophet Wardell Jeffs's voice slowly croaked in honest response despite the fact that he'd rehearsed the lies to the point where he almost believed them: "Exile. He's to be excommunicated, removed from the community and banned from the religion. Shunned."

"And why is that?" Insanity asked him. "After all, it seems like he is a good kid, better than most that I know. Why make him a pariah? Well, the official rationalization, anyway. I think we all know the real one."

"For wearing short sleeves in contravention of the written word," he swallowed hard on the lie that explained the official reason, and that hid the real reason of getting rid of competition for brides. The sandwich man looked at his own short sleeves and gasped, falling to his knees.

Insanity picked him up. "Wrong emotion, he's counting on that. Your fear and shame. You make it too simple for him when you do that. He'll just turn that against you, it's how he gets people to follow him—it isn't just me, I'm not that talented. What you need to do right now is get in touch with your anger. I don't have time for you to do it some thoughtful way like The Muse would do, so just, kind of, feel the anger, get mad." And he did, clenching his fists and readying himself for the attack.

Insanity stopped him, "Not yet, let it stew for a minute, it'll be better that way. Besides, there's more, isn't there Wardell? I don't even have to know this to know this! Too easy. How old's your oldest daughter?" he asked the sandwich man.

"Fourteen this month."

Insanity asked Wardell Jeffs what was to happen to this man's adolescent daughter.

"God will call her to be my eleventh wife in February," he answered.

"God's got no interest in that, I know, we play cards," Insanity said seriously. "So, whose idea is it for your friend's daughter to be your child-bride?"

"It was mine," he said robotically. "I made up the part about it being God's directive. I do that all the time to justify my earthly desires."

"And tell your friend why that is, why you want to marry his fourteen-year-old daughter. And please, just the truth, it's boring and not very fun to correct you."

Wardell Jeffs didn't want to answer, didn't want to tell the truth. It'd been hidden in lies in this community for years, and now he found himself blurting, "Because I think she exists to gratify my sexual fantasies."

The sandwich man, who was much larger and stronger than Wardell Jeffs, threw him on the counter and smashed his nose with a cast iron frying pan. He ran in the back to get a butcher knife, but Insanity stopped him and directed him to a five-gallon bucket of liquefied lard instead. The crazed man dragged the bloody Prophet out to the grass beside the road, doused him head-to-toe with the grease, and covered him in flour. An updated, fast-food version of the classic tar and feather.

Cars stopped to see what was going on, and a crowd of onlookers gathered and tried to stop their Prophet from being beaten senseless by a crazed fat man with a broom. Among those who tried to stop him were his wives, hysterical with shock and shame. They pulled on his apron and jumped on his back. But their husband was berserk, and he also hit them with the broom, sending them toppling onto their grease-battered prophet. The fracas may have continued, but Insanity put a stop to it.

"Hey sandwich guy, they say we're ready to go. Let's move out," he said as they got in one of the vans with his face painted on the doors. "I had this whole religion starting thing all wrong! Jesus didn't have nearly as much fun as he should have had, way too dour, I tell you. This is awesome!"

GOD

The breeze—the breath of God—is still—
And the Mist upon the hill,
Shadowy—shadowy—yet unbroken,
Is a symbol and a token—
How it hangs upon the trees,
A mystery of mysteries!

Edgar Allen Poe

God lives in Detroit. Well, at least God spends a lot of time there. It's not actually the case that God lives anywhere in a way anybody can really understand. God is everywhere and nowhere, selling bread in a crowded Palestinian market, needling Khrushchev to pound his Soviet wingtips at the United Nations, shooting comets around Alpha Centauri, adding spice to the primordial soup—a quarter cup bovine, two-thirds table-spoon ursus, half a sapiens, and a bit of last night's meatloaf—and all at the same time.

I wasted an otherwise fine millennia trying to understand when and where God is at any given moment. I don't get it, neither does Genius. Nobody gets it. Some people have come to grips with their inability to understand God's domiciliary dilemma. Others, like the Mormons, be-lieve God hails from a planet called Kolob. We laugh all the time about that one; even God thinks it's funny. A bit of advice: God needs an ad-dress like Bigfoot needs a toupee. Anyway, even though we don't know where God lives in the regular sense of the word, if we wish to commu-nicate directly with the Supreme Being we go to Detroit.

Don't believe me? Do you really think America's love affair with the automobile happened by accident? Not a chance. Divine intervention. Divine purpose actually, God loves the feel of creation whirling around a fully throttled convertible, and Detroit was the vehicle to the vehicle, if you will. Somebody had to make the cars ...

It was a late-spring morning, and I sat on a weathered bench in Hart Plaza looking across the river, losing myself in the colorful eastern haze that heralded the new day. I had been here awhile, enjoying my cof-fee and strolling around the sculptures in the half-light. The Horace

39

E. Dodge Fountain was my favorite. It showers water from a chrome halo suspended by symmetrical tubular escalators. Water, steel, and halo—humanity's attempt to bridge the natural, technological, and the divine—all watched over by the constant vigilance of the seven hundred-foot General Motors tower, lest people forget the pecking order.

I bought a local newspaper with my coffee, but it was still a little too dark to read it. Standing, I put my hands on the cool railing that separated me from the Detroit River. A homeless person shuffled in the bushes behind me, ruffling his newspaper blanket as he did so. I decided to give him my copy of the *Detroit Free Press*, he'd probably dig it out of the garbage later anyway. As I tossed it at his feet, I could just make out the headline: "Pistons Thump Nets, Advance to Conference Finals." Like it mattered, the Lakers would mop the floor with them. The Pistons were good, but too young to make 2004 their year.

"What're you doing?" the man asked before I had the chance to walk away. He looked like he hadn't had a full night's sleep in months. Maybe years.

"Adding to your blanket," I replied, and tapped the ground with my foot more for explanation than emphasis.

"Could see that," he said between coughs. "What're you doin' here? You kickin' me out?" Even in the pre-dawn dimness, I could make out the bloody spittle dripping down his chin. He sat up to get a better look at me, not entirely sure what to think of the daybreak meddler.

"Far from it," I assured him. "I hope you stay and sleep soundly." And I did wish that for him. It's hard enough to find a place to sleep in this world, even if your bed is only a pile of newspapers. He asked me if I was a cop, and I chuckled as I told him that I wasn't. I guessed that regular police harassment kept his guard up. Somewhat relieved, he asked me for spare change.

"Here." I took a fifty dollar bill from my pocket and handed it to him. It was all I had, and in a few minutes I wouldn't need it. He looked at the money and then back up at me, and shrugged his shoulders. Then he asked me if I knew that the president was his brother.

"I was unaware of that, but even in this light I suppose I can see the resemblance," I lied as I laughed to myself about the absurdity. Oh well, he believed it.

"Owes me money."

"He owes you more than that, my friend," I said as I noticed the sun's first rays striking the top of the General Motors tower. That building's shine will never touch this man; it will never illuminate his humanity.

"He's got this helicopter, see, and he's goin' to pick me up soon. I can't leave, 'cause if I do, he won't know were to find me. He can't find me if I'm not where he's lookin'," he informed me matter-of-factly.

"That much is certain," I agreed and told him that that would indeed make it easier to be found.

"Yah," he smiled, "you wanna meet 'em?"

"I'm sorry, I can't stay," I answered truthfully as I looked to the sunrise. "I'm waiting for God."

"Waiting for Godot?"

"No." I kind of liked the guy.

"I read that once, afore the voices," he muttered as he swatted a couple times at something near his face that I couldn't see and was pretty sure didn't exist. I turned to leave. "Have fun waiting for God," he bade me farewell.

"Good luck waiting for Godot," I called out over my shoulder. He was going to need it. He shuffled back into his make-shift blankets as I walked to the river's edge.

As I looked across the water, the still air shuddered, sending the trees into a frenzy, and then stopped abruptly. The sky turned an expectant shade of purple as the sun's first rays broke the Canadian horizon. An eager songbird greeted the daylight and quickly fell silent. Anticipation cut short the sounds of morning. God was coming.

On the river's southern shore, a dense fog crept out from between the trees, cloaking them with an unnatural gray mist as it moved over the water and approached Detroit. Soon it enveloped me, coalescing and swirling in hurried circles, and then just as quickly was gone. It left no trace that it existed, except a sublime calmness and the relaxed figure to my left who stood silently enjoying the sunrise.

"Beautiful morning," I broke the silence with unnecessary obviousness. God smiled and told me that it always is.

"Are you Godot?" the homeless man surprised us. I hadn't realized he was up and about.

"No, I'm not, but I can get him a message if you'd like," God replied with characteristically infinite patience.

"Then you must be the president." He was undeterred.

"No, I'm not him, either." God laughed out loud.

"Yah, I know it you are! I seen your helicopter stir up the mist on the river afore you got here. Didn't hear it though." He scratched a little dirt from behind his ears in a strange motion that he may have hoped would clean up the paradox of a silent helicopter. Easily accepting or ignoring that which he couldn't explain, he moved on, "Did you git my letters?"

"I saw them, yes." God played along.

The man held out his hands, "Then you come to give me my money?"

God said that the money was in the man's pockets. The man reached in and pulled out dozens and dozens of crisp, hundred-dollar bills. Looking very at ease with this surprising event, he said, "Thank you, Mr. President, thank you. I knew you'd come," and walked back to his bed and crawled under his newspapers.

"And the lung infection?" I asked God.

"I cannot change everything."

"Cannot or will not?"

"Don't and won't."

"Deist," I cracked. "Do you think he could see you for who you are?" I asked, having always wondered how God appeared to the world. "I mean, addressing you as the president shows he's at least more than a little off kilter, but sometimes people who have decreased sensual or mental capacities in one area are blessed with particular acuity in another."

"Not a chance, didn't you hear him? First, he thought I was the president, which evidences typical American leader deification almost as much as a depressingly comical lack of mental acuity." God chuckled contagiously. "Second, he addressed me as 'sir'."

"Yeah, but I just wondered."

Still laughing, God nonchalantly took my coffee and downed a big gulp. "Good coffee by the way," it was pretty hot and God sipped slower this time. "Anyway, you know most people cannot see past the gender issue. That man's a product of a long history defining me as a he." Motioning for me to follow, we made our way out of the park toward the city.

"Wait, that's my ..." it was no use. God took my coffee, again. Always does. I sometimes think that whatever reason I have to see God is just a manufactured coffee delivery device. Perhaps Insanity's on the loose only so God can get a good cup of joe. Just as I was thinking about finally addressing God's beverage pilferage, I felt something warm in my hand. It was a fresh cup of java. I shook my head.

"Sorry, I really don't think about it," God said casually. "And yeah, I know I do it all the time. I've been doing it for so long, I actually didn't think anybody would ever ask me about it."

"I didn't," I hadn't said a word yet.

God's eyes twinkled, "You would have."

"Anyway, back to how most people see you as a male—holy shit this is good! What did you put in this?" I exclaimed as I relished another sip.

"Little spice, you won't even find it on this planet." God travels a lot and says it's nice to be able to be everywhere at once. I stared dumbfounded at the cup that contained something that looked and smelled like my coffee but wasn't my coffee.

God had moved on. "It's mostly a social construction. Think about it: that guy's language doesn't even have a gender neutral pronoun by which to address me that doesn't refer to me as an 'it'. Most societies and religions have defined me either as mother creator or father protector; they peg everything into narrow dichotomies, black or white, male or female. Such definitions assist with explanations, but they also restrict if not completely negate their ability to transcend them."

"True, but it doesn't seem like everybody boxes you in like that," I said as I thought about all the world's divergent God views.

"A few religions don't, I suppose, but most do. The problem isn't that people can't understand me, but rather that they don't like the answer. The heart of the matter is that most people cannot understand me and confound the problem by refusing to accept it! They try to conceptualize me as they would be in my place, keeping people at the center of the universe. The importance of such a view is less my humanization than their deification. Made in my image? As if I'm human? Where'd that come from?" God laughed and feigned a look of revulsion. "As if I die or bleed. Or have a colon, for that matter."

Thinking that this was a little unfair to people, I noted, "It's a natural supposition that a child resembles a parent. Apples don't fall that far from their trees. More to the point, pumpkins don't ripen on coconut palms."

"I can arrange that," God chided.

Smiling, I said, "Nor have I ever seen you pregnant, although modern Christians have a pagan idea about you fornicating with and impregnating a young married virgin. But hey, the day's still early. Let's go to a fertility clinic and get you knocked up with a universe!"

"The day's not that long! Anyway, not all creations are births," God went on. "Christ, imagine me, pregnant with the universe! Assuming I had a belly, how could it expand into that which hadn't even been created? The amniotic fluid would have put out the big bang! Not to mention that about a tenth of the Universe would be afterbirth! I created physics and distinctly remember Red Shift and Blue Shift, but no placenta shift!" God scoffed, but was on a roll, "Imagine the starship conversations: 'Captain, we're three days and half a light year from Alpha Centauri, and about to be broadsided by an interstellar placenta, shall I sound the alarm and raise the stirrups?' Where do they get these ideas?"

I coughed as I spat coffee out my nose. "Don't look so shocked," I said. "You can't pretend that people's theological misunderstandings come as a surprise, you designed them! They could have evolved simply knowing."

"You don't even know, yourself," God laughed. "They'd be better served to focus on acceptance than understanding."

"I'm just saying that you knew what would happen, don't get coy on me now," I said, but God just shrugged and told me not to argue about philosophical necessities. We were at the street now, and God approached a gleaming, silver sports car the likes of which I'd never seen. It was a convertible and the top was already down. God told me to get in and get ready for a ride.

"Oh no, not again," I pleaded with the Supreme Being.

"You're not still scared after last time, are you?" God asked disapprovingly.

I couldn't believe what I was hearing! "You drove the car off the Hoover Dam! Seven hundred feet! With us still in it! You knew it couldn't fly."

"Look, that's not fair," God said. "First, we slid off the road at least one hundred feet above the dam! Don't short change me the extra height. Eight hundred feet's a personal record for this planet! Second, as I've told you more times than I can count, I knew it couldn't fly, but I thought it could make the corner!"

"But you also had to know that it couldn't!" I had thought long and hard about this, and still didn't believe it. God's omnipotent, for Heaven's sake.

God responded to my words and thoughts. "Ahrg, there you go again with your philosophical necessities! Sure, if I wanted to know, I would, but how fun would that be?"

Now I had God boxed in. "Okay, so now you're saying you can both know and not know something?"

"Yeah," said God while fumbling deep into pants pockets. "I can't even remember where I put the keys. I'd expect my Cognitive Dissonance to get that concept."

"Oh I get it!" I said, unnecessarily. "I get it in that I get that I accept it, but don't understand it."

"Some things people will never understand because they cannot understand them." God replied sensibly. "Quit whining and get in. You're fine. Anyway, one of Muhammad's kids redesigned the suspension; it's going to be awesome. There's no way we slide off this time!"

"Shit." I got in the car.

*   *   *

As soon as I buckled myself into the soft leather seat, we were no longer in Detroit, but instead heading south through central Nevada with breakneck speed, on U.S. 93, the Great Basin Highway. God loves this lonely stretch of two-lane road; it's almost always deserted, generally level, and frequently straight for dozens of miles at a time. In other words, a perfect place for a God with a speed complex to let loose. As an added cartographic joke at my expense, when followed south far enough, it leads to Hoover Dam.

The bright desert sun warmed my face while the wind rushed through my hair, and the valley floor sprouted a shallow sea of flowers that lightly scented America's Great Basin with the smell of spring. Pushing the western horizon ever higher, the snow-capped Ruby Mountains stood silent watch over God's joyride. In little more than a month, the burst of life from the snow and flowers would be gone, leaving a sterile and oppressive heat in its place. Gorgeous in its desolate extremes of frozen, windswept valleys and searing summers, only the heartiest stayed here year-round. A few, like Bing Crosby, met the vistas on their own terms, enjoying vacation homes on working ranches, avoiding the summer and the winter. But as it's most certainly in the middle of the middle of nowhere (a drive through, not drive to), most people never set foot in this beautiful, remote, and vast landscape.

A disheveled coyote stared at us above the sea of blooming sage brush, and then let loose a wonderful howl. She usually greeted us when we arrived, and told anybody who would listen of our presence. But the people in this valley who listened to her had long since left. The Native Americans were victims of an eastern interjection of western expansion, and the survivors were forced out on less than amicable terms to even more inhospitable reservations.

"Coyote's out there, should I stop and pick her up?" God stomped on the breaks while Coyote approached the car, her sly smile intermittently interrupted by her flopping tongue.

"I'm not sure it's the time," I answered truthfully, thinking about Insanity as I lurched forward, the seatbelt fortunately, if painfully, preventing me from playing windshield pancake.

"I know that, but she's great company."

God had a point, and since we had to go through Vegas anyway, it would be exciting to have Coyote around. Last time we were there, she tricked Mike Tyson into thinking Evander Holyfield's ear was a snack. Still, she slobbers a lot and has a habit of awkwardly sniffing everybody's crotches, and I had some serious issues yet to discuss.

As I wondered whether there was a way to smell somebody's crotch that wasn't awkward, Coyote lapped her tongue and nodded her scruffy head at us in forlorn acknowledgment before bounding off into the brush. God frowned at me, then peeled out as we sped south.

We didn't speak for a while as the world rushed by us, looking like a hyper-caffeinated impressionist painting. Losing myself in the colorful blur, I wondered if Monet raced horses.

It disturbed me that God still hadn't discussed why I was here, but when you're with God, you talk about what God wants to talk about. We chatted philosophy for a couple hours as we made our way across the sparsely populated high-desert plains of Nevada's Great Basin. I bristled when God mentioned Hobbes's Leviathan, and when I brought up Ayn Rand, God fell into a laughing fit and lost control of the car, unceremoniously introducing it to a rocky ditch. The danger of a joyride with God is somewhat offset by the fact that you never need a mechanic or tow truck.

Pretty soon, it was six o'clock in the evening and we were closing in on Las Vegas. Fighter jets on training missions from Nellis Air Force Base flew overhead, and the sun hung low over Mt. Charleston to the west, turning the pollution and dust into an oddly beautiful rusty haze. I love southwestern sunsets, the way the light steals the color of the rocks as it careens back to the sky. The southern Sierra Nevada Mountains frame the Las Vegas valley below in a manner that makes the rest of the world's geology green with envy. What happens in Vegas stays in Vegas, but the sunsets will stay with you forever.

*   *   *

Before I finished my thought, I found myself sitting with God on top of Sunrise Mountain on the valley's east side, four thousand feet above the metropolis below. Me, the Supreme Being and a view to die for. God had read my mind and gave us the best view for the sunset. In a few minutes the sky would undergo one of nature's most spectacular color transformations, only to be replaced by the city's tacky glitz that can never live up to its natural predecessor. Despite Bugsy Seigel's attempts to prove the contrary, terrestrial neon can't match celestial fusion for the spectacular.

There's not really a flat spot on top of Sunrise Mountain, and God and I sat with our feet dangling over a rocky precipice.

"Beer?" God suggested, popping the top of a Sierra Nevada Pale Ale, preoccupied with something other than the view, me, or the beer. The air atop the treeless mountain was cool, and I wanted something heartier than an ale. A dark porter appeared in my hand. "Vegas is a fun place. Or it was, at any rate. I used to have front row seats for Dean Martin, Frank Sinatra, and Sammy Davis, Jr. That was a great show, great show." God waxed reminiscent.

"You forgot Peter Lawford and Joey Bishop—"

"They don't count," God interrupted, laughing. "I can't believe they blew up the Sands Hotel. I was so distraught that it took The Muse a week to talk me down from turning Leviticus on the whole city council."

I had hoped to avoid one of God's infamous Rat Pack lamentations, as they could go on for hours, and no matter how much you'd like to, you just can't interrupt the Supreme Being. I took a swig of the beer, and immediately realized it was the best porter I'd ever had. Holy shit, it was good! Remembering the extraterrestrial coffee, I wondered what planet the beer hailed from.

"The planet Oregon," God commented on my thought with dry wit, tactfully ignoring my thoughts about the Rat Pack rant before returning her gaze to the kaleidoscopic sky. Suddenly looking forlorn, God took a swig and said abruptly, "So Insanity is loose and you can't find him."

"Jesus tried," I said. "He said that by the time he untangled the mess Insanity created for him, there was no way to track him down. We've got to find him; he's not meant to have that much freedom in the world."

"Jesus didn't tell you what happened," God said as more of a statement than a question; on point but evasive, distant but near.

"No, he didn't give us any details, but I get the impression that it was pretty bad." I thought about the fresh scars on Jesus's wrists.

Not looking at me, but instead staring intently ahead at something that wasn't the sunset, God said, "It was worse than that." The Supreme Being continued, hands fidgeting slightly. "They crucified him. Tortured him. Stabbed and beat him. The books about it are cryptic, don't do the scene justice." God quietly sighed.

I don't pretend to understand all the reasons for God's actions, yet I know you cannot surprise an omnipotent being, so I found this reaction more than a little curious. I'd seen God evasive and noncommittal, but never particularly bothered or brooding. This was both.

"Insanity really outdid himself this time," God continued. "He got the whole Middle East in a tizzy, too, for that matter, and in such a short time. It was a wreck before and it's even worse now. You know Jesus will never be the same, don't you?" God asked me, mournfully eyeing the valley's flickering lights.

"Yes," I responded, realizing full well that what I know isn't as important as what God knew. Had to know. Does know. God knew exactly what happened to Jesus Christ in a way that my tangential and second-hand understanding can never competently comprehend. Although we were together, I felt like God was alone.

To the west, Mount Charleston stands as a twelve thousand-foot sentinel above the valley, and we watched the sun's last rays dive beneath its perpetual watch, finishing our beers in silence.

Trying to lighten the mood, I asked, "Are you going to tell me how to find Insanity before or after you drive us off Hoover Dam?"

God gave me a raised-eyebrow frown—a patient gesture letting me know the humor was appreciated but would not be reciprocated. "No, I won't drive you off the dam this time. Turn around, we're going to watch the sunrise." I got up and followed God across the mountain's narrow rocky spine to the other side, and noticed that the sun was indeed about to rise over Lake Mead and the Mojave Desert, despite the fact that it had just set in the west. God is talented with time. The first light coming over the horizon blinded me, but God helped me see the spectacular view.

Stopping the sun and everything else in time, God said, "Look to the northeast." I did as I was instructed, and the object of my sight shone distantly like a celestially illuminated sandy copper table. "That is Mormon Mesa," God continued as I snickered about the name and the Mormon history in the founding of the Vegas area. Native Americans, Mexicans, and Spaniards had used the valley's springs for years, and John C. Fremont scouted the area in 1844. But it wasn't until nine years later that the first westerners permanently settled when Brigham Young, in his attempt to create an earthly Zion for his burgeoning flock, sent missionaries down from Salt Lake to convert the Paiute Indians. The fact that the Mormons eventually abandoned their fort does little to soothe the irony. Anyway, they came back in plentiful numbers and built a temple overlooking the city.

"Don't laugh," God almost let a smirk escape an otherwise severe countenance. Almost.

Looking at me intently and setting a new, firm demeanor to the conversation, God continued, "Pay attention. I will not get Insanity back for you. I'll no more involve myself in your affairs than I do humanity's. You all lost him, and it's up to you to find him and set things straight. To do that, you must go to the site of my Vulnerability, which lies west of the mesa."

"What is your vulnerability and why do the Mormons guard it?" I interrupted incredulously, setting aside my greater confusion that God wouldn't just "get" Insanity back.

"Don't be crazy! Listen when you want to speak and you'll often be better for it," God scolded. "Besides, I don't wish to draw this out." Sitting down, exhausted and crestfallen, God explained, "You humorously point out my detached deism, but do you know what price I pay for that detachment? What I simultaneously provide and ignore to give the world the gift of free will? I created evil in order to give them a choice. All-powerful monotheism cannot logically have it any other way." I didn't know what free will had to do with vulnerability and Mormon Mesa, and my look gave away my frustration.

God tried to explain. "The world's evil is a guilty scar on my omnibenevolence, a painful regret. And I keep the pain hidden and locked away." God paused and took another drink of beer, "Not all those who are detached are devoid of feeling."

Fearing that I didn't have enough cognitive dissonance for this, I implored, "Then just tell me where Insanity is—zap him here and be done with it!"

God looked at me with something approaching pity, "Contradiction, to some degree and in some manner or other, everybody keeps their vulnerability guarded, myself included. Some people cloister themselves in protective walls and die a lonely death in a crowded world without ever really living. But some barriers are worth having. Protective mechanisms can be healthy and serve a purpose; most people build plenty of healthy walls to protect themselves from predatory strangers or criminals from the outside world—but my walls shield me from my own necessary iniquity and protect the outside world from more. Why do you think I made The Devil?"

"To reconcile monotheism and omnibenevolence with the problem of evil?" It's what I had always assumed.

"No, that's your job as Cognitive Dissonance. People blame The Devil for injustices so that I remain above reproach. He is a scapegoat."

"Does he know this?" Although it went a long way toward explaining the horns, this was news to me.

"Of course he does, it's why he's such a petulant ass," God rejoined dismissively. I have to admit this cast Lucifer in an entirely new light. "You're lucky I'm even giving you direction. I could just let Insanity roam free and call it part of some master plan."

God gestured to the east. "Listen, below Mormon Mesa sits the Moapa Valley, bordered on the west by the Valley of Fire, wherein lies my Vulnerability. You must arrive from the north but enter through the south. Off the freeway sits a small Paiute Indian reservation tobacco shop; they will know who you are. Ask for Wovoka. He will guide you to the road that leads to the Great Seal, which is guarded, and for good reason. Wovoka may tell you that your shirt will protect you—don't listen—his shirt is bullet proof, but you needn't fear bullets, The Gate-Keeper is far more subtle."

This was getting worse in a hurry. I'd never heard God talk about vulnerability or remorse or good's concomitant and necessary opposite. Sensing that this task was a little above me, I didn't think I should just go to the Valley of Fire now, but instead thought I should go back and get help.

"You'll need help," God had read my thoughts again.

"How will I know how to find Insanity?" I asked.

"Insanity wants to be found, just not caught," God let me know tersely. "He's left a trail, and you'll find it there. Haven't you listened to anything I've said?" God got up without warning and made to leave suddenly.

I wondered exactly what was in the Valley of Fire. What did God keep hidden not only from the outside world, but from God's own thoughts? Memories of injustice and evil? Was there really something, anything that bad? What one thing of God's would need a GateKeeper to keep us from it, and it from us?

For the first time in quite awhile, God ignored my internal thoughts and didn't immediately speak an answer. Without fanfare, God returned the beer bottles to the ether from which they came, restarted time, looked at me sadly, and said, "Not one thing, Contradiction. There are four." And with this the Supreme Being vanished, leaving me as confused as I was alone in the cool morning air atop Sunrise Mountain.

THE MEETING REDUX

Standing outside Foresters and Lager Heads, I was terribly perplexed both by what God said and the strange delivery. God was distraught? What the hell was in the Valley of Fire? Why did Insanity leave a trail there? Why couldn't God just tell me where the crazy bastard went? Has Oregon always produced such good beer? Thinking about this made my head hurt—I could use a few more of those porters.

I wondered who I should take with me to God's Vulnerability at the Valley of Fire. Jesus didn't need more to think about right now; I wouldn't even ask. Genius was a given. While I can figure out most conundrums on my own, she can do it quicker and with fewer mistakes. Once, Evolution, The Muse, and I had spent years trying to put together a coherent theory accounting for nuclear, electromagnetic, and gravitational force, and had nothing to show from our efforts but some empty pizza boxes. Genius, however, produced a unified theory in two minutes. (We had eternity. We would have found the answer.) Of course, the only person she told was Sylvia Alverez-Shabaz, who isn't due to be born until 2146.

Leviticus and Deuteronomy were good in a pinch. I had been told that The GateKeeper wouldn't use bullets, but you still never know when the strength of God's Wrath will come in handy. I didn't plan on destroying any cities, but I'd feel more comfortable with them around. Then again, Leviticus picks on his little brother and they're prone to bickering, I'd better take just one of them.

The Muse—of course. Nothing in the universe is quite as useful as inspiration. That and if everything fails, her beauty can blind its object to all else, freeing the rest of us to do whatever needs done; when smarts, strength and inspiration fail, try smoke and mirrors. Plus, I really wanted to talk to her about God's behavior—if anyone would understand, she would.

Gabriel shirks work the way Dick Cheney avoided the military draft—effectively and without reprobation—which is just as well in this instance. We'll be expected and won't need the Vox Dei's exposition, or what I call unintentional death by verbosity. He's comic relief without the relief or the comedy. Raphael, maybe, but he doesn't get along with Leviticus. I wish Michael and Uriel were here; maybe they can meet up with us later on.

Shit! I'd been standing outside so long that I probably missed The Devil's reassemblage. He'd be past the Picasso phase and well into convulsing, angry gelatin by now.

*   *   *

"Wuhterrfuhk tuhk yuh suh lurg? Er's Inzanee?" The Devil spat incoherently as I entered. Awesome! He was still Picasso'd! He looked like a boiling pot of red, pustulant warts with eyes! It would be another ten minutes at least before he could speak clearly. I gawked in disbelief at the demonic train wreck, completely powerless to look away or verbalize my morbid fascination!

"Kit strrring, esshoe!"

"I'm sorry," I lied, "I don't understand you. Do you speak English? You know it's the official language? Besides, I flunked Cubism and Picasso."

"Fuhque."

"I'd also accept Surrealism—"

"That's enough," Jesus interrupted with a hint of a smile that quickly disappeared. "Where's Insanity?"

Realizing both that they would not like the answer and that I could not fully convey God's puzzling reaction, I opted for the cryptic. "I don't know, God only would tell me how to pick up his trail."

"What?" wondered The Muse, "That doesn't make any sense."

"I know," I answered truthfully, "I was surprised myself. God was upset and didn't want to talk about it anymore than was necessary." This stunned the group, as I was pretty sure that none of us could honestly say that we'd ever seen God in a mood that we'd describe as "upset."

"God was angry?" asked Leviticus seriously.

"Not so much angry as evasively curt," I said. "We have to talk to some mystic who will take us to see The GateKeeper in the Valley of Fire."

"What the hell is that?" Leviticus demanded, nearly apoplectic. "And who's 'we'?"

"God was upset?" The Muse reiterated, ignoring the vulgar interjection.

"Well, disconcerted, at the very least." I told her.

"That's strange, really strange," mused The Muse as Jesus and Gabriel shook their heads. Even the supremely bellicose Leviticus paused his assault. Genius sat in reflective contemplation; this wouldn't be easy like her unifying force theory. Nobody spoke or made a sound. Nobody, that is, except Satan.

His face began to bob like a plump and overripe tomato trying to flee the vine. No longer cubism's personified nightmare, his head's shape had returned to normal, but maintained an unnerving sheen the deep color of a fresh scar. At first his discordant laugh was only audible because a silk napkin could have shattered the silence, but it grew quickly into a hellish cackle that was so bizarre none of us dared interrupt. Even Leviticus looked astonished.

"Heh ... heh ... Ha ha ... He hee, HAA HAAH!" laughed The Devil with maniacal gusto. "One hell of a mess you've got there. Better you than me. If you're not careful, you're in for one hell of a ride, that's for sure!"

"What are you talking about, Lucifer?" Genius demanded icily, obviously wishing he hadn't regained articulate speech.

He didn't reply. He just kept laughing and lit up another fat cigar.

"This is getting nowhere," Gabriel whined, congratulating himself for stating the obvious. "As usual, The Devil doesn't know what he's talking about. Contradiction, you have God's instructions, let's go find Insanity."

"Can't talk your way out of this one, Voice Boy," mocked Lucifer, pointing his cigar at the Archangel and raising his eyebrows in gross punctuation.

"He's right, Gabriel," I said, "we're expected. No annunciation required." I didn't feel like soothing his ego. The Devil's reaction also bothered me more than a little, but I wanted to just get going. "Genius, Muse, Leviticus—let's go," I said, motioning toward the door.

Pushing back from the table to get up, The Muse gave Genius a confused glance indicating that they were as much in the dark as I was. Gabriel looked like a scolded puppy.

"Hey, I want to go too!" Deuteronomy spoke up.

"No need, kid, you'd probably flood the wrong city," his doting older brother teased without hurting any feelings.

"Aw, come on, you never let me bash anything."

Patting him on the shoulder, Leviticus instructed, "Stay here and brain The Devil's new hue out of him, even I find it unsettling. We'll raze Sodom again when I return. It'll be just like old times. And don't go off with Jesus again! He'll just try to muscle the venerable vitriol out of you with his peace and love bullshit."

Jesus and Leviticus had an openly acrimonious relationship. It began when Jesus talked Deuteronomy out of killing everybody in tenth-century Europe by proving to him that he'd be murdering exponentially more innocent than guilty people, and that in addition to the terrible bureaucratic inefficiency, it was patently unjust. Leviticus, always good with a grudge, had never forgiven The Christ, and glared as he growled, "People will tire of your message soon enough. Stay away from my brother."

Ignoring their spat, I thought about taking The Devil with me. Obviously, he knew something about the Valley of Fire we didn't. Plus, if things didn't go well, we'd have a scapegoat. "Lucifer, you want to come along and put your sarcasm to good use?" I asked.

"Nope," he replied, "I do not." I didn't feel like staying and trying to change his mind. He looked pretty resolute, and anyway, his grotesque, newly empurpled melon gave me the shivers.

As we left, The Devil's mangled-beet-of-a-neck belched a mushroom cloud of smoke as he commented menacingly, "Send my regards."

"To whom?" I asked as I turned around to face him.

"You'll see. And tell Wovoka he owes me twenty bucks."

WOVOKA

Genius, The Muse, Leviticus, and I rented a car at Las Vegas McCarran International Airport on a scorching July afternoon. As we walked to our air conditioner on wheels, I noticed a waxy green splotch on the sizzling asphalt. At first I thought somebody sneezed antifreeze, but upon closer inspection I realized it was a melted crayon. I imagined it had committed solar hari-kari, diving dishonorably from its coloring book in the back of a minivan to its blacktop death. Either that or the Wicked Witch of the West had lost a finger in a squirt gun fight. You never can tell in these situations.

The soles of my shoes stuck to the road like warm gum under a table. The lady at the counter said it was 115°. She lied. I figure after you add up the heat from the asphalt, the real temperature was more like 135°. Dry heat, my ass. This sucked.

"Who's driving?" asked The Muse, having already gotten in the backseat. I told her that I would because I was the one who signed the rental contract. Genius and I bickered about it; she likes to be behind the wheel.

"Come on," I made my case, "I spent a day driving with God. I'd really feel more comfortable driving. Consider it post-Supreme-Being-Vehicular-Occupant-therapy. You remember when The Muse and God drove across Russia; she spent a week in the Betty Ford clinic."

Leviticus broke the stalemate. "I'll drive!"

The Muse playfully chirped, "Huck, just deny to yourself that you want to drive and get in already." She had taken to occasionally calling me that after we prodded an opus from a brilliant, witty, and superbly mustachioed erstwhile Mississippi riverboat captain in the 1800s. Anyway, she had a point, so I got in the front passenger door, and we began our short drive northwest on Interstate 15 to the Moapa Tribal Enterprises Smoke Shop and Fireworks Shack.

"Who is Wovoka?" I asked Genius as we drove.

"Well, for starters, he also went by Jack Wilson. He was born sometime around 1856 into the Paiute Tribe near the Smith Valley southeast of Carson City, Nevada. His father died when he was in his young teens, and he was taken in by a white Christian rancher."

"You sound like an encyclopedia," I told her, still not happy that I wasn't driving and blaming her for it.

"Fuck you. Do you want to know or not?" she said, and I nodded. "Anyway, he prophesized that through a ritualistic 'Ghost Dance', white conquerors would disappear, game would again be bountiful, and the native dead would rise and reunite with their living kin."

The Muse interrupted, "He preached nonviolence and pacifism, but not all who heard this message listened. Some people who Ghost Danced saw it as a symbol of militant resistance, particularly because it unnerved the whites."

"He also said that Ghost Shirts would ward off bullets," Genius added in her best deadpan.

"That's not really true," said The Muse, "be fair."

Genius looked moderately annoyed, but continued, "Wovoka probably had training as a Shaman and was known to perform a little magic now and then. One of these tricks apparently involved something akin to dodging gunshots."

"Anybody looking to justify native nationalism in the face of horrific odds could be forgiven for spreading the rumor that Ghost Dancing shirts stopped bullets," said The Muse. "You've got to find hope somewhere, even if you have to make it up."

Made sense to me. "What's he have to do with God?" I asked. I mean, he sounded like an interesting guy, but plenty of interesting people never personally serve the Creator.

"God's always had an affinity for Animists," thought The Muse aloud. "And Pantheists. Something about how they embrace complexity rather than shoe-horned simplicity. Doesn't Wovoka have a Paiute connection to the area?"

"Actually," Genius answered, "he's Northern Paiute from the central Great Basin a few hundred miles north, more associated with the Shoshone, whereas it's Southern Paiute around here, who are generally more affiliated with the Utes. It's possible he never set foot in this area."

"So let me get this straight," put Leviticus, "Wovoka was an American Indian who thought that some flowery verse and a soft-shoe would defeat brutal Anglo hegemonic oppression? What's more, people believed performing his dance could stop bullets? Sounds to me like he spent too much time with Insanity in the sweat lodge drinking the wacky mushroom tea. Probably peyote, too." Like so many bigots, Leviticus blamed his inability to understand another culture on their shoddy morals or drug use. Usually both. Skin color was another of his favorites.

"And Gandhi was high, I swear it. Natural hallucinogens and marijuana always turn people into blubbering pacifists," he continued his rant. "LSD and PCP are alright I suppose; hallucinations are only worth-while if you're jacked-up."

"When you put it like that," commented The Muse, ignoring every-thing he said after 'bullets', "it doesn't make any sense."

"Not at all, but it's funny," Genius chuckled.

Leviticus was only partially dissuaded and continued muttering to himself, "And Martin Luther King, too. Who put them up to that? I didn't put them up to that, fucking freeloading pacifists. If you won't fight for it—or more to the point if you won't kill for it—then you don't deserve it."

"I don't know, it seems to make sense to me in that not all reasonable actions outwardly make sense." I tried to bring the conversation back to the topic at hand and away from the angry grumbling. "God and I were talking about that, I mean, reason's limited ability vis-à-vis creation. Humanity cannot live by math alone, but needs a clear place for inexpli-cable magic, or at least something beyond reason."

"Inexplicable magic is kind of redundant," Genius berated my logic.

"No, it isn't." I responded, sure of myself in the face of my learned friend's pedantism. "All real magic is inexplicable, but not all that is in-explicable is magic."

"Faith is kind of like a belief in magic, I suppose," Genius carried on. "Well, as long as it doesn't descend into dogma. Real faith is a belief in the beauty of the inexplicable. Whereas dogma usually does little more than justify ecclesiastical orthodoxy, vainly attempting to prove the improvable. You see, people confuse dogma and faith all the time, but it's not an accident. Church leaders throughout history have perpetu-ated this conflation to legitimize their hold—"

"Anyway," Genius would have continued this tangent forever if I didn't put a stop to it, "God said most people don't get reason's limitations. May-be this Wovoka character does."

Looking up, I could see that we were approaching the tribal smoke shop, the only building for dozens of miles that challenged the endless sea of desert chaparral for supremacy. Provided that your eyes worked even marginally, you'd have to try to miss it. As we turned into the over-sized parking lot, the wavy mirage above the pavement announced to any visitors that, "yes, it is still too hot for you." I wondered if I could fry an egg on the pavement and promised to try it someday.

Standing outside the car, I was struck by the building's resemblance to an orphaned, overgrown tin shed. It was as if a metal shed had a tryst with a box of Marlboros and this was the resulting love child. Awkward in adolescence, this shack had "video poker" and "slot" signs for pimples. Because it was on tribal land and not subject to many state and local taxes and regulations, Las Vegans came here often to buy cheap smokes and illegal fireworks. Acne cigarette signs on the outside, pimpled teens buying smokes and firecrackers on the inside. One-stop shopping. An oblivious teenager nearly ran me over on his way out. He had an armful of bottle rockets and cigarette cartons, and rushed off with his illicit stash. The Mojave Desert isn't generally known for an abundance of flammable materials, so when the kid blows his fingers off, at least he won't start a fire. The only victim in that crime is the match. Maybe slow lizards and snakes, too.

Genius looked at me and shrugged her shoulders before we followed Leviticus through the glass double doors. I had expected to feel a cool rush of air carrying the smell of greasy hot dogs, and wasn't disappointed on either account. We walked toward the counter, not really knowing what would happen next. Looking down an aisle pregnant with fireworks, beef jerky, and cigarettes, I noticed a small table near a self-service soda dispenser. Although the table was empty, the surrounding shelves overflowed with knick-knacks, dream catchers, miniature headdresses and peace pipes that were all labeled "authentic" but nearly all made in China.

Nearly seven feet tall and wearing tight-fitting, modern clothes that added to his absurd musculature, Leviticus demanded, "We are here to see Wovoka."

"I thought you'd be taller," cracked the young, braided man behind the counter, clearly unimpressed with God's Wrath. Leviticus actually smiled, and replied that he was as tall as he needed to be.

Raising a finger and pointing behind us, the clerk indicated, "Wovoka is behind you, at the table next to the soda machine."

This time as I looked across the store, an old man sat at the table in front of five glasses dripping with beaded condensation. He hadn't been there just moments before. Smiling from under his black and round cowboy hat as we neared, he wore a heavy black suit from the 1920s and a bandanna around his neck to soothe the heat. He looked like Johnny Cash sounded, and I liked him immediately.

*   *   *

"Take a seat and help yourself to some iced tea," said Wovoka in an accented baritone, weathered and gruff with age. He squeezed a lemon wedge into his tea and politely wiped his hands on a paper napkin.

"No peyote in it?" mocked Leviticus.

Wovoka shook his head and smiled. "You're as forward as they say, but I thought you'd be taller."

Looking more annoyed than angry, Leviticus replied, "And I'd hoped you'd be less of a pacifist."

"If you resort to violence, haven't you already lost before you even begin?" asked the Shaman.

"If you resign yourself to pacifism regardless of how it's met, haven't you already given up?" answered God's Wrath.

Lifting his hat so he could meet Leviticus's eyes, Wovoka said wistfully, "Peace brought my people the same death that violence brought the Lakota who corrupted my movement. I had faith in human kindness and yet I shared the fate of those who lacked the sentiment. Coyote says since peace and violence both exist that they must naturally have their respective places, and that it's the smart being who knows when to use which. But Coyote is a trickster, and so I remain as unsure as I am unwise."

"But—" Leviticus began as The Muse cut him off.

"Wovoka, we're glad you can take us to The GateKeeper in the Valley of Fire."

Taking a big drink of the tea, he said, "Of course, you must be in a hurry. Insanity has probably created a big mess by now."

"You know Insanity?" I asked, fascinated by this friendly, charismatic man.

"Oh, it's not that I actually know him so much as I'm unfortunately familiar with his work. Bearing witness to the systematic genocide of my people taught me all that I need to know about him."

"How do you know he's loose?" asked Genius. She avoided discussing the massacre of his people because really, what is there to say?

"The wind speaks to those who listen," he said sagely while Genius looked at him incredulously. "Nah, I'm kidding you, Coyote told me." He got up and indicated for us to follow him to the exit. "She keeps secrets well enough, but she also has a nasty habit of using them as currency when we play poker." Was I the only one not in on the poker games? Oh well. Amazing how little I'm bothered by that which I don't know.

In the parking lot, Wovoka led us to a beat-up truck with a rusted camper shell. We couldn't all fit in the cab, so Leviticus and I got in the back, which contained a small mattress above the front of the truck and two small benches on either side of a central table. It was terribly hot, and Leviticus sardined himself on a bench looking as frustrated with the seating conditions as with the stifling heat. Opening the small window that provided access to the cab, I heard Genius ask Wovoka about The GateKeeper as we drove off.

"We really don't know what to expect," she said. "What kind of trail is Insanity supposed to have left that we'll find? Is there an actual seal we have to open? Does The GateKeeper have the key?"

Answering plainly, Wovoka replied, "The GateKeeper guards a seal—more of a gate, really—that divides two worlds. Nobody goes in or comes out without his assent."

"Do you mean permission?" asked The Muse.

"Yes," he said.

"And if he denies us entry?" asked Genius.

"Then you must convince him."

"How do we do that?" she followed up.

"I wish I could help you, but I don't have an answer to that question. I will say, however, that Coyote tells me years of guarding God's vulnerability have left The GateKeeper scarred and frustrated. Even more than he outwardly appears. She calls him The Crimson Seraph, and told me to tell you to approach cautiously. Something about him having a shorter temper than he used to have."

"Coyote knows him, too?" wondered The Muse aloud, hoping to gain some psychological insight.

The GateKeeper is a Seraph? I thought to myself. I had always figured they were just made up, like so much dogma, as a way for people to understand their relationship with God, to give it a tangible story. "You're telling me that we're going to meet a six-winged Angel of the highest order?" I asked, rather curious now, if not plainly excited.

"Although I've met him many times," Wovoka said, "I really don't know The GateKeeper as well as Coyote. She made up a song about him that she sometimes sings to the moon. I can't really sing it like she does, but I know the words:

> *Highest of Angels on timeless rocks Red.*
> *Silver white Vestment corrupted with Red.*
> *Crimson Red born of evil and the dead.*
> *Blood slowly seeps anguish deep from his pores*
> *Providing a choice that is truly yours.*
> *Painful is the gift that is truly yours.*
> *The Good Angel paid the ultimate price*
> *In a Faustian twisted sacrifice.*
> *An unwanted, regretful sacrifice.*
> *For this, Crimson Omnibenevolence*
> *Deserves honor and deepest Reverence.*
> *Entreat as supplicants with reverence.*

Wovoka finished the words to the song and grinned. "But Coyote is less than reliable. To heed her word is perilous, to ignore it is equally so."

Genius was nonplussed, "That's not a very straight answer."

"Not all answers are straight, and the more you bend the curves out of them, the less the words contain their original meaning," he said.

Wovoka turned into an empty, small parking lot, indicating that we had arrived. Standing outside the truck while Leviticus smoothed the right angle out of the place his neck would be if he had one, Wovoka motioned toward a narrow but clearly visible trail in the red sand. "Follow that trail about a couple hundred yards. You will know when you are there." Getting in the truck, he said, "I trust you can find your way back to Foresters and Lager Heads without me when you're finished here." Although Genius knew a lot about him, none of us knew how he knew so much about us. We'd never seen him before.

Hanging his arm out the window and waving as he pulled out of the parking lot, Wovoka said, "I wish you well. Oh, and don't believe The Devil if he tells you I owe him money. I don't owe him anything. There are only four aces in a deck." With that, the four of us stood alone on an island of blacktop surrounded by a sea of red sand, redder rocks, and a brown sign that read "Elephant Rock."

The Valley of Fire

We looked up at a rusty, copper-colored mountain that jutted about two hundred feet above the valley floor; craggy rocks the size of houses lumped precariously on top of each other. Occasional chaparral and sage brush hung onto whatever piles of sand were firm enough to hold them. For countless millennia, wind, ice, freezing nights, and relentless sun chiseled these formations, made largely of petrified dunes, giving them a strange and otherworldly appearance. The trail quickly disappeared among the winding steps and outcroppings. A desert horny toad lizard watched warily, nearly impossible to see when still. Either its camouflage was fantastic or it thought itself too cool to be seen, I couldn't decide which, and its half-shut eyes weren't giving anything away.

The effect of the bizarre geology bored its way through my skin and left an eerie feeling deep in my bones. I understood why the Anasazi who farmed the nearby Moapa Valley came here for religious ceremonies. Something about this place that lay just beyond your mind's eye demanded reverence.

"I don't like this," commented The Muse as we made our way up the sandy trail through a soft breeze. We walked a level hundred yards or so before coming to a steeply bouldered face. A fat, aloof, black and orange Gila monster greeted us by ignoring us as it sunned itself on top of a hot stone that contained etchings of some sort.

"Can you read it?" I asked Genius, "is that an Anasazi petroglyph?"

Furrowing her brow, she replied, "No, it's not Anasazi, and yes, I can read it. It's a mixture of Latin, Aramaic, Aztec, and Urdu, with a smattering of a dead language that bridged Arabic and Hebrew."

"What does it say?" interrupted Leviticus in a huff.

Genius traced the words with her fingers as she read aloud:

> I guard a door that most can't see,
> Keep me from you and you from me.
> Ignore what's on the other side
> The part of me I can't abide.
> Contorted on a bristlecone
> Silent He waits yet not alone.

"It's gibberish, there isn't a bristlecone tree for hundreds of miles. Let's go," barked Leviticus as he began to scurry up the rocky steps, annoyed at what he considered our unnecessary dalliance with desert graffiti.

"Leviticus, I'm not so sure," The Muse noted reflectively.

He stopped climbing and came back to face her. "How do you figure?"

"Well, for starters, I think it's obviously written by The GateKeeper."

"Who cares?" he responded. Beginning to climb again, he shouted, "If it were important, it would be understandable."

Following as close as we could behind the extremely agile Leviticus, we scrambled to a narrow promontory where the trail decided it had enough of the sun and hid itself among the shadows. We no longer needed it, however, as about one hundred feet above us, perched in a way as to protrude above the horizon and dominate the sight line, was what could only be Elephant Rock.

The behemoth geologic art project looked like a four-story elephant made of rusty, interlocking rocks that had been frozen in motion between standing and sitting on its haunches. A narrow, red-rock trunk stretched precariously from its head forward to the ground, creating a tilted rectangular window between trunk and body through which you could see earth and sky beyond. Except the view through the trunk wasn't red rock and blue sky; instead, the portal showed through to an eerily black-and-white world on the other side. This was the gate through which we must pass to find Insanity, the seal dividing the two worlds.

As we made our way between gigantic boulders to approach the preternatural pachyderm, we were stopped dead in our tracks by the sudden appearance of a tall, six-winged angel standing ominous guard. His hair, wet and sticky with blood, hung low over his face and shoulders, dripping blackish-red globules on his wings. Robes that must have once been glorious and flowing now hung heavily on him like draperies soaked in cabernet gravy. Although he seemed to be in a great deal of pain, he projected a manner of dejected resolution.

"So you're The Crimson Seraph?" demanded Leviticus, characteristically eschewing any attempt at conversational pleasantries.

"I am a Seraph, yes," replied The GateKeeper somewhat less than patiently, ignoring the reference to his attire's color. Following Leviticus's conversational clues, he dispensed with pleasantries in kind. "Why are you here?"

"What's on the other side?" Genius blurted, completely failing to respond to the Seraph's question. Her natural inquisitiveness sometimes overrode tact, and occasionally got the better of her.

"Besides something that you obviously seek," said the Seraph cautiously as he looked at us each in turn, "is something which you unknowingly do not."

"What's that?" gruffed Leviticus, "you don't know what we seek."

The GateKeeper took a step down and sat on a large sandstone. The Muse pulled on Leviticus's sleeve indicating for him to back off. "Please forgive our manners, but we know what we seek is through the portal, and we know as little about that as we know about you," she entreated.

He crossed his legs and responded derisively, "To know me and see my present predicament should remove the shroud over the other side."

"God said the other side was a blight on goodness, a festering scar on God's omnibenevolence," I spoke up, surprising myself.

"I am God's Omnibenevolence, and that would seem to be an accurate description," he replied in a manner I can only describe as sarcastically matter-of-fact. He didn't seem too happy that God's description fit him so well.

The Muse gasped, and Genius pursed her lips in thought. They, like all of us, had always assumed that Jesus, as God's Love, was the purest Good.

The Seraph continued, "I am the ultimate goodness, benevolence perfected. I am one of only two universal moral absolutes." Pointing toward the portal with unabashed disgust, he continued, "And my bloody robes attest to the iniquity and injustice that reside through and emanate from behind that door."

Genius had a quiet, reflective epiphany. "Free agency," she whispered, comprehending something that I didn't.

"Right. This is the price I pay for humanity's free will. Their choice, as it were, is my agony. I wrench with each injustice they choose, every evil act perpetrated gnashes and grates on my wounded goodness."

My expression gave away the fact that I didn't understand God's structuring of the philosophy, so the Seraph continued, "Perfect Goodness and Evil's existence cannot be reconciled as easily as you would have it, Contradiction. Free agency necessitated my opposite, and he resides through the portal."

"All that is good is but a reflection of me," he went on. "And all that is evil is but a reflection of my opposite. You may not see us directly in each action a person takes, but you needn't see an object to see its shadow; to observe the shadow, to examine it, is to glean something about the object that casts it, if you are both inquisitive and astute. Some goodness may occasionally exist in the shadows, of course, but people shouldn't confuse the shade with the tree that caused it."

"And all shadows have penumbras," The GateKeeper continued. "And just like a ray of light carries more in its electromagnetic spectrum than you can see with the naked eye, God's light carries both The Good and The Evil, even if you cannot always see them. But whereas I diffuse The Good like a prism, my Evil twin shades it out. And to carry the analogy further, all spectra have varying degrees, so yes, there are shades of gray. But my purpose is not to play shades, it is to provide clarity of palette."

Genius was getting it now, and I wasn't too far behind. She spoke up, "God knows that on your own you would destroy free will for the sake of The Good, and left to its own devices Evil would destroy everything for destruction's sake. So God created a prison for Evil, the likes of which only you could guard, knowing that no matter what evil shadow was cast upon the world, you wouldn't leave your post for fear of a greater Evil." She beamed in appreciation of the concept's design, "That's spectacular in its simplicity!"

"Right, again," he answered sullenly. "Because Evil wants out, I will not leave; and because I will not leave, Evil cannot escape. The rest of the world lives in this shadow. God keeps us close to each other in part to keep us at bay from the world; necessarily powerful, but neutered by our predicament, everything lives in a well-designed shade of gray. You may not realize this, but this also includes all of you."

"I'm fine with a shade of gray," I responded honestly, "and think that they're absolutely necessary for anyone to exist in the world." Imagine if you had to kill, enslave, and stone everybody the religious books told you to; there wouldn't even be time to go to the bathroom. Leviticus and his brother would be fine with this, I suppose, and Insanity, too, he likes the senselessness of it. In fact, one of Insanity's favorite tricks for getting people to do his bidding is to make them believe in moral absolutism and the unquestioned definitive correctness of their actions. He says people will do all sorts of crazy stuff once you get them to ignore complexity and to think simplistically. Logic by sound bite, he calls it. And he swears by it.

Leviticus had had enough, "I don't like your erudite squawking! I've got business to do!" He puffed his chest in an exaggerated show of intimidation, like an angry chimpanzee. "We've lost Insanity. We have to go through that door to find him. You will let us through." This was not a suggestion.

The Seraph met Leviticus's eyes and chuckled, answering the impolite challenge in no uncertain terms: "First, my condolences on your lost sanity." He keenly played up the double entendre. "Although it's comically obvious you two were never close, I can see you clearly miss it; second, from what I know about him, you would most likely pick up his trail on the other side; and third, I will not, under any circumstances, let you through."

"What?" Leviticus howled.

"Genius," The GateKeeper confidently asked, "did he have a problem with the numbering, the substance, the volume, or is he just a complete obstinate and insolent fool?"

"Actually, he's often a completely obstinate and insolent fool precisely because of those reasons," she said while glaring at Leviticus. "Perhaps you could just open the door long enough for us to go in, shut it behind us, and then let us out when we're ready. You can let us in and still stand guard."

"You don't have to leave or do anything rash," The Muse added. "I don't know how long it will take, but we'll do our best to hurry."

"It's just that easy, is it?" the Seraph sighed.

"I believe it could be," The Muse hopefully implored, "it's really up to you."

He paced a bit, looking as if he were mulling it over, considering the freedom of a world without this gate; a world in which he did not have to suffer for humanity's ability to choose evil; a world in which God's goodness wasn't a walking schism. I could sense that he was frustrated, that he would have liked to help us, but that he couldn't. "Well, you're right about that, that it's up to me."

"No," growled Leviticus, interrupting the Seraph, "you do not have a choice in the matter, I'm damn sure of that."

Angry but patient, as one who is holding all the cards and knows it, the Seraph retorted, "You mistake your certainty with objective morality! And you, my simpleminded, acrimoniously choleric muscle with a head, should consider this point in greater detail. Your strength means that you usually have the last word in any dilemma. But being definite and final seldom make anybody morally correct. If argument volume bore any relation to validity, I'd have greater faith in your moral certainty."

"I'm certain I'm never wrong," barked Leviticus as foam dripped from the side of his mouth.

"But if you'd listen to other ideas once in a while, especially when they're handed to you on a silver platter, you'd have just heard that I and my twin are the only moral certainties. We are as the Platonic Forms of moral certainty! And because of this Red Rock Paradox in which we're standing, you, my hypertensioned dimwit, and everything else that exists, are but capable only of realizing mere shades of moral truth!"

"Enough!" demanded Leviticus as he leapt up the rocks intent on smashing the portal. The GateKeeper only slightly looked up to better see this frustrated battering ram's impotent attack. With each connection of Leviticus's fists, the ground quaked and rocks tumbled down the mountain, but the Elephant and its portal remained steadfast in their disinclination to oblige God's Wrath. Rabidly hysterical after attempting to break the trunk/rock with a force that would easily shatter diamonds, he resorted to biting, frothing, and screaming. I made a note to risk asking him later about the finer gastronomic qualities of sandstone.

After crushing his canines and reducing his molars to throbbing nubs, Leviticus finally released his jaws. He then rained fire down as uselessly as his thundering blows for ten terrible minutes, before turning his berserk wrath on the Seraph. Making his way at him with venomous malice, he howled, "How do you open the goddamned gate, you bloody, winged paradoxical shit?"

"It stays shut," The GateKeeper met this insult with confident brevity.

At this, Leviticus jumped high into the air to attack, fully intent on beating the Seraph into ground chuck steak, only to stop abruptly in mid-air, and then slam to the ground two feet in front of his intended victim. He was unconscious, lying on his back with a contented smile across his twitching face.

"Leviticus!" Genius yelled and ran toward him as he lay paralyzed by an unknown seizure—a twitching, helpless mass of muscle flopping on the rocks. But Genius only made it to within a few feet of him before wretchedly succumbing to her own epileptic fate.

I looked at The Muse, unsure what to do next. She looked at me with terror in her eyes as they rolled back into her head and she collapsed. I waited to fall into a heap like the others, but it didn't happen. Looking at the twitching, convulsing, and sobbing figures before me, I wondered why I hadn't been overtaken as well. Mulling it over, I noticed the decidedly befuddled GateKeeper staring intently at me with equal confusion.

THE MUSE

The Muse shook herself from an amnesia she couldn't explain and looked down on a lush, tropical island. She didn't remember how she got here or what happened before she found herself floating gently above a beautiful lagoon, but she felt at ease. A refreshing breeze guided her to a strip of powdery sand separating the calm water from an impenetrable line of coconut palms. She saw snorkelers around a reef one hundred yards out in the shallow, waist-deep water, and heard the shouts of the people playing volleyball and children frolicking. A flittering memory threatened her serenity, but she felt relaxed as she touched down at the deserted end of the crescent beach. Before exploring, she took a refreshing swim and smiled underwater at an inquisitive fish. Back on the beach, she put on a bikini and sarong she was sure were hers.

She hummed while walking toward a bar hiding among the coconut palms, appreciating the soft sand between her toes. An attractive couple emerged from the lagoon, and The Muse saw her own hair turn blonde and her hips fill out in the boy's eyes. The Muse laughed, because when his girlfriend looked at her, she saw her best girlfriend from college.

"What'll you have, Miss?" asked the surfer behind the bamboo counter. The Muse blushed when she realized that she looked like this boy's mother. This evidenced either a healthy and loving relationship or unaddressed Freudian issues. Or both.

"Coconut water and black rum over ice," she smiled as he handed it to her.

She savored her favorite tropical drink and made her way along the beach, noticing that there were fewer people than she thought there had been. She approached a good-looking, youthful group splashing in the waves and playing volleyball, and was struck by their extraordinary beauty and paused to consider the concept in greater detail.

Beauty had always been a difficult idea for her. She thought it strange for a universal concept to be without a universally agreed upon definition; to be without objective reality and instead to depend entirely on the observer, even if culturally collective.

Wondering what God thought was beautiful, The Muse concluded that she really didn't know. Worse still, as she only physically existed as others saw her, she didn't know if she thought herself beautiful. As her appearance is entirely dependent on an observer—it is without its own form—in a very real way her physical existence is predicated upon an observer's opinion of it. While this idea wasn't at all foreign to her, it usually was only a passing discomfiture; an occasional itch that couldn't be scratched but only ignored. But on this gorgeous beach, surrounded by what she considered obvious beauty, she had a sudden, hollow feeling that everything had intrinsic beauty except her. She became frightened by the insane thought that her worth, herself as a being, didn't have any purpose except to glorify others' desires.

She felt sick and swooned. She quickened her pace toward the few remaining people on the beach. But the volleyball game vanished! Desperate, she ran toward sunbathers who disappeared as steam before she could make eye contact or get their attention. One by one, all the people on the beach faded into nothingness.

Now standing alone on a deserted beach, The Muse began to sweat and her heart pounded a rapid requiem for her sense of self. She looked down at her sarong and noticed that nothing was underneath it! It waved gently on an invisible breeze from an invisible and unknown hanger. Nor could she see her arms or feel her hair or see her legs!

In a panic, she threw off her clothes and dove into the water, hoping that a fish or dolphin or some creature would catch sight of her and help her define herself. But the water refused to acknowledge her torment, and the sea was as empty as she felt inside. Now wading waist-deep in a lifeless sea and sobbing uncontrollably, The Muse was terror stricken.

"There have to be more people on the shore or behind the trees," she thought and turned toward the island. But the beach was as effervescent as its occupants, fading through her tears into the sea. Hanging her arms that she couldn't see at her sides that she couldn't see, she spun completely around in the shallow lagoon that now extended forever in all directions.

She tried to think herself back to Foresters and Lager Heads, but couldn't, and instantly knew she was stuck. Screaming and yelling with as much muster as her hysteria would allow in a blank and toneless voice to an empty sea, she pleaded for another living creature—any creature—to make itself known.

Between sobs, she saw a flickering, straight brown line in her peripheral vision hovering a few feet above the water. Turning to directly face the apparition, she noticed that it had a long, vertical, rectangular shape, about ten feet tall and three feet wide.

"It's a hollow wooden frame, and no stranger in its appearance than everything else's disappearance," she thought in frustration as she looked through the empty frame at the endless sea. Reaching up, she attempted to put her hand through the frame, but instead encountered something completely unexpected—a glass mirror. It wasn't a transparent windowpane through which she could see out, but instead a window meant for looking inward. She touched the mirror gently where her face would be if she had one and utterly lost her will. She cried again, not gasping sobs, but a slow, disconsolate, and endless cry.

Standing alone and naked, waist-deep in an endless sea, The Muse stared into an empty mirror. And stared. And stared. And stared ...

LEVITICUS

Seven bulls and seven rams, seven crows and seven lambs. Seven bulls and seven rams, seven crows and seven lambs ... Leviticus repeated the words seven times, one for each of the seven lines of seven lines of animals to be sacrificed according to his Law and his penchant for numerology. The animals stretched out the temple doors, beyond the city walls, over the horizon, and past the sea of salt. No matter how many he sacrificed, there'd be more. There would always be more here; he need only command that it be so.

Leviticus understood how he came to be in the Middle East during the first millennia BC only slightly less than he cared for the animals he slaughtered. It's not in his nature to ask questions, especially when imposing the Law. Questions only get in the way, cloud your thinking. The value was in doing things the way they'd been written, the way they'd been done for countless centuries, not in examining the propriety of those dictates. Besides, this was his time, his era, his temple, his throne. These were his sticky, drenched robes, and this was his sacrificial alter. Here he was king, here he was God. No tolerance, no forgiveness, no endless reasoning. His Law built this temple. And now, after more than two thousand years of dormancy, its gruesome fountain erupted again!

He dipped his hand into the still-throbbing entrails of a bull and splattered the blood seven times about the alter, in accordance with his will. There was enough blood iron in his raiment to make steel, and the blood poured down the steps onto the feet of the chanting crowds and hoofs of the terrified animals below. The whole building reeked of briny metal as the next bull's belly spurted onto Leviticus's contorted face, which was by now gory enough to be nearly indistinguishable from the carcass. The lines blurred in the extremity of the situation; the more he killed, the more he looked like one of the dead.

The scene was as loud as it was visually macabre; the animals bleated and mewed in an anxious cacophony. They smelled the temple, they smelled each other's fear, and they smelled their deaths. The shrieking people being stoned to death outside added greatly to the horror inside. They were (accused) adulterers, fornicators, sodomites, blasphemers, menstruating women who'd defiled temples with their presence—you know the types—and they all pleaded for their lives before stones crushed their skulls—stones as guiltless as nearly all of the people being murdered. You might think that at this pace he'd eventually run out of people to stone, but that's the great thing about defining and punishing sin that's original: there's always more.

This is what I am, I don't belong with the others, and neither does my brother, Deuteronomy, Leviticus thought while splashing ram's blood on a bull's horns. He wasn't going back, no way for nothing. Screw Insanity and the Seraph! Why leave this place again? If he got bored or tired from sacrificing seven lines of seven lines of animals, he could just go outside and stone people or tell them what to eat and how they could eat it. Or stone them for eating what he told them not to eat. This felt good, this felt right. The modern world just made him mad. He was happy as he twisted an owl's neck and drizzled the remains on a bull's remains. No Jesus talking of love and forgiveness, no Genius trying to reason with him, no Contradiction pointing out his inconsistencies, and no chasing down that fool Insanity. Forget that, forget them. And he did.

Seven bulls and seven rams, seven crows and seven lambs ... Seven bulls and seven rams, seven crows and seven lambs.

GENIUS

Genius looked at a freshly sharpened number two pencil in her hand. Although she momentarily wondered where she was, it seemed natural that she should be here, in this desk with a blue test booklet. She didn't remember entering the boringly monochromatic lecture hall— beige walls, beige carpet, beige dais—but uninspiring interior aside, any concern she may have had about how this situation came to be quickly faded—this was an academic test, and they were her element. Genius was excited.

A two-sided exam sheet sat on the desk next to the answer booklet. She set out to answer the two questions on the front before getting to the question on the back.

1) Discuss singularity from a human perspective:

Singularity is the point at the center of a black hole at which all of the black hole's mass is reduced to zero volume, zero height, width, or length. Singularity's gravitational pull and density are infinite. Thus, we are left with a problem of a great and ever increasing mass with no volume—an inherent contradiction. In an effort to save the General Theory on Relativity, some scientists have claimed that the point of singularity actually rips the space-time fabric and emits the matter into an alternate reality. Others call foul on the concept and maintain that the gravitational pull of the black hole's event horizon evens out and prevents matter from falling into actual singularity. Recently, however, scientists have theorized that black holes do not and cannot contain a singularity, but instead shoot jets of matter out in an amount equal to or near that taken in. Of course, this ignores the fact that the gravitational pull of the black hole must equal the speed of light, and the ejected matter cannot travel faster than the stellar speed limit. Yet, this appears to be an observable theory.

Some physicists have realized that forces stronger than gravity may be responsible. Nothing should emit from the black hole based on its gravitational force, but the stronger nuclear and electromagnetic forces are able to eject matter irrespective of the gravitational pull. At least this is the newest working theory. Human observance and description of singularity is ultimately hindered by: 1) their inability to see more than shadows of the extra dimensions in which they operate; 2) a stubborn belief that nothing can exceed the speed of light; and 3) a fundamental misunderstanding of gravity in relation to the other forces. Singularity, in the end, is a name for a theory that attempts to explain a physical phenomenon they do not yet fully understand.

2) Discuss love from a human perspective:

Discussing love from a human perspective is quixotic at best and impossible at worst. By its very nature, love alters perspective; it is designed to override the heretofore overtly rational. Through a biological system of chemical and pheromonal tools, love replaces rote rationality with a new form of logical thought, at least as far as the objects of that love are concerned. Consider Shakespeare's Juliet: an outside observer may rationally consider her love for Romeo a heretical act of irrational teenage exuberance that will end in her demise. Yet, love bears a subjective rationality wherein Romeo provides an outlet from a banal and violent world, and represents a better and more peaceful future for herself and her family. And this is every bit as rational as the outside observer's contradictory conclusion. Indeed, if Shakespeare was in a lighter mood that day, this may have been the outcome of the story.

Love also adheres humans to preserve the species. Adam Smith correctly noted that people care most about those closest to them, those they see everyday in their homes, neighborhoods, and communities. Love is a hyper-attenuated feeling of affection for those nearest to them that allows for familial and cultural perpetuation. Ultimately, love exists as a gift and a tool. The genius of love is that it is both.

Genius smiled and turned the test over to see the final question. She was on a roll!

3) Whence came God:

She stared at the question with angry disbelief and gnawed on the pencil's eraser, then tapped the misshapen nub repeatedly on the desk. Sweat appeared around her temples and her heart's previously rhythmic tempo now pounded an incoherently frantic beat. Panic-stricken and wondering if she could stall the inevitable, she noticed that the room's clocks and her watch were frozen. Good. She was going to fail, but at least she could put it off while time stopped. She tapped the pencil more fervently and bit through the wood, breaking it in half. The sound of her sweat falling heavily on the desk echoed through the otherwise silent lecture hall.

It was bad enough that she didn't know the answer, but at least she could delay so that nobody else knew she didn't have a clue. What would people say when confronted with the insanity that Genius did not have an answer for this most basic of questions? Since failure is to forestall as unknown is to unadmitted, she sat ... and sat ... and sat ...

Meanwhile, Back at Elephant Rock ...

"Well, Contradiction, you've got some serious talent," the Seraph spoke dryly, surprised but not wanting to appear unduly so. "The others were easy to take care of. I gave the angry one a dream of his perfect world, from which he'll never willingly wake; Genius is caught trying to use reason to figure out something that reason cannot figure out; and The Muse, well, she's trying to figure out who she is. Piece of cake. But you? After what I hurled into your head, most beings would be little more than histrionic gelatin." He fluttered his wings and put his hands on his waist. Smiling without smiling, he said, "You should be proud of yourself."

"I am," I said.

He chuckled at his futility. "I hit you right between the eyes with two absolute and opposing moral certainties."

"Easy to deny," I told him. "For a split second I debated whether it would be easier to ignore the fact that they were clearly opposing principles or simply to reconcile them."

"Well," he asked, "which did you choose?"

"Actually, it's a pretty easy process for me, so I did both," I replied. After all, this was one of my specialties.

Much to his mouth's consternation, his lips betrayed him and he grinned, "That blinding white light should have taken care of you."

"You mean the calm blackness?" I asked.

"I wouldn't have considered it calm by any means," he said. "I figured you'd be wandering around in the darkness for at least forty years."

"I just borrowed a little of your white light to guide my way," I let him know how I used his own ruse against him.

The GateKeeper's response showed more surprise than confusion or frustration, "I thought—incorrectly—that you could not handle both."

"Shades of gray, my friend," I said as I tapped my noggin for emphasis. "It's all a matter of perspective."

"You certainly are a handy fellow, aren't you?" he said, genuinely appreciative of my skills.

"Yeah, I never cease to amaze myself." I feigned disinterest as I looked at the bodies still flopping on the desert floor. "Look, I appreciate that you've got a job to do, but I've got one to take care of myself. God even sent me here! If you care so much about goodness, then you'll let me through so we can find Insanity."

"My job isn't a duty, it's who I am." He ambled forward and took a seat near me on a flat boulder. "Even if I was so inclined, and rest assured, I'm not, I could no more leave the gate unguarded, even for a second, than I could starve a child."

We sized each other up in silence for a minute before a completely unexpected and cheerful voice broke the stalemate. "This is quite a pickle, isn't it?"

We turned around and saw Coyote bounding up between us, smiling and wagging her tail in a playful frolic. Even her most joyous and bizarre dreams could not have conjured up a more perfectly comic scenario. I greeted her with a nod.

"Wovoka told me I'd find you here. Said that I might have some fun if I watch," she sung impishly as she sat on her haunches, looking back and forth between myself and the Seraph.

"As you can probably tell, there isn't much to see," added The Gate-Keeper with sarcasm and genuine familiarity.

Coyote looked at the convulsing bodies stirring up dust, "I don't know, it's pretty funny that you turned that blowhard Leviticus into a smiling slobber-beast," she lapped.

"He deserved it," The GateKeeper said.

"Yeah, I suppose so," she thought aloud. Abruptly turning to me with a gleam in her eye, she barked, "Why don't you just wake him up?" The GateKeeper stood, nostrils flaring, but Coyote continued undaunted, "Look, The GateKeeper's strong, but he's spending a lot of energy keeping all three of your friends emotionally paralyzed like that. Give your biblical blowhard a little cognitive dissonance to deal with his predicament and I bet he'd perk right up!" She jumped to her feet excitedly and hopped up and down, tongue flopping ridiculously. "Probably be pretty pissed, too. Do it! Do it! I want to watch!"

"You shaggy canine rabble-rouser!" the Seraph roared as he chased Coyote away, stumbling over the rocks.

"You owe me twenty bucks and you know it," she yelped as she deftly avoided his grasp. "Five aces beat a full house."

"There aren't five aces in the deck!" the Seraph screeched as he threw a rock in the general direction of the disappearing Miscreant. Angrily dejected, he stopped the chase. He couldn't leave the gate area and he knew he couldn't catch her quick enough. She'd find a place just beyond sight and out of reach and taunt him with ear-splitting howls. She always did when she wanted to annoy him.

By the time the Seraph turned back around to the scene of his emotional chicanery, I was standing above a wide-eyed and furious Leviticus.

THAT'LL BE AFTER THE FIGHT

Leviticus glared at The Crimson Seraph with controlled rage. He filled the angry silence and short distance between them with fuming malevolence. He never took his eyes off his target as he strode up the hillside, intensely stalking his prey. Rocks cracked under his feet. The GateKeeper boldly unfurled his wings in their bloody entirety to meet the upstart challenger. If he had any fear, I didn't see it.

With two explosive leaps high into the air, God's Wrath and God's Goodness collided into each other one hundred feet above the Valley of Fire with a schismatic crash. A thousand terrifying lightning bolts from the Seraph met a thousand fireballs hurled wickedly by Leviticus. I quickly prodded The Muse and Genius from their frightful stupor and led us to cover in a rocky alcove. The violently quaking ground tried to force us into prostrated submission with every wobbly step.

We huddled together and watched the melee in horror for five minutes before an ear-splitting crack precipitated the end of the contest. The ground convulsed, mountains crumbled, volcanoes erupted, tidal waves formed, and at least three stellar systems were born in that instant. The air smelled like boiling metal. As I struggled to see through the smoky cloud, I could taste burned copper and iron, like bloody pennies.

A hot breeze slithered down the rocks and blew some of the smoke away—enough so that we could make out Leviticus standing battered but confident above the defeated Crimson Seraph. With a charred forearm, he wiped the dirt and sweat and blood and bits of bone and feathers from his knotted brow. He looked derisively at his vanquished opponent and commanded with severe authority, "Now you will open the gate!"

The Seraph writhed painfully while coughing viscous blood from his mangled and broken mouth. Two of his six wings were missing, a third grotesquely broken, and the other three clinging to badly scorched tendons. It hurt to look at the sadistic asymmetry, and I winced. The Seraph stoically turned his nightmarish stare toward God's Wrath, then quickly looked away and made a pitiful attempt to roll over and slink into grievous retreat, but he could no more right himself than he could fly. Leviticus held his foot high above his victim's chest and prepared to deliver a final, fatal blow.

"Leviticus, wait!" shouted Genius. "God damn it, why don't you ever stop and think? Killing him won't open the gate! And he'll just come back angrier than before!"

"Then I'll keep killing him until he changes his mind and does what I tell him to do," he spat, and viciously stomped his boot through the Seraph's chest. His ribcage collapsed with a sickening crack and his heart exploded under the massive force. Leviticus contemptuously picked up the carcass and hurled it into the distance and just out of sight.

Before I could process the grotesque display of barbarism before me, a deafening roar brought a powerful vortex. Leviticus, The Muse, and I had one quick second to see the terrified bewilderment in each other's eyes before being savagely sucked into and flung across the desert sky.

"Shiiiiiiiittttttttttttt!" I heard Genius howl as we all tumbled helplessly through the shattered gate. She knew then that the Seraph literally was The GateKeeper—the closer he was to the gate, the stronger it was. And seeing as how he was dead and far away, at least for a few minutes, the portal had been obliterated.

At that precise moment, she was thinking about the gate's ingenious design and the beauty of the engineering. I was thinking about how much it was going to hurt when we landed, and where the hell the yellow sun went.

THE BAD

(MOST ASSUREDLY)

Broke on Through to the Other Side

In the midst of flailing through something that resembled the sky, I saw fields of undulating human shadows in the gray desert valley below. Since it was obvious we would soon crash unceremoniously down to earth, I hoped that the shadows were really big, fluffy black pillows. Perhaps a bean-bag farm. If I was going to drop from this colorless grayscape-recess of God's mind, what would be the problem with a comfortable landing? Or maybe I could maneuver Leviticus between me and the ground; he was big enough to break my fall, and it's not like I cared about his ribs that my fall would break. In the end, however, I didn't land on God's Wrath, and the shadows with which I inelegantly collided weren't comfy bed accoutrements. They were two stoners.

"Ahhhh! What the fuck, man! Why the fuck are people rainin' down on me?"

I collected my thoughts and disentangled myself from the two specters that were unwittingly kind enough to stop my fall. A cursory physical inventory revealed that contrary to all known probabilities, I might have survived the fall relatively unscathed; even the stoners seemed unharmed. If you ever find yourself plummeting from the upper regions of the stratosphere, land on a stoner.

The others had landed nearby and were making their way toward me. Still listening to the two frightened and possibly inebriated shadows, I realized that while I was unbroken, I couldn't say the same for their treatment of the English language or the morbid surroundings, for that matter. They were clearly human. Or at least they looked and acted like humans. Mostly. They were like everything else in that place—a contorted form of something that wanted to be something else, that once was something else, and rightly still should be something else. The sky wasn't at all blue, but instead a bleak, diaphanous gray. Bushy apparitions that appeared to be chaparral and desert grasses were anything but. Mountains that on the other side of the gate stood timeless in fiery ochre had been co-opted by a color-blind palette—sterile white, thick black, and depressing gray. Everything that should have color didn't, and everything that should be alive wasn't, or didn't appear so, anyway. Aside from myself and my companions, this place was a colorless bastardization of a world that wanted to be anything but what it was, but couldn't. Bereft of color. Hopeless and lifeless. And judging by

The GateKeeper's predicament, entirely inescapable.

The acrid wilderness and everything in it was like a shrouded yet acutely painful memory that you cannot extinguish. You might banish it to your subconscious, conceal it behind a lie, drown yourself in banalities, hide it in a bottle of scotch, or even deny its existence. But no matter how desperately you implore yourself to forget, you can never completely expunge the purulent gash from your mind. Neither can God.

My skin crawled as the stoners continued their anxious bickering. "I dunno, man, maybe shit's flyin' out of the sky for the same reason that you jus' went 'n shot me through the back of my fuckin' head!" answered the shadow-stoner in a strangely metallic voice, poking a gaping hole where the back of his head should have been. He picked himself up and shook the dust from his black clothes that weren't actually black and weren't really clothes.

"Dude! We've been through this like a million times already. I don't know why I shot you, and I don't have any fuckin' clue why people are fallin' on us from outta thin air!"

He kept ranting through dusty tears, "I dunno, I dunno! I don't even know why I shot myself. It's not like I wanted to give my car to some strange appear-out-of-nowhere man and kill myself in the middle of fuckin' New Mexico! Fuck man, who was that guy and how did he get in the back of the car? Why did I shoot us? Jesus this is messed up—this is freaky scary man. I don't want this trip!"

He swatted wildly at the air around his face, afraid and unable to comprehend the incomprehensible. "It's goddamned insane! It's fuckin' insane shit! Stop! Stop! It's insane's what it is."

"Actually," I interrupted, nodding at Genius and The Muse, "it's probably Insanity; he's kind of a coworker of ours." Sometimes he's almost a friend, but I didn't think it a good time to admit that. The three of us faced the confused and wasted apparitions, while Leviticus stared at a smoky dot on the horizon that I could barely see.

"That's what I just said, dude, it's insane!" He continued witless and terrified, "Who are you anyway? Do you know where the fuck we are? I jus' wanna go home, man."

The other one frantically talked over his friend, "How come you four Technicolor dudes just came flyin' through the sky?" Although I was aware of the fact that we were the lone bastions of color, I hadn't thought about how striking we must seem against the colorless backdrop.

As much as I tried to pay attention to the stoners, I struggled to hear them over a rapidly approaching metallic cacophony. A flock of eerie drapes shaped like people began to gather around us with curious fear and lamentations—people of all ages and predicaments—ruefully sucked of life, stripped of color and ultimately robbed of hope.

Except they weren't people; they endured a horrifying state between life and death, between living as people and existing as God's personified guilt. A toddler with what looked like a raw and large abscessed tumor bursting from the side of his neck wailed uncontrollably—an extended, ear-splitting, and miserable sob. He was wildly searching for parents he'd never see again and screamed more horribly when he realized we weren't them. Looking across the immense valley, I guessed that somewhere in this wasteland his mom and dad were helplessly looking for him, too; forever searching and never finding. Rusty iron shackles jangled languorously over the sand, pulled with great effort by the slaves that could never remove them when they were alive. A bulbous man with a bullwhip followed closely behind them. He had no interest in the whip or the slaves, other than to banish the memory that he ever owned either.

It was an ocean of nightmarish epiphanies. As far as I could see, there were interminable waves of groaning scars that would never, ever heal. Many had obvious grotesque physical wounds that shaped their shadows. Others, who looked otherwise normal, kept their trauma hidden internally within a deeper shadow. Nobody escaped misery here, it's what brought them.

Leviticus held the crowd at bay while we pried the stoners for information about their previous whereabouts, hopeful that if Insanity wrote their tragedy we'd be able to pick up the author's trail.

"Please," said Genius sympathetically, "You said you were in New Mexico when this happened, but we need to know when this happened."

"What?" the stoner replied like he'd misheard the question.

Genius asked again, undeterred and unable to decipher his confusion. "Not what, when. When did you shoot yourself in New Mexico?"

"What? What do you mean when?" He wasn't getting it. "It happened when it fuckin' happened, that's when!"

"When, not what!" bellowed Leviticus. "She said when!"

"What?" the poor kid said it again.

Leviticus roared and the ground began to rumble, "When! When! When! Not what! When! You ignorant son of a bitch."

"What!?!?" He shook his head as if it still hurt him, clearly not understanding this line of inquiry.

"Say 'what' one more time and this place'll be the last of your worries! Say it again and I'll torture you for a million years, I'll string you up by your own entrails, I'll—!"

"At sunset! It happened at sunset, I swear to God," his friend screamed. God's wrath took an angry step forward to carry out his threat, and I sighed at the thought of having to witness him string up innocents by their innards again. No matter how much he does it, I never get used to it.

"Leviticus!" The Muse yelled, placing herself between him and the pitiful shadow to stop the assault. "Please," she turned to face the young men, "we're trying to help. People come here from all sorts of places, but they also arrive from different times and dates. So please, tell me the last date and year you remember?"

"You've come to help us?" he implored abjectly.

The Muse looked at me, and I could see a thick veil of sorrow cover her eyes in the form of barely restrained tears. We knew these people were beyond our help, that we couldn't undo the wrongs that had been done. The Muse might have appeared to them as a bright ray of hope, but the hot coals sitting in her stomach painted a fresco of futility.

Swallowing her words with great difficulty, she whispered, "We've come to help." By leaving off "you" at the end of this sentence, The Muse had parsed her words just enough so that the guilt of a lie wouldn't join the guilt of agonizing impotence. It is a terrible thing to be helpless to the helpless, and it is doubly so when you must tell them this to their faces.

"1978," one of the stoners said. "We live in Arizona and were drivin' to Texas for a concert. I don't think we'd been in New Mexico very long, probably less 'n an hour. Both of us were really high, just enjoyin' the ride, you know. Then for no reason my skin began to crawl and itch, like from the inside. My brain felt like it had little worms inside tryin' to eat their way out. Then this guy just appeared in the backseat—I don't remember picking him up or anything like that or how he got there—an' he started talkin' an' we just did what he said. We couldn' stop ourselves. It was like we had to do whatever he said, you know?"

The Muse nodded empathetically, and he continued in controlled desperation. I thought about his fear and the sorrow of the others pleading for help. All together it was the tortured and baleful whimpering that accompanies misery. And when I considered the depth of the hurt and suffering, a wave of nearly debilitating panic struck me deep in the gut. In some way I realized at that moment why God kept these injustices and tragedies safely locked away in a nearly unreachable memory. Hell is well-hidden and firmly ensconced as a state of God's mind.

"The next thing we know, we're here in this place," he sighed heavily.

"Isn't it 1978?" a histrionic voice screeched from directly behind the stoners. "What do you mean it isn't 1978? How can it not be? I don't recognize this place or understand how it cannot be 1978. I don't follow any of this. Please help me. I can't find my children. I looked everywhere and can't find them! I have to find them, please help me find my children!"

"Ms., please just hold on for a second," The Muse instructed patiently. We were all fully aware that we couldn't respond to everybody, and we had a good lead regarding Insanity from the Arizona stoners. But the hysterical woman wouldn't wait, and she continued between shuddering cries.

"But this looks sort of like home except it's a different color, or without color. I don't know how I got here! I don't belong here. It has to be 1978 and this is Utah and I have a husband with three sister-wives, and eighteen beautiful children and my husband didn't take the older ones to follow that charlatan who came and ruined our town. I have to wake up, to wake up now! Wake the others up, too!" She put her wretched arms out and begged The Muse, "Please stop this dream. Please! If I can just wake up, my children and husband will be home again!" She kept wailing, and soon the crowd joined the sorrowful refrain so loudly that I could hardly make out what she was saying.

"Shut up!" Leviticus roared, causing the earth to tremble violently and stunning everyone into a petrified silence.

Genius, as is usually the case, had seen the fish for the scales, and addressed the disconsolate polygamous woman, "I'm going to ask you a few questions that I need answered as best as you can. They may not make sense to you, and you will probably wonder why I'm even asking such strange things. It's okay to feel that way, but I don't really have time to explain everything right now. Please, I need you to think clearly, and to calm down so that I can help." The woman stared at her expectantly. "First, how long have you been here in this colorless place?"

"In this dream?" she sputtered.

Genius cleared her throat and decided to play along, "Yes, in this dream."

"I don't think I've been here very long. I cannot keep track of the days here. The light never changes, and I cannot tell night from day."

"As best as you can recall," Genius tried to be patient, "what was happening right before you came here?"

"I remember falling into a rocky gulch in the desert a mile or so behind our ranch house. The young children had just gone to sleep when I went off to try to find the others. It seems like just an hour ago."

"What month was it when you went into the desert?" Genius asked.

The woman thought about it for a moment before replying, "August."

Genius turned to the stoners, pointing without pointing, "You, the two Arizona boys, what is the last month you remember?"

"July," they responded in unison.

"Okay," Genius again turned to the woman, "please bear with me, Miss, and tell me where you were when you went into the desert."

"At home." This question confused her greatly.

"Okay, that's not quite what I meant." Genius shook her head. "Where is your home?"

"My home is on my street." She was trying to answer, but Genius wasn't exactly clear with her questions.

Leviticus had enough, "Good God, woman!" The Muse cut him off with a look that presaged a stiff jab to his ribs.

"Please, in what city is your house?" continued Genius, annoyed but undeterred.

"Monticello, Utah," she said.

I thought that Monticello was Thomas Jefferson's plantation in Virginia. Geography's not my strong suit. "Do you know where that is?" I asked Genius.

"Yeah, south-central Utah," she answered, "not too far from Canyon-lands and Arches national parks, realizing that 'not too far' out West is nothing like 'actually near.' By the looks of it, over a month or two, Insanity took the stoners' car, drove west on Interstate 10 into Arizona, then made his way north on U.S. Route 191 into the middle of the Colorado Plateau. If we get out of here quickly, we might be able to catch up with him in that area."

"But we don't really know where he is at this moment, do we?" The Muse pressed. "He could already have left Utah or 1978, for that matter."

"True, I suppose," admitted Genius. "Maybe he's in Colorado or Wyoming or some other time and place altogether. But he's been there long enough that hopefully we can just follow the oddities, and if we're lucky, we'll find him or his trail. I don't know that we have any better options right now. Plus, it appears like he's gathering people or followers of some sort and that doesn't sound like he's going anywhere on the quick." I thought of the hysterical woman's husband and children, haplessly doing Insanity's bidding. This would not end well for them.

"Why followers?" demanded Leviticus with oddly timed truculence. He had been staring so intently toward the horizon that I didn't think he was paying attention to our conversation. "What does he need people for? Is he going to build an army or something?"

"Who knows? He probably needs them to make his sandwiches," I answered in complete seriousness, thinking back on how difficult it was for us to find a good one in Jerusalem.

"What did you say?" he blared like a convoluted trombone. "Did you just say sandwiches?"

"You know him," I said, exasperated with Leviticus's bellicose attitude. "He'll do just about anything for some good sandwiches and beer. Well, provided that doing anything doesn't mean actually doing something."

"What are you talking about?" Genius looked at me.

"It's not like he ever makes a sandwich himself." I went on, knowing that I was onto something. "Hell, he can't even think about putting one together without getting mayonnaise all over himself or open a beer without the head blowing up in his face. He loses half his beer every time and throws a fit! You've seen it! A good sandwich is too structured and ordered for him to prepare; it's beyond his powers of comprehension—it would be like a bird designing a birdfeeder."

Leviticus's expression had changed from anger to disbelief. "Look here," he barked, "aside from a couple of accidents, we've kept him shackled longer than any of us can remember. You know how much he hates and detests that. He wants revenge, and I'd bet he's building an army right now to march on us!" He quivered with disgust as he continued, showering us with spit as he choked on his words, "Most likely homosexual shellfish eaters, too!"

"Gay lobsters? That's a bit much." Even now I took the opportunity to mock him. For the life of me, I cannot understand what he and his brother have against shellfish. "So not only do you hate gay people, but you hate straight ones who eat gay crustaceans?"

"Fuck you," he shot back.

"I'm serious about the sandwiches," I said again. "Genius, Muse, you both work with him a lot, too, and know it's true. Ten-to-one says he's sitting somewhere having lackeys fan him while he nibbles on a Reuben and downs a perfectly poured beer. A sandwich may not even have been his initial goal, but once he got hungry I bet that's what happened. Sandwiches, mark my words."

"So, what?" Genius asked, incredulously. "The end of the world is *rye*?"

"I don't know," I continued. "But it's not like he wants power or money or anything that we would think makes sense. Nor is it like he wants to torture people until they go insane—they just get in his way. Logic and reason won't give you answers here. He didn't care one whiff whether those stoners shot each other or went bat-shit crazy, he just wanted their car and that was the quickest route he knew."

"Quickest route to a snack?" Genius shook her head. "I don't know, what do you think, Muse?"

"It's possible, I suppose, even if far-fetched. To tell the truth, I've never been able to figure out what makes that guy tick—and believe me I've spent centuries trying. But I agree with Contradiction that he's probably not deep enough for organized retribution. I guess we'll find out when we get there."

"I don't give a damn if Contradiction is right or not about sandwiches," railed Leviticus, "we've got to follow Insanity's trail either way. Whether he's scarfing hoagies while downing ale on Cleopatra's barge or jerking off on a cheeseburger in a highway rest stop, I'm going to bash that bastard's brains in and—"

He stopped mid-sentence, and turned to face a thunderous buzz saw from a ball of smoke racing toward us across the desert floor. It was the same dark blotch that he was staring at earlier, but none of us had noticed its approach until it came within earshot.

While the four of us gawked at the billowing cloud as it neared, the shadow-people scattered to the surrounding hills—they disappeared in a flash. What had just been a sea of personified sorrow was now an empty dry lake bed, and we were a solitary bull's eye of color for a dark and ominously roiling missile.

"What is that?" I asked Genius.

"Something or someone is coming, and quickly. Maybe it's the Depraved Seraph," she said.

The Muse broke in, "Well, the shadow-people know what it is, and they lit out fast. I think we should do the same." She shuddered, "This doesn't feel right."

Leviticus popped his knuckles, stretched his neck, and aggressively yelled, "Let him come! I kicked the shit out of his omnibenevolent twin and wouldn't mind going two-for-two."

"Let's go back to Foresters and Lager Heads," said The Muse, "the sooner the better." Genius reminded her tersely that we had to get to the other side of the portal before we could go anywhere.

I looked toward Elephant Rock and figured that it was at least a couple miles away. "I don't think we can get there before that thing—whatever it is—gets to us," I told them just above the impending apocalyptic clamor.

"Bring it on," growled Leviticus.

The ground rumbled underneath three dark shapes racing just in front of the cloud, causing it, in fact. Their stampede churned the dry earth, spitting it up behind them in hellish, fuming arrogance.

"Horses," Leviticus spat. "They're horses, but I can't make out the riders."

As they closed the distance, I saw three magnificent stallions, the first an unblemished white, the second midnight black, and the third fiery red.

"The Horsemen of the Apocalypse?" Leviticus shouted incredulously. "Hah! I thought the Book of Revelation was a legend! Didn't you?" He looked at us, "Oh yeah, this is going to be one hell of a fight. Are you all ready for a fracas of seriously biblical proportions?" He flexed his muscles and the veins popped out of his forearms and, more grotesquely, across his temples.

"Revelation isn't truth and it's not exactly a legend, either," Genius shouted to be heard over the thundering three-horse herd. "It's one of John's crazy hallucinations—craziest, in fact. Jesus told me that he let Insanity too close to John and that he was completely incoherent for months. The Christ was stunned when they included that fantastic gibberish at the end of his life's work, he felt it controverted the message of the rest of the book. Insanity thought it a masterpiece, though. I think he has an original copy."

"So there's no Apocalypse as written in Revelation?" I yelled.

"Of course not, don't be daft," she continued, "it's absolute rubbish. Think about it, seven hills, Babylon, Rome! It's John's delirious phantasmagoria of Rome's downfall overlaid with a standard, if incredibly bizarre, final judgment/end of the world fable."

"But those are the Four Horsemen, coming right at us," Leviticus shot back. "Seems to me like the Revelation is about to be revealed."

Pointing at them as she spoke, The Muse said, "For what it's worth, it looks like there are only three. Anyway, like many legends and myths and religious stories, some of the characters and places are real or at least marginally sprinkled with the factual."

She had a point. The existence in fact of some people, places, and occurrences doesn't add a bit of proof for the fantastic predictions and wild claims people make about them. Evidence that Jesus was born in Nazareth and had a ministry in Galilee does absolutely nothing to confirm his divinity as God's son—zip. Yet, dogma-driven zealots make that incredible conclusion all the time! People should not mistake a myth or legend or parable's fragmental truth for its actual occurrence. The inability to grasp a parable for what it really is usually indicates an inability to comprehend the message it's trying to convey. It's like Leviticus's boy Jonah. Sure, he actually existed, we all knew him—and we also know full well that he was no more swallowed by a whale or "great fish" than any of us. He's not fucking Gepetto.

"Revelation-type Apocalypse or not," I told them as I looked at the oncoming riders, "this is going to be interesting."

The wicked, frothing beasts stopped about fifty yards away and were quickly overtaken and enshrouded by their own dust cloud. I heard metallic jangling when their boots hit the ground as the Horsemen dismounted. A creepy breeze cleared the air as they walked toward us, removing a physical cloak from the scene and replacing it with a sinister preternatural aura.

The Horsemen said nothing as they coolly advanced in straight lines from their muscular mounts, the man in the middle confidently a few paces ahead of his companions. The red and black horses to the left and right mirrored their masters and stood one length behind the magnificent white steed between them. Their saddles were of beautiful, worn black leather with faded platinum buckles inlaid with an intricate archaic lettering.

The imposing, muscular Horsemen were completely adorned in black. Heavy black motorcycle boots, wide black belts, fitted black T-shirts, all covered by immaculate black dusters with long, draped hoods. In fact, in almost every way, their dress was indistinguishable, except for their brilliant platinum belt buckles.

The man on the left with the red horse wore a seven-inch broad sword for his buckle, its handle elaborately encrusted with ruby roses that formed opposing crucifixes. It proclaimed that power had been given to him to take peace from the Earth and declared that his name was War.

The man on the right who rode the black horse wore gleaming daedal balancing scales for his buckle. Ghastly diamond skulls gnawed on platinum chafes of wheat, smiling ghoulishly from each balance pan. This proclaimed that power had been given to him to rob the Earth of nourishment and declared that his name was Famine.

The lead Horseman with the white stallion wore an ingeniously intertwined crown and archer's bow for his buckle. They were twisted in such stunning impossibility that you had to stare to make sure the design was real. This dazzling clasp proclaimed his given power to conquer and declared that his name was The Antichrist. With the exception of The Muse, he was the most beautiful creature I had ever seen.

We had all read chapter six of the Book of Revelation, but none of us was prepared for the overwhelming dominance these charismatically sinister men exuded. They were born into existence fully confident of their divine, unmatchable, and immeasurable strength. Fear was a disdained and entirely foreign concept. A shield of reverence for their power filled the air before them and hit me like a hot gust of wind. Even Leviticus felt their commanding presence, and in that instant his eyes betrayed him, providing The Antichrist with the initiative.

"You've done me quite the favor, Leviticus," he indicated toward the open portal and spoke in a sublime voice. Although I knew he was only talking, the sound I heard was pure song. "I'd be remiss if I didn't stop and offer you my most sincere appreciation. And since I'm nothing if not a mannered man, I'll do you a favor in return—"

"I'm not letting you give me shit, you fucking roach!" snorted Leviticus, cutting off The Antichrist.

If the coarse insult stung, he didn't show it. He merely smiled and waved his hand dismissively. "I should have thought as much. Genius, Muse, Contradiction, I suggest you take my advice and leave quickly."

"Why would you do us any favors?" I asked, not swayed by what I took to be his mock manners and faux attempts at reciprocity.

At first he ignored my question, shrugged his shoulders, and made his way with the other two back toward their mounts.

"You're not going anywhere," Leviticus howled. "You'll go through that seal and get into the world over my dead body." He didn't want to be responsible for letting the Horsemen get into the world, and he was practically salivating at the thought of fighting them. His eyes were fireballs and his fists stood at the ready to call forth a fierce barrage of lightning.

The Antichrist stopped and calmly turned to face us again. "First, Contradiction, I offer you a favor because there's naturally something in it for me. Ask Genius, she'll figure it out soon enough. Or ask The Gate-Keeper if you get out. Rest assured, however, that your instincts regarding my selfishness are entirely correct. Second, I needn't trample over your dead body, Leviticus, or really even give it much of a thought," he raised an eyebrow at War, "when it's so far from my path!"

The look of surprised anger hadn't even fully formed on Leviticus's face before War ran him through the chest with an enormous, serrated, double-edged broadsword, lifting him completely off the ground and twisting the sharp blade through his ribs to inflict the maximum possible pain. Leviticus stared blankly forward, and his mouth poured blood onto the sword that his arms feebly tried to extricate. For a few seconds, War triumphantly held his trophy high in the air like a bloody piece of skewered meat. With a guttural cry, he kicked him off the sword, sending him tumbling and spraying blood one hundred yards through the sky before he came crashing back down to earth with a sickening thud. War stared at us while he took a black handkerchief from his coat and wiped the blood off his sword.

"And with that, I bid you a good day," sung The Antichrist, bowing, before he and his henchmen mounted their hell-horses and rode headlong toward the open gate.

Genius and The Muse hurried to the mangled and twisted pile of crumpled flesh that just a moment ago had been Leviticus. I stood with my mouth impossibly agape, unable to move and utterly in shock to have seen God's Wrath thoroughly bested, and so quickly at that!

I watched powerlessly as the riders neared the portal, and then gawked at the wreckage that was Leviticus. I might have kept staring, unable to move, but a flashing apparition suddenly appeared at my feet and stole my attention as well as my gaze.

A dark-skinned woman with dreadlocks lay on her back, convulsing and coughing. She wore a loose, orange and purple floral dress that blinked black and white, flickering between the color of her previous world and the lifeless sterility of this one. The length of time between flickers grew and her color waned. Her terrified eyes looked at the black spittle shooting from her pursed lips. She was dying, painfully and unexpectedly.

"Please, call 911! Hurry," she coughed at somebody in the other world, apparently unable to see me, or unwilling to give in to death.

"Mommy, we called, they're on their way!" a terrified little girl's voice cried. "Daddy's coming, too. Please don't die! Don't die, Mommy!" I found it strange to hear the child's sobbing through the void, but I was too taken with the sorrow of the scene to give it much thought.

"I love you so much," the woman cried and reached out to hug her daughter that I couldn't see; from my perspective in God's guilty conscience, her arms appeared empty. "I love you so much," she repeated and sobbed, her breath getting shorter and shallower with each plea.

"Mommy!" her daughter shouted. "Mommy!"

Her mother's spasms abruptly stopped as her body succumbed to the inevitable, and she gently caressed the space where her daughter's face must have been. "I love you, don't you ever forget that, Alexandra. Promise me. Promise me you'll never forget how much I love you."

"I promise, I promise, Mommy," Alexandra wept furiously. Her mother took another painful breath, looked up and saw me for the first time, her eyes wide with calm resolution. "I can see the other side, it's okay, it's okay, Alexandra. There's an angel above me, it's okay. Tell your father I saw the angels, Alexandra. I see an angel."

"I'll tell him Mommy, I'll tell him," her daughter wailed.

She heaved one final, wheezing breath. "I love you so much, I love you, Alexandra." And then she lost all her color and lay motionless. Dead in her world and unconscious here.

"Mommy! No, no, no, Mommy, you can't leave, the ambulance is here with Daddy!" the child shrieked. Although I couldn't see her, somewhere a little girl had just watched her mother die a horrible death. I bowed my head in reverence to her misery, to her unimaginable sorrow.

While looking at the woman at my feet, I jumped as a child's caramel colored hand somehow injected itself into the scene and grabbed her mother's arm, shaking it violently—it appeared disembodied, only the arm came through to the Valley of Fire. "Mommy, I can take you, I can take you! I won't let you go! Don't stay there! Take my hand!" she screamed and pulled, but the girl was powerless to pull her mother back.

Someone took her away, and her hand disappeared, but I could still hear her haunting lament: "No! No! I can't leave her! I can't leave her! Let go, Daddy, I can't leave her—it's so dark there! Can't you see? Daddy! Daddy, I couldn't help her, I couldn't stop it, Daddy."

I listened to her crying, wondering what her father could possibly say to console her at that moment, grief stricken as he must have been himself. Her voice trailed off and I was glad the scene was over. But I felt ashamed and dirty, and wanted to be gone before this woman awoke to another nightmare.

This was a lot for me to absorb. I needed to round up the other three and get the hell out of there before things went from worse to worst. As I spun around to face the others, I could see, however, that "worst" was in fact on his way, and Hell followed with him.

"We need to go, now!" I yelled as I frantically ran to them. "There's another rider on the horizon! There's another horseman coming!" I stopped right behind The Muse, almost plowing over her as she crouched close to Leviticus's crumpled and broken body, which, much to my surprise, sat up and shouted.

"What fucking color is it?"

"Leviticus!" I shouted. "What the hell? You scared the bejesus out of me! You can't be alive yet, not after that!" There was no way he had recovered already from such a savage slaughter; it should have taken an hour at least just for his heart to start pumping again!

"God damn it," he hollered with indignant viciousness, "what fucking color is the goddamned horse?"

"You don't look so good," I stammered. It was all I could think to say. I mean, I knew he asked me something about a horse, but it's hard to really listen to what somebody's saying when that somebody is a seven-foot, three hundred-pound volcano with a writhing heap of boney ground beef where his chest should be.

Genius and The Muse stood up and scanned the valley for the new rider while I reluctantly swallowed the vomit that had found its way up to the back of my throat.

"He missed my heart, you idiot!" Leviticus coughed as he stood up, wobbly but generally stable. "I saw War's sword coming and moved, not fast enough to avoid his attack, but quick enough that I made him miss his intended target."

"I think the horse is kind of a pale, off-white color," said Genius as she turned to face us, "and there's something floating in the air above the sickly beast. It looks like the Horseman is just hovering and not actually riding. Either way, it's moving steady and quick, but not nearly as fast as the other three."

The Muse motioned to Leviticus's hideous wounds, "I think Genius, Contradiction, and I can make it to the Gate before he overtakes us, but I'm concerned about you. Do you think you can run?"

"I don't run," he belched through bloody slobber that his quivering mouth couldn't expectorate quickly enough. "I have decimated the strongest armies and obliterated entire civilizations." His attitude had obviously survived War's onslaught unscathed and his arrogant posture belied his severely wounded health. "I left The Crimson Seraph a mutilated mess, and would have defeated War, too, if he hadn't run away."

"Leviticus!" I shouted. "He absolutely clobber-slaughtered you! He kicked your ass halfway through Hell and you're lucky he didn't do worse!"

"His upstart arrogance would have been his undoing. He would have thought me dead, and I'd have played possum, and then beat him into oblivion as soon as he came within reach."

"Let's go," Genius interrupted, pulling his shirt for emphasis. "Now."

"How do we know the fourth Horseman just won't speed up and catch us?" I asked the logical question as Leviticus gruffly pulled away from Genius's ineffectual grasp.

"We'll have to take that chance, because I don't want to wait around to meet and ask him," Genius answered.

"I told you I'm not going anywhere! I've had enough with this shit! These insignificant neophytes need to learn some respect, and it starts now!" He couldn't be serious!

I nervously looked at the rider and back at Leviticus. Then my neck snapped back toward the pale horse and the freakish apparition suspended a few feet above it! While it was still maybe a quarter to half mile away, even at that distance I could see a mangled tree in the distinctly recognizable shape of an upside-down cross! This gruesome, gnarled crucifix had to be forty feet from top to bottom, and perhaps thirty feet wide. We all stared, temporarily paralyzed by the surreal monstrosity coming our way. Genius thought of impending death; The Muse was reminded of Dali; and I thought of cream cheese and steamed clams and American pale ales and lots of other innocuous vittles that took my mind off the approaching arboreal abomination.

But Leviticus was the beneficiary of superior eyesight, and he saw quite clearly what we saw only as a blur. "It's the Seraph's twin," he said evenly. "He's hanging upside-down from a misshapen, contorted, bristlecone cross. It's hard to see him though, because it doesn't look like he reflects light. It's rather akin to looking into a black hole. You can only make out the shape by looking at the contextual material that surrounds it." I could see the wheels spinning in his otherwise Precambrian intellect. He kept staring as he continued, "It's odd to look upon him— almost disconcerting—if that's how you describe this feeling. I think his form feeds off my mere observance of it."

"Is the horse wearing a silver saddle?" I asked as I squinted to get a better look. "I've never seen a metal saddle before. Talk about saddle sore."

"That's not silver," Leviticus said. "The Horseman appears to be bleeding quicksilver from a chain embedded in his head that's slowly dripping onto the horse's saddle. It's like a barbed-wire crown is gnawing into where his skin must be."

I thought back on my conversation with God about Jesus's time on the cross and shuddered. "Genius is right. Let's go."

"Suit yourselves. I'm staying right here," growled Leviticus.

Genius had had enough, "Leviticus, you can't beat him! And even if you do, The GateKeeper will reawaken soon, and there's no guarantee that he'll open the gate to let us out!"

The Muse gently took Leviticus's hands and impressed upon him that even if he won, we all might lose. He was unmoved. "I won't stop you cowards from leaving, and you're not about to stop me from staying," he remarked coldly, jerking his hands free and smacking his fists together.

"Let's go," Genius exclaimed as she, The Muse, and I moved toward the gate.

"I'm not going," he replied icily.

"Well, we are," she shot back.

"Good riddance, ignoble and craven cowards," he spat.

"You stubborn bastard," she yelled over her shoulder as we sprinted for the seal. "Do me a favor and read a good tragedy before I see you next; I'd suggest *Oedipus* or *Coriolanus*."

"You'll thank me soon enough," his voice trailed off as we put him behind us.

The three of us had run almost to Elephant Rock, tripping over shadowy tumble weeds and panting wildly. Suddenly, the sky behind us cracked an ear-splitting, infuriated display of voltaic force.

"Didn't Oedipus and Coriolanus die?" I asked Genius while I watched Leviticus hurl fireballs at the fourth horseman, who was called Death.

"Yes," she replied, gasping for breath, while Leviticus's fiery missiles fell harmlessly into the shadow of Death, "they did." As we approached the gate, the ground heaved and the air spewed sulfuric sparks in every direction.

When we reached the safety of Elephant Rock, The Muse dove headfirst through the seal without stopping to make sure it was still open. Luckily, it was. Genius and I pulled up and turned back toward the ongoing battle.

"I won't watch him destroy himself," Genius's low whisper gave her emotions away. I hardly turned as she despondently passed through the portal to another world.

The combat raged below, and the explosions provided the only color against the otherwise funereal achromatism. Death had righted himself in his gory magnificence and pushed Leviticus further back and closer to the gate and myself—so much so that I could now see that Death's feathery wings were a million obsidian blades slashing back and forth. He was much taller than his twin and twice as imposing. Towering at least twenty feet above his pallid and miserable mount, he resembled nothing less than a nightmarishly demonic locust. Devoid of eyes or countenance and frighteningly bereft of sympathy, he maintained a steady advance and merely guffawed as Leviticus's attacks careened futilely into his abyss.

Death straightened to his full height and grandiosely unfurled all six of his butchering wings in a hellish display that ensnared its prey in a convulsing shadow of evisceration. Leviticus quit his feckless assault, and his expression turned from twisted vitriol to epiphanic resignation. For the first time in an ageless life, he felt the fear he had brazenly inflicted on his hapless victims—fear that he was going to be unceremoniously vanquished and fear on top of that fear that he was entirely incapable of doing anything about it.

"Contradiction!" he yelled, attempting to run toward me and the gate, but he didn't take more than two steps. The last two he'd ever make. The whites of his wide eyes seared my petrified psyche as six slicing and gashing evil wings enveloped him. Leviticus howled in protest, but his scream was quickly muffled by the heavy, swooshing shears.

Death pulled his menacing wings close toward his body, then let them fly loose again; Leviticus wasn't there—he had been swallowed by the void. There should have been a bloody mess on the ground or something to reanimate; it's not like we can actually die (or so I thought). But there was no trace of him. He was gone, and although I didn't have any idea how it happened, I had no doubt about its permanency. He'd been erased.

Death's grim shadow rose triumphantly into the sky, casting its pallor directly over me, and an immobilizing fear transfixed my feet firmly in opposition to my brain's desire for them to fly through the portal. "I am about to die," I thought, as a living nightmare began to envelop me. Closing my eyes, I waited for the inevitable, when a strong hand unexpectedly clutched my shoulder and yanked me quickly across the threshold, which snapped shut as soon as I was though. Against all probability, I was safely on the other side.

"Hey! Commander Mike, what are you doing here?" I said to the Archangel Michael, who had rescued me but looked like he did so with a great deal of reluctance. He and Uriel glared at me disapprovingly, with Genius and The Muse at their side. The Omnibenevolent GateKeeper glared through the closed transparent seal at his vacant, demonic, and equally incensed opposite twin.

You've Got Some Explaining to do

The Muse put her hand on my shoulder and asked if I was all right while Genius helped me to my feet. I checked myself for any damage and patted the metallic dust off my singed clothes. I don't think I was harmed, at least not physically, I told them. I squinted to adjust my eyes to the bright colors—the Mojave is kaleidoscopic compared to dichromatic Hell—and my eyes burned.

"I think Leviticus is gone," I quietly said. "Death slashed him into a million pieces and there's nothing left to put back together or reanimate. He's just not there, and he didn't leave a trail anywhere either, at least not that I saw. I couldn't even move. Death casts a paralytic aura about him." Genius and The Muse said they tried to help me but that they had also been frozen. Looking at Death is like being the wallpaper in Poe's *The Raven*. You're stuck, glued in place, and powerless to avert your gaze. Since Michael and Uriel hadn't been on the other side, they were unaffected. They arrived just in time.

"We could see everything, though," Genius whispered. Her demeanor bore a melancholy acquiescence. In a strange way, Genius was close to Leviticus, certainly closer than me, and generally would play it off when I asked her about it. I think now, however, that the freakish mania with which he defended the senseless fascinated her rigidly structured logic. He was like an intellectually wild beast for the taming; the inanity of hating people for eating shellfish, for example, vexed her to no end and would satiate her curiosity for centuries at a time. She loved him, in her own way.

The GateKeeper cursed and kicked the dusty ground, sending a confused beetle hurling toward a hungry lizard. He was frustrated, but I was so shaken that I confronted him, "Did you know we're not immune to Death? You saw that, right? Did you know that Death can just ... just erase us entirely?"

"Of course," he responded.

"And you didn't bother to inform us?" I said. "Even though you knew we'd meet the only person capable of actualizing such a fate?"

"I told you not to go through the seal," he answered. "And if you had heeded my instructions, you wouldn't have needed to know." It was pretty hard to argue with that logic, so I sensibly let it go. Our foolishness had cost us dearly.

Genius may have known the answer to her next question, but she proffered it anyway. "Then it's true that Leviticus is completely gone?"

The GateKeeper, while still angry, hadn't lost sight of who he was, and was empathetic as he explained, "All that exists is a thought of God's, including ourselves. As such, we are all subject to God's perception. Although our existence is epistemically very different than a human's, it is nonetheless predicated upon God. In other words, we cease to be when God wills it so—Leviticus's time was at an end. There is nothing we can do to change this course of events."

All of this was new to me and I was agitated, so I asked him crudely, "God just up and says 'fuck it, I'm through, no more Leviticus'?"

"In a more polite manner of speaking, yes," he said. "Death exterminates everything it can. But remember, God has backup plans in Deuteronomy."

"Can God reconsider?" I wondered.

"God can do anything," the Seraph responded kindly, realizing that in my exuberance I'd forgotten the obvious. We sat quietly for a few minutes, alone with our thoughts, awkwardly avoiding each other's direct gaze but craving each other's presence at the same time.

I felt depressed and dirty, and wanted to rid myself of the feeling, so I tried to change the subject away from my mortality and Leviticus's death. I asked the Seraph, "If Death is God's eradicator, then why would he tolerate all the company in Hell? We saw all sorts of people—we even talked with them."

He seemed happy for the deflection. "In the Valley of Fire, they exist only as a shadow; they are God's painful memory of injustice and the world's evil. They do not actually exist in that Hell in the way we think of existence. It is not a place for them, it is God's remembrance of their pain that God allowed them to endure. They may exist in Heaven, or in a happier place somewhere. Maybe reincarnated. I really don't know."

"So Death cannot kill them because they don't physically exist?" I asked him.

"Correct," he answered, "and it drives him crazy, too, that he has to share his eternal detention center with constant reminders of what he cannot change, cannot alter, and is powerless to expunge. Rest assured, however, that could he escape his prison, he'd wipe out anything and everything that currently is, ever was, or will be."

"Then why doesn't he kill the other three Horsemen?" asked The Muse. "They weren't specter-people and presumably he could have wiped them out."

"True, he could have, but they have a purpose, and that purpose is to help Death achieve his ultimate goal of existence's annihilation."

"But aren't his goals different than theirs?" I thought aloud. "I mean, Revelation had the first three Horsemen wreaking all sorts of Old Testament havoc, and Death as you describe him would have no business with that."

Genius answered for The GateKeeper, "I see it now. You're right, Contradiction, in that the goals are different, but the Three are harbingers and necessary precedents to the Fourth. Their desires seem independent—and in a very real way they are—but they exist only as subsets of a coherent whole."

"So they're like Pawns to Death's King?" It was beginning to make sense.

"Not so much Pawns," replied The GateKeeper. "Famine and War are rooks and The Antichrist is the queen."

"I hate chess," I sighed.

"And this is the answer," Genius explained, "to your question about The Antichrist's motives: their purpose is to create famine and war and hate, and they require humanity to do this. To free Death is to destroy humanity, to destroy their playground. They were probably hoping this would happen, that we'd get out and shut the seal before Death could escape."

"Huh?" Sometimes I'm a little slow on the uptake.

"Put another way," said Uriel, "they have no interest in Death escaping. In the long run, they cannot realistically stop him, but they also chose not to help him directly."

"That doesn't seem to help Death achieve his plans," I noted.

"No honor among thieves, I suppose," Michael deadpanned. "Anyway, whether they want to assist Death or not is immaterial to the fact that they cannot help but to do so. The chaos and disorder they create in the outside world is intended by Death to open the gate. It's bait. Bait that Death hopes The GateKeeper will take to leave his post."

Uriel spoke and looked ready to leave. "Luckily, what Famine, War, and The Antichrist lack in thieves' honor they made up for in leaving a trail."

"Were you already here when they escaped? Did you see them?" The Muse asked.

"We got here just as they came through the seal." Uriel pursed her lips and turned her head.

"We only saw them long enough for Famine to flip us the bird." Michael finished her thought. "War just scowled." Turning, he admonished us brusquely, "Christ, you caused a lot of trouble. Why didn't you wait for us at Foresters and Lager Heads?"

"Why? What do you mean why?" I asked. I had direct instructions from the Supreme Being. "God told me to come here!"

"Did God tell you to go alone?" he sensibly replied. The Muse changed the subject and asked where the Horsemen went, and he told her that they went to 1978 on the Highway to Hell.

"Where's that?" I asked. It sounded like a roller coaster. Genius told us that it was the old Route 666 that starts in Gallup, New Mexico, and heads north to Monticello, Utah. In 2003 they changed the name to Route 491 to assuage the locals' concerns that numerical highway denotation is tantamount to approval of the number of the beast.

"They're after Insanity," I blurted in surprised recognition. "The Arizona Stoners and Monticello Polygamist wife were both from 1978, and it fits our guess to his trail perfectly!"

"The Horsemen could have known Insanity was on the loose," The Muse added, "and if what The GateKeeper says about their motives is true, then using him as their captive flunky would fit their designs exactly."

I thought about this for a moment and exclaimed, "They're good."

"Yes, they are," Uriel agreed, rubbing a little gritty sweat from her brow, "and Michael and I have to leave now to try and get to them before they do too much damage."

"Do you think you can stop them?" The Muse asked. After what they did to Leviticus, she shared my doubt.

"Probably," Uriel answered, "but we've got to hurry. Go back to the meeting and tell Raphael and Gabriel to meet us in 1978 on The Highway to Hell near Monticello. We'll need their help. And you three have to try to get to Insanity before the Horsemen of the Apocalypse get their hands on him."

"What do we do if we run into the Horsemen before you do?" I wondered, realizing that the only obstacles we'd present to them would be soft and pliable targets.

"Go back to the meeting, and fast," she replied. "Deuteronomy can help."

"And if they follow us? We've got to tell Deuteronomy about his brother, and he's unpredictable as it is. I don't want to have to rely on him right after such a shock. He hid in Assyria for a week when his dog died, and I figure now he'll be completely inconsolable."

"I don't think they'd risk an attack on Heaven's Gates for Insanity." Uriel leaned in and whispered something to Michael, and he nodded his head. "But if you're sure Deuteronomy is going to be out of commission, get Orrin Porter Rockwell, the Danite Chief."

"The Destroying Angel and Mormon avenger? The illiterate western outlaw and ruffian?" The Muse exclaimed as she folded her arms tightly around her chest. "You've got to be kidding! I mean, the Danites were a secret Mormon sect in the 1800s that believed so fervently in Joseph Smith's prophecies and the Book of Mormon that they committed all sorts of atrocities for him without so much as blinking an eye!"

"The Danites may have been misguided regarding the veracity of their theology," Michael retorted, "but you can't doubt the veracity of their tenacity. Don't be so hard on them. Look, I'll bet you don't know that the Danites formed in self-defense—Missouri Governor Lilburn Boggs issued what came to be known as an "extermination order" against the Mormons. And he practically refused to prosecute any of the numerous violent crimes committed against the Latter Day Saint settlers. In fact, he flat-out told people to take their property and possessions. It didn't take long for a few of the tougher sort to band together to fight back, which is exactly what you'd expect from hardy people of the frontier."

"But they killed innocent people and tortured their own flock when they threatened to go astray or reveal church secrets. They did Smith's and Brigham Young's dirty work; we all know it!" She was already torn up about Leviticus, embarrassed by the whole outcome of events, and didn't want to have to deal with another loose cannon.

Genius added her encyclopedic knowledge. "Both sides committed some admittedly dastardly acts, but in the end half the crimes attributed to them are unsubstantiated and baseless. Religious bigotry, mostly. They were neither as saintly as Mormon history would have us believe, nor are they as villainous as their reputation. As is often the case, the truth hides between the extremes."

"We can debate their morals for years, but that's not important right now," Michael said. "The Danites fight like wolverines, and they won't think twice about fighting dirty. Tell Porter that your instructions come from Joseph Smith and give him the second token of the Melchizedek Priesthood so he'll know who you are, and he probably won't ask too many questions."

"What the hell is a melkezdik priesthood token?" I asked, thinking it was some sort of coin used to operate skee ball and video games, or even proprietary laundromats.

Genius answered, "Mormons had all sorts of secret handshakes and rituals, most of which Joseph Smith pilfered directly from the Masons. Anyway, you clasp right hands and interlock little fingers, and place the index finger of the right hand on the underneath center of the other man's wrist. Oh, and it'll have to come from a man—no women in the Mormon Priesthood club—all that preaching might take blood from the uterus." She shook her head in disgust at the last comment.

I tried the handshake unsuccessfully with The Muse. I'm pretty sure if we kept it up, we'd either break our fingers or be married. Michael continued, "Old Port has been waiting for something like this to go down for years. In fact, even though he doesn't know it, it's why we've kept him around. Since you're going to Utah anyway, you should have him serve as your guide."

For my part, I didn't think this made a lick of sense. "War dispatched Leviticus like he was no more than a lethargic fly. And you're telling me that an ancient and delusional Mormon outlaw can hold them off?"

"Doesn't he think he's Samson or something like that?" asked The Muse.

"He is," chuckled Michael as he gave Uriel a knowing glance.

"What?" Genius, The Muse, and I responded at the same time.

"Well, it's not as if he's actually Samson," Uriel tried to clear things up. Still, the raised eyebrow that capped off her expression let us know that she thought the whole situation was, at the very least, a little bit funny. "We don't have time to give you all the details, we can't let the Horsemen get too far ahead of us, but Genius can fill you in about Porter."

"Where are we supposed to find him?" I asked.

"The Dead Goat Saloon, on West Temple Street in Salt Lake City. It's a couple blocks from the Mormon temple and is quite the local icon. You can't miss it. Don't ask for Porter Rockwell though; it's a safe bet that nobody will know who that is. Even if they've heard the name, there's no reason to associate it with the Dead Goat. He goes by the alias James Brown, and you'll probably find him behind the bar. He's owned the property for around one hundred years, but that's as secretive as his real name."

"When?" I asked. "What year should we go?"

"Um, around 2001 was the last time I definitively knew him to be there. So, perhaps 2000?"

"Go," commanded The GateKeeper, his voice tired and gruff.

As we left the Valley of Fire, The GateKeeper took his seat on a boulder and kicked the sand absently. Holding his weary head in his hands, he stared intently at absolutely nothing in particular; his frustration blurring out everything on the horizon. Everything, that is, except for a small, shaggy fuzz ball that appeared to loup effortlessly across the desert floor toward him.

"You want to play poker? Wovoka's on his way," Coyote chanced with a dumbly innocent affect, her tongue flopping wildly about her jowls. "It looks like you've got some extra time on your hands."

"Sometimes I really, really don't like you," he sighed and picked up the cards, "I'll deal."

LEST WE FORGET

Insanity didn't like his shackles, so he broke free. But freedom didn't really suit him either, so he started a religion in a sandwich shop. Because he could infect people's minds, he was used to people doing whatever he wanted, but this experience was entirely different. Once his flock believed he was their Prophet, the rest flowed naturally and they followed him almost entirely of their own accord. They unflinchingly did whatever he asked and believed anything he told them, no matter how crazy or absurd. They even started doing stupid stuff on their own, like organizing committees to fill the inevitable holes in Insanity's doctrine. They replaced their sorrow and panic from Monticello with enthusiasm and zeal.

Although this removed much of the fun, it also removed most of the work, Insanity thought as he munched on a sandwich and downed a beer atop his throne in the canyonlands, calmly enjoying the beauty of the desolate. At his sandwich man's advice, he established a base on Island in the Sky, a desert peninsula two thousand feet above the canyons of the Colorado and Green rivers at their confluence in eastern-central Utah. The cliffs below him fell a thousand feet to a tightly confined ledge about a quarter mile wide, and then another thousand feet to the rivers on either side. There were cliffs to the south, west, and east, and only a narrow isthmus of land connecting it to the northern highlands—like a desert Florida, with the Colorado and Green rivers as the Atlantic Ocean and Gulf of Mexico, respectively.

It was an excellent defensive redoubt from which he could see for miles in nearly every direction. Even better, there were only two roads in or out: a threadlike stretch of pavement from the north; and from the east, the Shafer Trail was little more than a one-lane dirt path carved into the side of an otherwise impenetrable cliff.

He looked down at the White Rim trail, a dirt road that ran along the slender ledge between Island in the Sky and the river canyons below. It provided access to the Shafer Trail and, since he lined the northern road with dynamite towers, the most consistent point of attack for the local authorities that had been trying to root him out. Upon arrival, Insanity toyed with local law enforcement and recently graduated to the National Guard. A detachment of clueless soldiers stirred up a column of dust as they approached.

Insanity gathered a specific group of well-armed zealots around his throne during these feckless assaults. Some were men, some were women, and some were children. All were now irrevocably insane, and all were good shots. "It's another group of those green guys. Those, what do you call them again?" he smacked a man to his right who he ordained St. Paul the Pockmarked.

"Army men. National Guard." St. Paul the Pockmarked was honored to be touched by the Prophet. "Skeet."

"Skeet? What's skeet?" Insanity asked but didn't wait for an answer. "Whatever. They're coming to take me away. That's bad for you. Shoot them."

"All of them?" a burly man asked evenly. He was middle-aged and had a thick beard without a mustache and intense, hate-filled eyes. He used to be clean cut. His eyes used to sparkle. He used to be the Mayor of Monticello.

"God hates you," Insanity replied, upset that they still had a hard time understanding what needed to be done in these situations. His acolytes' groupthink was good for getting things done, but it usually precluded any intelligent initiative on their behalf. Mindless followers do not provide thoughtful leadership. "Just the ones that are unarmed. The drivers and such."

"What about the others?" The erstwhile Mayor asked.

"We need their weapons. Weapons are always good, and they can't bring them to us if they're dead. You'd have to go down there and get them. You should thank me." They praised him in unison while Insanity beckoned for a man to fan away the heat of the morning sun. "Let them scale the cliffs. When they get to the top, I'll convert them. I'll keep their souls. Well, for God anyway, I actually don't care about them. Or you either, really. Come to think of it, I don't think God cares either. Seriously, I don't understand how you can face each new day of your pointless existences. I'd go crazy. All your lives are meaningless."

"Amen," the Mayor snapped to attention before leading his group to massacre the latest wave of National Guard troops called up to extricate the cult colony. "Our lives our meaningless, and it is only through obedience to our Prophet that we have meaning. Through the Prophet's thoughts we are perfected, through his deeds we are saved. Through him we know God's love." They lined up, took aim, and fired.

Brigham and his younger sister Verily were busy making sandwiches in an adobe hut about a mile north of the Prophet's throne when they heard the latest round of shots. They exchanged nervous glances, but so inured to the violent sounds had they become that they no longer jumped or even flinched. They realized people were dying, but they also knew that they couldn't do anything about it, so they ignored it as best as they could. The two discussed their miserable situation in their father's absence and could only come to the conclusion that they really didn't know why they couldn't go home. Nobody had ever given them a good answer. On more than one occasion, they'd tried to leave on their own, and found that despite their health and desire, their feet simply refused to carry them beyond the compound's threshold.

They missed their mothers and their siblings and each night knelt beside their bed-rolls and prayed to God that they would one day be reunited as a family. Brigham heard that one of their mothers died, but since he was unsure if it was true, he didn't tell his sister. He didn't think he'd tell her even if it was true—he wanted her to have that gleam of hope and would do nothing to take it away. It was all she had. Once, Brigham asked their father, who everybody now called The Sandwich Man, if they should go help their younger brother Lehi with the family business and the work on the ranch. His father replied tersely that God had separated them from their family, and that their lot was now with the Prophet. He told them that the Prophet delivered them unto the wilderness, and only their faith in the Prophet would deliver them from it.

Over the next few weeks, Insanity saw to it that the military repeated its miscues, and as a result his cult swelled with well-armed denizens. He had his freedom, a cadre of bodyguards, a personal brewmaster, and all the sandwiches he could eat. In effect, he had everything he thought he wanted. But he is insane, after all, so instead of enjoying the situation, he got bored. It was all too easy, too predictable. His flock was crazy enough now without his influence, and the National Guard never had posed a serious challenge. He missed his friends. Well, at least he missed the chase. He had put too much distance between himself and Jesus. Next time he'd leave a hotter trail.

"They should have been here by now," he murmured under his breath one morning while the sandwich man brought him his breakfast. The sun was just beginning to rise as he scanned the horizon and found, much to his pleasant surprise, a lone vehicle approaching from the east on the White Rim Trail. "There they are! They're here! They're here! Get everybody and their guns together; we need snipers on the ledge. Hurry!" he smiled and sang as he ordered the assault. "Snipers on the ledge!" He had to wait longer than he thought he would, but it was turning out just like he planned. Now he would watch his followers kill his friends, and then he would zap himself away.

In the middle of dancing a jig and ordering some sandwiches to go, a series of explosions robbed the smile from his face and replaced it with a fearful scowl.

"Somebody else is coming from the north. They've exploded the barricades," the Mayor shouted as he ran up to them.

Insanity felt a chill in his bones and immediately tried to zap himself out of there, but his body was frozen in his mind's fear and he remained on Island in the Sky. He glared awkwardly at Elmer, his sandwich man, and said, "Well, this isn't good."

THE UGLY

(MOST POSITIVELY ABSOLUTELY)

THREE THINGS WICKED THIS WAY COME

"Lehi! Please answer the door! Didn't you hear the doorbell?" Edna shouted to her oldest child who remained in the house, the words sounding as tired and desperate as she felt.

"Lehi, I'm tending to the baby. I know you're busy too, but please do as I ask." She knew he could hear her. With much effort and no help, she had just put the remaining children to bed, except her youngest, Nephi, whom she was stroking and nursing softly in a wooden rocking chair. The chubby infant wasn't biologically hers, neither was Lehi, but nobody had seen their mother, Sarah, since the night their sister-wife El-laDawn killed herself. The authorities considered her dead, and nobody saw any reason to disagree with that conclusion. That was right after her husband, Elmer, joined most of the city and took their older children and followed the strange man to Moab. So much had changed in that brief time, but she had too many children to look after to consider the enormity of the situation or even really consider Lehi's stark behavioral changes. She was too busy swimming for her life to ponder where the tidal wave came from.

"Lehi!" she pleaded again with the boy. But her formerly inquisitive, good-natured and outgoing thirteen-year-old son was busy at the kitchen table not paying attention to the lesson book he was supposed to be reading. His teachers had called earlier this week to tell Edna that he had been brusque in class and often simply refused to do his assignments; they said for the first time since they'd known him he didn't seem to care one whiff about his grades; he was there but wasn't there. At least that's what the message said. She couldn't answer the call because she had spent all day in town trying to get the family restaurant back and running again to bring in some sort of income. It's hard enough to make a living selling tacos, and even harder when the only people who really knew how to do it left.

If Lehi had lost interest in his studies, he showed even less an appetite for his casserole that night. Instead of devouring his favorite dish like he used to do, he made aimless designs in the crusted mashed potato topping and ate little more than a bite or two. He'd been losing weight and had even begun to look peaked and a bit gaunt. His exterior shell withered and disappeared as his interior shell grew. He hadn't just lost one mother, he'd lost two, and the funeral played over and over in his mind like a repeating chord in a song he couldn't force from his head. How was he supposed to act? Should he smile and pretend that this hadn't happened? It seemed everybody had their own ideas as to his behavior, and nearly everybody wanted to ignore its real causes. School? That didn't matter now. Surviving each minute without breaking down mattered. Putting one foot in front of the other, gingerly taking each new step in this world that had crushed him took all his effort.

Their comfortable ranch house sat alone at the end of a tree-lined, dirt driveway a few miles outside of town. The sky was starry and still that late summer night, and Lehi heard the roar of the approaching motorcycles die to a low, idling hum before they finally came to a gurgling stop at the front gate. The kitchen was near the front door, and he listened to the spurred boots jingle their way across the lawn before the doorbell rang.

But Lehi's motivation to greet the strangers was as gone as his mother, and nothing about the jangle of approaching spurs was about to change that. Lots of people had come to see his family recently, and although he tried his best most of the time to be polite, he didn't involve himself with them any more than was necessary. They didn't say anything that punished his father or brought back his mothers and older brothers and sisters to his Monticello home. They didn't come to return a life and family he had no decision in forfeiting. People were more than willing to discuss with him the lives his mothers had lost, ignoring the fact that in a very real way, he had lost his, too. All they did was force upon him another situation wherein he'd choke back his tears to hide his emotions lest others know he couldn't control them.

He hated to cry and hated it even more when he did it uncontrollably in front of people. They'd tell him that they knew how he felt, that he should smile, that he should go out and play with his friends. Or they'd tell him that he'd feel better if he went to church more often. He wanted them all to just go far, far away. He had been robbed of his entire world, nearly everything he'd ever known and loved. He didn't particularly care for constant reminders of that fact. And everything constantly reminded him of that fact.

"Please, honey!" Edna begged, exasperated.

"Yes, Momma," he finally responded evenly. It wasn't a rebellious response, but wasn't enthusiastic either. Inconsequential. He set down his pencil that had become dull from twenty minutes of ceaseless doodling in his otherwise empty lesson book. He pulled up his suspenders as he stood and plodded to the door. His mind was full of fear and anger and sorrow, and his heart was as empty as the expression his blue eyes wore under an increasingly greasy mop of sandy blond hair. He was spent from trying to make sure that nobody else saw this, that he was spinning emotionally out of control.

At his exciting age he should have been happily playing games with his brothers and sisters and playing baseball while laughing with neighborhood friends like he used to. But he wasn't. Not that he really could play with neighborhood friends, anyway. All of them went to his church, and after the scandal his dad caused, their parents wouldn't let them see him. He'd become a pariah practically in his own backyard, and this had been the cause of more than a few fights with his erstwhile companions, so surly had his demeanor become. He now had two types of friends: those whom other people kept at a distance and those whom he kept at a distance.

He kicked his kid-sister's doll out of the entryway as he reached for the door. But he paused. He hesitated. His hand remained motionless, suspended only an inch from the knob. The air suddenly seemed thick and almost electric as he struggled to inhale, and the door actually looked warm to the touch—as if it were inviting an opening and begging to remain closed at the same time.

Lehi was frozen with panic; his heart pounded, face flushed, and hands turned moist with sweat. He almost had to gasp for breath, and his head swooned violently. It was the same panic feeling he experienced when he went to bed every night and forced his eyes shut to the darkness, when he was forced to be alone with his thoughts, devoid of distractions; when he anxiously lay in bed and thought of killing his father for the death of his mothers and for abandoning him and putting what was left of his family in this horrible position; and when he thought of committing suicide for thinking such horrific thoughts about his father, one the Commandments ordered that he honor; when he couldn't control either thought even though he knew he'd never actually harm his father; when he thought people would think he was crazy for thinking these things; when he thought authorities would lock him away and throw away the key for being irrevocably insane. He was too young to realize that being the victim of Insanity didn't make him insane.

He swiveled his head and looked to his mother for reassurance while a heavy spur rustled up the gravel on the other side of the door. It was the only sound to mar the eerie silence, even Nephi had stopped suckling.

"Please, Lehi, they've been waiting." She was emotionally and physically drained, and she struggled to see each day through. She'd cry herself to sleep each night after putting the children to bed.

Lehi gathered his courage with a deep breath, said a little prayer as he let it out, twisted the knob, and opened wide his front door.

Three imposing, statuesque men wearing full-length, black leather jackets towered above the frightened youth. The man on the left grinned maniacally but said nothing. The man to the right stared sternly at Lehi, and then turned his eyes to the house's interior, cataloging his surroundings. But the pretty man in the middle squatted down to meet Lehi's face, and said in a beautiful and gentle voice that assuaged his fears and comforted him greatly, "Good evening, young man, I most sincerely apologize for interrupting you like this—"

"Who is it, Lehi?" his mom called from the other side of the room.

"Lehi, is it?" The Antichrist asked, his eyes gleaming above his sincere, wide smile. "Lehi, I'm looking for your father."

"If you're here looking for Elmer, he's not here." Edna yelled from her chair. There had been so many bill collectors and police and church people stopping by here of late that she could hardly keep track of them all. This is to say nothing of the gossipy gawkers. Although she still loved Elmer, she wanted to strangle him for the shame and betrayal he heaped upon her; for destroying her family, leaving her to bring up and provide for the kids. And that's even setting aside how he humiliated the Prophet.

The Antichrist spoke to Edna over Lehi's shoulder, "I'm sorry then to have bothered you."

He confidently shook the boy's hand, looked into his eyes, and whispered with great empathy: "I'd guess that you've had a rough lot lately, and that a great deal has happened in your life about which you have little control and are none too happy. You and your mothers have been lied to and cheated out of a life you think you deserve. That you do deserve! I know also that one of your mothers is dead and another missing, that your father took your older brother and sister. He is the reason they are dead; he is the reason they are gone. You are angry, and I can see it, and I'm here to tell you that it's good! It is good to be angry with those who hurt you, Lehi, to hate them for it! Yes, you mustn't ignore it or confuse it with sorrow! And it is also good to punish those same people. Yes, Lehi, it is both necessary and just that you harm those who harm you! For you are the man of the house now, and I can give you the chance to do what is right, and I'm asking you to protect your family. For it is your family now." Lehi nodded sadly.

"I can do this, and more, Lehi. You can help me stop your father, to put an end to this madness that keeps hurting you and your family. Your anger is a gift! Let me help you transform it into something more than frustration! I can deliver unto your father tenfold what he has visited upon your family—I can pay him back where you cannot, I can hurt him where you cannot, and I can end the pain he causes, where you cannot. I can put an end to him as you cannot! To end him is to end your pain. But in order for us to help you bring righteous justice, you must first tell me where I can find your father.

"Do not listen to your mother, for she is tired from crying and weak from caring for the household, whereas you must be strong in your anger. Do not listen to your sorrow or pity, for these are feelings heaped upon you wrongly, and you will be doubly sorry if you listen to their advice! You would not ask a disease for a cure, would you? Of course not, you are far too smart for that! Of all your emotions, anger alone is the cure, and you must now be a man and heed its advice."

He put his hand on the boy's shoulder as he patiently waited for an answer.

Lehi was amazed! As depressed as he was, he hardly even acknowledged to himself that he was mad at his dad! He'd turned his guilty anger into self-abasing depression. It was hard for him to be angry at someone whom he so desired to return home, with whom he desperately longed to be once again. His desire for normalcy had overridden his feelings. But now that this stranger had put it so plainly, it felt good to realize that he was mad, that he could be angry, that he didn't have to hide his anger in order to protect his dad! It felt good to hate his father instead of himself! Deep down, he knew his father had gone insane, that he didn't care about hurting him and his brothers and sisters. He could push back. Yes, he should push back. And he had to protect his family and mother. It was his responsibility now, and he couldn't run from it. He would tell this man where to find and stop and punish his dad! He would say it proud and strong, for he knew it was the right thing to do. Yes, it was the just thing to do. Most people came to his door offering apologies or platitudes, but this man offered a way out of his pain, and he did it with the healing sword of divine justice!

"Moab," Lehi muttered meekly.

"You have done a good thing here," The Antichrist said quietly, cupping the boy's face gently in his firm but soft hands before leaving.

"Shut the door please, Lehi," his mother instructed.

But he didn't shut the door, at least not right away. Instead, silent tears streaked down his face as he watched the men walk across the lawn. Lehi thought it strange that the grass died where the man with the skulls and grain on his belt buckle walked. It was like he left a trail of death, which seemed oddly appropriate to him. Their motorcycles rumbled through the darkness as they rode off into the unexpectant night.

I Ain't Dead, I'm Just at the Dead Goat

"It feels like I'm walking around in an oven out here," Genius complained. "How is it that this place is arctic in the winter and yet blistering in the summer? It needs to make up its mind, either fire or ice—not both. I'd even settle for something in between. No city should be able to host the winter Olympics and Dante's Inferno in the same calendar year."

"I don't mind it at all, really," The Muse said happily. "It's a dry heat, and plus I think the view of the mountains is spectacular." I didn't find the weather too oppressive in either extreme here, and looking up at the majestic Wasatch Mountains, I heartily agreed about the view.

"And the fresh air is also nice," I put in. "I love Salt Lake City." Utah's capital sits about four thousand feet above sea level, and from where we stood downtown, less than ten miles separated us from jagged granite peaks nearly three times that altitude. I craned my neck and noticed that their tops still wore a sprinkling of glistening snow, even this late in June.

"I could probably live here, except I get annoyed at the inane liquor laws—"

"And we're going to a bar within spitting distance of the LDS Temple, the holiest of Mormon holies!" The Muse laughed, "Owned and operated by a Mormon, no less!"

Genius rolled her eyes, "Don't Mormons realize that Brigham Young operated a liquor still, and Joseph Smith had a full-blown bar downstairs in his home in Nauvoo, Illinois? In his house, for Christ's sake!"

"Nothing a helping of cognitive dissonance doesn't fix," I answered, slapping my chest in a gesture of exaggerated self-importance. "Anyway, I come here often to camp and ski in the mountains, and there's actually a fairly large non-Mormon population that keeps the booze flowing, thank God. In fact, there are some awesome breweries within walking distance of the temple!"

"Ooh," The Muse exclaimed, "have you had St. Provo Girl or Polygamy Porter? I tried them last time I was here in 2004."

"Yeah, they're some excellent beers," I said as I thought about a good, ice-cold Polygamy Porter. "I tell you I just don't trust people who don't have any vices," I added as I thought about teetotalers, alcohol, and the spicy cigar in my pocket.

"Or pretend they don't," The Muse observed sarcastically. "Anyway, Genius, tell us about Porter Rockwell."

"Well," she began, "you know how God sometimes likes to stir the pot a little, to spice things up?"

The Muse and I nodded, and I laughed to myself about my experiences with God and Coyote. God's got a great sense of humor. Don't believe me? Just look at the platypus.

Genius told us how God thought Joseph Smith was a riot and followed him during the Mormon leader's transformative years to see what kind of shenanigans he'd get into. First Smith got people to give him money by telling them he could find gold and valuables in the ground by putting stones in his hat. After that stopped panning out, he renamed some of his rocks "seer stones" and put them into the hat. These new stones allowed him to translate some golden plates that nobody else ever saw into the Book of Mormon. The book has self-serving attestations of authenticity at its beginning, but history has shown these statements to be dubious at best and outright lies at worst. Some of the listed witnesses later recounted their statements that they had actually seen Smith's golden plates, but they remain part of the book nonetheless. In the end, Joseph's literary venture proved lucrative enough that he eventually ditched the stones altogether. He'd pulled a religion out of his hat. Literally pulled it out of his hat.

"Why would the Supreme Being think it's amusing that an imaginative and resourceful man was designing a religion that millions of people would follow for hundreds of years?" The Muse inquired astutely.

I explained that it was probably because God was hanging around a lot with Coyote at the time. For example, Coyote was with God, Insanity, and me for Moses's magic staff that turned into a serpent. In truth, Moses and Aaron made one hundred fifty crazy predictions to the Pharaoh that day regarding the consequences of not letting their people go. Since God is a little like Puck, a few of these predictions came to pass. Of course, the Bible leaves out the baseless prognostications and only includes what they got right. In fact, Moses erroneously instructed the Pharaoh that if he didn't let his people go, interest rates would rise sixteen percent in the next week. And Aaron told him there'd be a plague of square-dancing oxen. Coyote and I told God to enact the pandemic of the prancing bovine, but Insanity and God thought covering Egypt with frogs was kinkier. Those were good times. Before the scientific method you could get anybody to believe anything, provided it was only marginally inexplicable.

"At any rate," Genius continued, "Joseph Smith was having a difficult time with his nascent flock and was running out of money, threatening his foray into theocratic oligarchy. So one Christmas, God, Coyote, Deuteronomy, and Leviticus, incognito, of course, attended a party in Joseph Smith's home in Nauvoo, Illinois, when Porter Rockwell made an unannounced and surprising visit. He'd just spent a year in a Missouri jail without the benefit of barber or razor, and he and his mangy hair and burly beard demanded entrance to his friend's house.

"Now, Joseph had known Porter for some time and was rather fond of him as one of his earliest friends and converts. They grew up together. But at times like these, he had trouble reining him in and explaining the disheveled ruffian to his more aristocratic friends. Smith was desperate not to let his belligerent friend ruin his party in front of those on whom he relied for all his monetary and political support. So he proclaimed boldly to Porter: 'I prophesy, in the name of the Lord, that you—Orrin Porter Rockwell—so long as ye shall remain loyal and true to thy faith, need fear no enemy. Cut not thy hair and no bullet or blade can harm thee.'

"The crowd thought this nothing more than another boast in a long line of terrible boasts, and God could see that it might bring the proscenium crashing down over this divine comedy. Coyote perked up and said, 'God, why don't you just have Leviticus and Deuteronomy give Porter Samson-type powers. You know, like you did with Samson.' God saw the brilliance of proving the prophet prophetic and empowered Porter Rockwell forthwith. Smith was once again a trusted sage to his people, Old Port took on Herculean powers, and God and Coyote made some popcorn for Act II."

She finished up just as we arrived at a heavy black door emblazoned with a goats' skull, surrounded by an old, nondescript reddish brick building. We were standing on West Temple Street in downtown Salt Lake City, and about to enter the Dead Goat Saloon.

I pushed the door open casually, and since it was three o'clock on a Monday afternoon, none of us was surprised that it was empty. Empty, that is, except the bartender, who looked at me and Genius with friendly but mild suspicion and then beamed a wide smile at The Muse.

He wasn't overly tall, maybe five feet and ten inches, and that's with the biker boots he was wearing. But what he lacked in height he made up for in a rugged stoutness. His loose jeans hugged his trim waist, and the worn, gray Smith & Wesson T-shirt tucked in them did little to hide his wiry, muscular frame. He looked about forty, and crows feet snuck up on his brilliant gray eyes, giving an extra layer of intensity to his steely gaze without unduly adding years to his countenance. He had the eyes of a crazy man. Not the vacant gaze of the sociopath, but rather the penetrating stare of the fearless. Orrin Porter Rockwell was the toughest person anyone who met him had ever met, and he knew it, and his eyes reminded you of that fact every time you looked at him.

Yet, for all that, he didn't strike me as mean or vicious. In fact, I sensed just the opposite; he projected a quiet sense of amiability, at least to those who showed the same to him, and we certainly bore him no malice.

And his hair! Two thickly serpentine, salt-and-pepper braids fell from either side of his neck over his chest, stopping just short of his belt. The ends were frayed and clearly hadn't seen a scissors blade in eons. Between these two impressive braids, three tightly wound smaller braids fell from his incredible beard, held snug at the end with elastic bands. Taking a clean, white bar towel from his belt, he absently wiped down the bar that wasn't at all dirty, even though it may not have known varnish or polish for thirty years.

"Y'all members?"

He was asking us if we had memberships to The Dead Goat. At that time in Salt Lake, all bars that served hard alcohol had to be private clubs with their members paying annual fees. No fees, no membership, no booze. Some say it was originally meant to scare Mormons away from the pubs by putting a paper trail on who was drinking, but had been kept around mostly as a revenue enhancer. Just try abolishing a tax from a state's plate once it's tasted the meat.

We had already decided that in light of his religion's historical bias against women in authority, I would do the talking, at least at first. "We're members of a club, but not The Dead Goat, Mr. Brown. Or should I call you Porter?" I clapped my right hand to my right thigh, then raised it quick to my right temple, thumb extending behind my ear. Genius had taught me this as a Danite symbol by which unacquainted Sons of Dan would identify themselves.

Porter's eyes grew bigger than basketballs, then squinted tightly. "Who be you?" he said with more reservation than anticipation.

"Anama," I repeated the answer I had been taught to the secret question and walked across the sticky floor extending my hand. It meant "friend." He looked at me warily, but nevertheless we shook hands using the second token of the Melchizedek Priesthood, the "sure sign of the nail." Never once did his eyes fail to squarely meet mine during this ritualized, exclusively male Mormon greeting.

"This's the inernet age, son. Lots o' people know lots o' stuff, an' 'n this town evry ex-mormon's lookin' tuh talk large by showin' off stuff they swore not to. Sellin' books 'n stuff."

"That's probably true, Old Port," interrupted The Muse, "but none of them was sent by Joseph Smith bearing a special errand for his friend and personal bodyguard, his Destroying Angel."

He smiled out the side of his mouth as he lit an unfiltered cigarette and poured himself a shot of cheap whiskey. "First, over uh hunnert years I did 'ventuly learn tuh read'n write. 'Tween book learnin' 'n what I knowed personal, I know better'n most that Old Joe wuz full'f more shit 'n a well-fed hibernatin' shebear." He came around the bar and sat facing us on a dirty stool, one muscular arm on the bar.

"Although thar's some stuff that's plain 'nexplicable 'bout Mormonism—my still walkin' 'n this here earth fer 'xample—Joe warn't no prophet, that's fer shore. Leastways no more'n I am, I reckon." He took a drag of his cigarette and let the smoke out through his nose.

"Still, Joseph wuz uh friend, mebee the best one I ever had. The only one, 'n fact. So iffits all the same tuh yuh, we don't need tuh do no pretendin' 'n puttin' on hoaxes'n such that demean my dead buddy Joe."

"I'm sorry, Porter," said The Muse sincerely, "but I thought—"

"Pretty lady, I don't want tuh innerrupt yuh no more'ns necessary, cuz I do love the soft melody'f yer voice'n the way yer purdy blonde hair curls 'round yer mouth's yuh talk, but yuh didn' let me finish what I wuz tryin' tuh say.

"Secon', I ain't heard nobody call me my given name'n near uh dozen decades, so I figyur y'all mus' know somethin' that I don't know how yuh know! What Ima gonna do's pourus all uh drink, 'nvite yuh tuh take uh seat'n cut the shit, cuz I got uh feelin' I might like yuh, but I don't want things 'tween us started on no ruse. I've had more'n my share'f 'nemies 'n this world, 'n would rather have friends. I won't lie tuh yuh, but I gotta ask the same courtesy'n r'turn."

Genius, The Muse, and I looked at each other for a few seconds, shrugged our shoulders, and sat down at the table where Porter had poured the whiskey. None of us was prepared for his frank response, and since surprise seemed to be the theme so far for the encounter, we decided to keep it up by simply being honest.

"Porter," Genius began, "this is going to sound strange, but—"

"Stranger'n immortal'n nigh 'ndestructible mounten man tendin' bar three blocks from the Mormon temple'n Salt Lake City?" Porter cut her off.

I chuckled and downed a shot, "Well, since you put it that way, no, it's not so strange. My name's Contradiction, this is The Muse, and the cantankerous looking lady next to her is Genius." Porter poured me another shot.

"Interestin' names, but go on, I'm ah-listenin'."

I lit my cigar with Porter's lighter before I continued. "We're friends of the Archangel Michael, and he sent us here because he needs your help. We need your help."

"Well now, thar's one fer uh whopper'f honesty! It's just so 'mprobable that't might even be true! Awright, I'll play 'long fer now, what does the exalted Commander'f God's armies want from yores truly?"

"He wants you to protect us and serve as our guide," I said.

"Where y'all goin'?"

"Utah," I answered.

"Yore already there, son. That was easy!" he laughed boisterously. "Fer serious now, what'd' y'all need protectin' from?"

Genius replied this time, "Three of the Four Horsemen of the Apocalypse have escaped their hellish prison, and they're after a comrade of ours."

"Insanity's really more than a comrade, well, at least sometimes he is," I nudged her as I cut her off. "But that's not so much the issue. If the Horsemen find our ..." Come to think of it, I didn't really know what to call him. He wasn't exactly a friend or enemy, but you spend a few thousand years together and you're more than just a coworker.

"Friend?" asked Porter.

"For the sake of time," The Muse answered, "yes, a friend. The three Horsemen, Antichrist, War, and Famine, are after him, and if they get to him before we do, they'll use him to unleash all sorts of cataclysmic mayhem on earth. Michael and the other Archangels are hot on their trail, and we are trying to capture their prey, Insanity, before the Horsemen do."

Genius took up the conversation, "The point is that because all our muscle is chasing the Horsemen, we need extra protection in the event that we should accidentally run into them before the Archangels catch up to them."

"Sounds uh mite bit far-fetched. How do I know y'all're not tellin' me no bull? Y'all gotta give me more tuh go on than this here yarn."

"Simple," I said. "You asked where we were going, but you didn't ask when."

"True 'nough, I s'pose, I didn' think it necessary," he said. Normally he'd be right, but we're not exactly normal, so I told him that we were going to Monticello, Utah, during the late summer of 1978.

He looked at me slightly askance but keenly interested. Taking another belt, he smiled, "Ifn I didn' b'lieve yuh b'fore, tellin' me we're goin' back'n time won't help yer case much, son."

Genius instructed The Muse to go back in time to last Saturday and tell Porter to expect us today. The Muse nodded and disappeared.

"That's uh fair trick, it shorley is! Where the hell'd she go?" Porter demanded lightheartedly as he slapped the table before polishing off his most recent shot of whiskey. He stared at the bottom of the glass as if he half expected to find something unexpected. Although I always heard he drank quite a bit, I've never seen him drunk or boozed up. History shares this sentiment. He just likes whisky better than water and seems largely immune to its effects.

Just then, The Muse reappeared in her seat across the table. Porter's expression instantly changed from disbelieving surprise to excited acceptance. "Ya'll're tellin' the truth, I reckon! Leastways somethin' close tuh it. After I found out Joe wuz mostly uh shyster, I still wuz awful confused 'bout my own pruhdicament, but now that I've been charged by Archangel Michael with uh godly task, it's startin' tuh all come together."

"So you'll help us, then?" I asked.

He looked intently at each of us in turn. "Yes, yes, I will. But strong's I am, I still might need some help. Can I go home'n git my guns first? I take that I can do whatever needs doin' tuh protect y'all 'n yuh won't try tuh stop me from killin' someone that needs killin'?"

"Yeah," I replied, "if anyone tries to harm us, feel free to commence the killing. And there is a bit about us, however, that you ought to know before any fighting. We don't really die, our kind, that is, including the Horsemen." He gave me a look of disbelief, but I continued. "You can shoot us and we'll bleed and the like—we may even fall and appear dead—but we'll reanimate in due time. The more damage done to us, the more time it takes us to come to again."

"No problem, I'll cut The Antichrist's head clean off'n toss't down uh well'r somethin'." I had to hand it to him, he understood the rules.

I was beginning to like this guy a lot! "Genius, go with Porter to get his, er, arsenal, and meet us at the Foresters and Lager Heads. And try to hurry, will you?"

"Why do we have to go to the bar?" The Muse asked me.

"Because we've got to tell Deuteronomy about Leviticus. Believe me, it's not that I want to, but I figure that we should be the ones to tell him because we were there when it happened. Also, if he heard it from anybody else first, he just might raze a few cities."

"You don't think he'll do that even if we're the ones to spill the beans?" The Muse prodded me. "I'm not sure that the messenger is as important here as the message."

"Sure, he might go apeshit, but in this case at least we'd be there to try to talk him down off the ledge."

Be Careful for Old Deuteronomy

"Where's Insanity?" Gabriel's indignant shrill bounced off the paneled walls. "You were distinctly charged with bringing him back under your control."

We weren't in the mood for his boorishness, not that we ever were, so I said quickly, "Michael and Uriel need you. They're in 1978 on the Highway to Hell, route 491 in Utah, near a town called Monticello." His eyes beamed wide! Everybody likes to be needed, Gabriel more than most everybody else. "Raphael, they'll need you too." And they would. Considering the damage War was sure to inflict, they'd need all Raphael's celestial healing powers. Plus, he's fast with a sword.

Regaining something nearing composure, Gabriel remained undaunted. "Well, we'll go soon enough, but you haven't given me any information yet about what is obviously your total failure to capture and deliver Insanity. I demand an explanation and am not about to leave this bar until I have it." He tapped his feet and twiddled his fingers as Raphael made his way around the table to get his compatriot to leave without further making an ass of himself.

"Well," I answered sarcastically, having recently gone through too much to deal with his crap, "that's an interesting demand, Asshole the Annunciator, but I've got—"

"Where are Genius and my brother?" Deuteronomy broke in with more than a hint of the obdurate. It ran in the family.

The Muse answered patiently, "Genius will be here in a minute and—"

Gabriel exploded, "I say again! I demanded an explanation for your failure, and you provided me with little more than mocking!"

"No," I said calmly. "You mistake my insult, it contained absolutely nothing more than mocking, in fact—"

"I order you explain yourselves to me this instant!" Gabriel cut me off.

"I have a better idea," I told him as The Muse indicated to Deuteronomy to hold his thoughts for a second. "Why don't you tell Commander Mike and Uriel that, even though they need your immediate assistance to hunt down three of the Four Horsemen of the Apocalypse who have escaped, you chose to stay here instead and drink a piss-filled cup of your own inflated ego? Just say that you didn't want to heed their call to capture The Antichrist, War, and Famine because you are impertinent! How's that for a plan of action, Voice Boy?"

He straightened his back so much beyond his usual rigid posture that I thought he'd invert himself. "The Horsemen? Of the Apocalypse? From The Book of Revelation? They're loose?" he exclaimed as The Devil chuckled.

"Yes, yes, yes, and yes," I answered his questions in the order in which he posed them, the better to avoid confusion.

The Muse mediated our quarrel, "Gabriel, Raphael, we don't have time to explain the particulars of everything right now. Suffice it to say that the Archangels Michael and Uriel need you and are counting on you. There is no time for delay."

"Then I'm going too!" Deuteronomy included himself, "I've read enough about the Horsemen to know that the Arcs are going to need my help." He started to get up from his chair.

"Please wait, Deuteronomy," The Muse asked him. "Contradiction and I need to talk to you, and then you can decide what is best." As usual, she could put things in a way most suited toward achieving her desired results, and he sat back down.

The Devil perked up and raised his eyebrows, stretching his newly colored skin so that it looked like fire-engine-red patent leather. And I thought he looked unnerving before!

"You don't always have to be such a jerk, you know," Gabriel lobbed his wittiest jab at me on his way out the door. I ignored it and its echo.

I responded to The Muse's disapproving glare, "You know how much he bothers me sometimes. The only thing that makes him tolerable when he's like this is if I'm an ass right back to him," I told her as we finally took our seats at the table.

"What happened?" asked The Devil with a feigned disinterest that his keen eyes belied. "Just what did the four of you get yourselves into that you freed the Horsemen?" He knew that he'd eventually take the rap for this fiasco—that actual fault in cases like this mattered little to the people who would inevitably blame him—but he nonetheless wanted the particulars. Still, considering the fact that it was a real possibility that Deuteronomy might pound us into chuck steak when he found out about his brother, I was less interested than I otherwise might have been in any fit The Devil might throw.

I exchanged looks with The Muse before she spoke up. "In short, we know where to find Insanity, or are at least pretty sure. We first met with The Crimson Seraph, and then found the trail in the Valley of Fire. Regrettably, our entrance through the seal provided the Horsemen with an opportunity to escape. Now they appear to be after Insanity with the idea of using him as an unwitting partner in their twofold plan to cause hell on earth and free the ultimate evil, the Fourth Horseman Death. Either way, we have to stop The Antichrist and get Insanity back. The Archangels are working on the former and Genius, Contradiction, and I are on the latter."

"Is my brother with Michael?" asked a genuinely befuddled Deuteronomy.

The Muse's spirits lowered but her empathetic expression remained resolute. "No, I'm afraid he's not with them."

"Then he's with Genius. Where are they, anyway? They're not having all the fun of ruining people's fun without us, are they?"

"Genius will be here soon," she said. "She's getting someone who can provide us with protection should the Horsemen attack us."

"Huh? Why?" he asked. "That's what Leviticus and I are for, isn't it? I don't think you'd need more help than us."

The Devil chewed his cigar, twisting it with his teeth before inhaling the spicy smoke. I wasn't entirely sure how he knew what was on the other side of the Gate, but he did. It was probably from his regular poker games with Coyote, Wovoka and The Crimson Seraph. And Lucifer also knew by our reticence that Leviticus was dead and gone; it's not that he's particularly insightful, but rather he understands nuance better than Deuteronomy. Actually, ordinary rocks understand nuance better than Deuteronomy and Leviticus.

Lucifer wanted to see where this conversation would go and didn't mind waiting. He looked like a bit player in a Sergio Leone spaghetti western, squinting through the smoke while deciding whether to draw his pistol.

"Deuteronomy," The Muse addressed him solemnly, "inside God's Vulnerability at the Valley of Fire, we were attacked by the source of all evil, the Fourth Horseman of the Apocalypse, who is called Death. Genius, Contradiction, and I barely escaped. I'm very, very sorry, but Leviticus didn't make it."

"I don't understand? Where is my brother?"

She continued, "I know this is as difficult to hear as it is to understand—believe me, none of us even knew it was possible—but your brother is dead. Death killed him and he's not coming back."

"Dead, as in 'people dead'?" he asked suspiciously with an icy glare. "That doesn't happen. We don't die! It can't happen; we all know that! Even if it could, nothing could kill Leviticus, nothing! I don't believe you. Why are you lying?" he screamed.

I took a turn, "I saw it with my own eyes, Deuteronomy. I wouldn't have believed it had I not seen it myself. Death has the ability to erase whatever comes in its path, ourselves included."

"No!" he yelled in disbelief as he pounded his fist repeatedly on the table. "It's not true! It can't be true!"

"Dead?" The Devil asked calmly for clarification. The Muse and I nodded soberly in unison. "Hmmm," he muttered and scratched his chin.

"It's your fault!" Deuteronomy shot out of his chair and shouted at Lucifer. "You knew what was on the other side! I know it! You didn't go with them to find Insanity because you were afraid! You let my brother get killed because you were too scared to do anything about it!"

"Incorrect, my choleric Bible Book." The Devil said, "I didn't go because, as you are proving so well, I will get blamed no matter what I do. And since I'm going to take the rap, I'm not about to take the risk. If you have a problem with that arrangement, I suggest you take it up with God."

Deuteronomy hovered menacingly above The Devil, "You could have stopped this!" he shouted as he knocked him halfway across the room. Deuteronomy was cracking. And Lucifer, who had righted himself off the floor, was about to make it much, much worse.

"You really are a fool, you know that?" The Devil said as he wiped some blood from his lips. "It wouldn't have mattered what anybody said to Leviticus. Your brother was an obstreperous megalomaniac and was bound to get himself killed. You'd have to be illiterate to miss the writing on the wall." Lucifer was cool and exacting in his prescience. "I'll bet you anything that Genius and The Muse and Contradiction begged him to stop, that they were afraid his unthinking anger would get them all killed."

"Shut up! Shut up!" Deuteronomy pleaded, but Lucifer would not give any quarter and actually backed him down.

The Muse tried to cut The Devil off, but he brushed her aside and kept up his taunt, "You're too angry to realize that the world has changed and that you have no place in it. You and your brother were born when Genius and Inspiration mattered little compared to simple survival and superstition. Your angry castigating is simply anachronistic to today's world. Your time is up, you are a living relic, out of place, out of time, and completely out of your mind. Since it's too late to explain the obvious to your brother, I'll spell it out for you, and you'd be well advised to listen carefully: either you and your brother had to adapt to a new world or God had to do away with you. Since Leviticus refused to adapt, it seems to me that he actually did God a favor by getting himself killed."

Deuteronomy didn't move, and I couldn't tell whether he was in deep thought or about to blow up the building. He had been trying for some time to reconcile the divergent and often contradictory messages of the two Testaments, and now his brother was gone. Could it really be true that God wanted him out of the way? That this was all part of some greater plan of which he had been unaware? If so, what did that mean for him as the lone remaining representative of Old Testament enmity? Would he meet his brother's fate? He looked at Jesus, who simply met his teary-eyed gaze empathetically in return.

"ARRRGHHHHH!" Deuteronomy howled as he punched the table, exploding the old wood. He heaved uncontrollably; it was clear he'd lost it.

"I'll kill you!" he shouted and strode fiercely toward The Muse and me. For the second time in a very short while, I felt absolutely sure that I was going to die—or at least go through a terribly painful beating at the berserk hands of God's Wrath. But, as before, something entirely unexpected happened.

The front door burst open, as Genius and Porter Rockwell arrived none too soon. Porter might have been awe-struck by the imposing religious and mythical personages sitting at what was left of the table, but if he was, he didn't let it show. It took him little more than half a second to size up the situation and come to the fortunate conclusion that The Muse and I needed immediate protection from the menacing madman bounding toward us.

Porter Rockwell deftly matched Deuteronomy's speed and more than exceeded his resolve. In one lightning motion Porter jumped to block his path and pulled a powerful pistol from his belt, the business end of which he pressed into Deuteronomy's grimaced forehead. God's Wrath swung a powerful right that Porter easily caught with his free left hand.

"Yore quick, son," Porter said, his rugged voice overflowing with signature intensity, as Deuteronomy struggled in vain to free his hand, "'n strong, too. If yore smart's ya're fast, you know the only way I can stop yuh from connectin' with uh punch from yer left hand's tuh shoot yuh 'n the face with muh right. Just so we're clear, I'm more'n prepared tuh do it."

"Go ahead and pull that trigger! Throw it down, you hairy coward! You cannot kill me, and when I reawaken I'll pop your head like the bloated, pustulating goat testicle that it is!" Their eyes met in cold calculation while we sat paralyzed and speechless. "Throw down, I said!"

"Yer 'finity fer squeezing swollen goat balls notwithstandin', I've got tunz'f bullets, n' all the time'n the world. If yuhwanna wake up'n drink lead coffee, it don't make no diffrence tuh me."

"I know you," Deuteronomy let an angry smile slip through his teary face. "You're the Destroying Angel of the Danites. My brother and I made you. We turned you into Samson. We watched you avenge numerous atrocities against your people when you shot Governor Lilburn Boggs of Missouri in cold blood as he sat in his house. We were there with each punch you ever threw at anybody, deserving or not; we guided every shot from your revolver that blasted God's fury at a heretic or those who would harm Joseph Smith and Brigham Young. We filled your miserable life with righteous indignation; we gave it meaning. Before us you were a crazy louse wandering lost through the Missouri frontier, content to live on whatever scrap Smith would throw your way. You need me to be who you are. If you think about what I've just said you'll realize that you've got me on the wrong side of your gun."

For all that, Porter Rockwell remained unmoved. "Makin' uh person 'mortal gives 'em plenty'f time tuh think 'bout what the world's 'bout, 'n their place there innit. 'N that thinkin's made it so I'm not the man you knew. The strength you put 'n me tuh thrive 'n your worldview also put 'n me the will tuh move b'yond it. Now, I know full well I don't have all the answers—probably never will—but I reckon there's uh reason I'm here'n this room with uh gun tuh yer head'n Jesus ain't jumpin' up tuh stop me.

"I'm comfterble with the changes I've made through the years—'n from what I hear, half uh dime says yuh should be doin' the same sort'f reflectin'. Yeah, Genius tol' me all 'bout yer big brother, 'n if I was yuh I wouldn' wanna make the same mistakes. His death should give ya'all the 'nformation yuh need tuh make uh better decision'n he did. I feel fer yuh 'n this here moment, 'cause I've been 'round long 'nough tuh bury my wife'n kids. But while I shorely do xten' my sympathies to yuh fer yer bad loss, I'm fixin' tuh keep my shooter aimed right where't is. The choice's yores."

Deuteronomy's fingers twitched and they ached to reach up and crush Porter's stern and grim face; his fists burned with grief's impotent angst. But while his strong hands yearned to bring this physical confrontation to a quick and violent resolution, his mind mulled over everything he'd heard this past hour. It's true that his piercing sorrow tried to override any concern he may have had for his personal safety—he didn't particularly care if he lived or died right now—but he also didn't want to die for the wrong reasons. He backed up slowly, removing his arm from Porter's iron grasp and putting some distance between himself and the gun's barrel. Porter didn't flinch and kept dead aim.

Deuteronomy looked at me, passed over The Devil, leered at The Muse, and his bloodshot eyes finally came to rest squarely on The Christ. Things quietly stayed this way for what seemed like minutes but was probably no more than a few seconds. Then his shoulders fell as he turned around and plodded out the door and into the lonely, cold night.

Jesus surveyed the scene while I looked for somebody to say or do something that was more than giving a befuddled glance. Sawdust from the pulverized table covered Jesus's legs as he stood and smacked bits of rubble from his clothes. Turning to The Muse, he said, "You four do what you have to do to get Insanity back. I'm going to go see if I can talk with Deuteronomy."

"Why?" I asked. "He'll be all right, don't you think? He's probably going to go raze a village or start a plague or just blow something up. You know how he and his brother are, or were, as it were, or is, I suppose." I fumbled my words. "You don't believe that he'd be stupid enough to try to go after Death, do you?"

"I don't think so. He's slightly more of a thinker than Leviticus was, not that that says much, but hopefully his thoughts may lead him to carefully consider his predicament. If that is the case, he could use my help. There's still a place for constructive anger in the world, even if it's not his antiquated, bigoted vitriol. Anyway," he said as he opened the doors, "I have a hunch we're going to need him before all this mess is put behind us."

THE HIGHWAY TO HELL IS
PAVED WITH BAD INTENTIONS

Bushy cedar and juniper trees dotted the parched landscape on either side of Highway 666 between Monticello, Utah and Moab to the north. They sprouted from the white and red sand with a sporadic regularity and clung to the bases of the distant purple mountains. The sun shone brightly on that warm summer morning and illuminated the painted desert for anyone who wanted to take in the view.

The two-lane road was deserted except for a Volkswagen bus heading south, and neither of the occupants cared about nature's spectacle blurring past them; the five-year-old girl with the caramel skin slept silently in the passenger seat, clutching her teddy bear tightly, as if it could provide her the emotional security this world denied her. And her father, who'd hardly slept in the week since his wife unexpectedly died of a pulmonary thromboembolism, was far too occupied with how he'd lost the love of his life and how he'd have to raise their daughter without her to admire the whirring scenery.

Tears flowed from his eyes and he pounded the air next to the steering wheel. He wanted to hit it, to pound out his frustration, but he didn't want to wake Alexandra.

They were a strange match, Connor Gallagher and Alex's mother, Serwa Akosua. He was tall, broad, and pale, with lush red hair and a smattering of freckles surrounding his friendly smile. Her skin was the purest ebony, and she had a strong, curvaceous musculature and bright, engaging eyes that he found irresistible. They met eight years ago, in 1970, at a New Mexico artist colony fair near Santa Fe.

She'd come from Ghana to study landscape painting in the O'Keefe style, and lived in an enclave on the outskirts of town. He'd traveled from Dublin to learn the lost technique of blackened Pueblo pottery. He was born too late to study directly under the revival's matriarch, Maria Martinez of San Ildefonso, but a couple of her students had agreed to take him on as an apprentice.

Initially, Serwa and Connor had some problems communicating. Her English was broken at best, and his accent made his nearly unintelligible, although he repeatedly promised her that it really was his native tongue. She'd always tease him about it, but she loved it, and he knew it. When they'd first met, he'd asked her out for coffee or tea, and she'd thought he'd asked why she was a coughing tree. One of their closest friends relayed the story during a toast at their wedding. It was a touching story that their daughter never tired of hearing. They'd tell it to her over and over, embellishing their accents to Alexandra's delight. Connor looked at his sleeping daughter and cried so hard his chest hurt. His whole body hurt. His heart ached; it was empty.

Their love was deep and immediate, passionate and intense; an enthusiastic songbird in an often quiet forest. She called him her breath, her air; he called her his brilliant sunshine. To nobody's surprise and to everybody's delight, they married within a year of meeting. They purchased a small stucco house on two acres in central Utah where they set up their studios. Admittedly, their house wasn't much, but they considered themselves lucky that such an inspiring landscape came at a price two fledgling artists could afford. Although the general area was sparsely inhabited, there were plenty of likeminded artsy types interspersed among the largely amiable Mormons who made up most of the population.

Connor and Serwa laughed and loved and grew as people while happily building their lives in their small plot of Camelot. Though they weren't rich by any stretch of the imagination, they did well enough to make ends meet, to pay for their modest home and necessary occupational supplies. They even managed to coax much of their food from their rocky land. He laughed at her Ghanaian affinity for okra and fufu made from pounded yams, and she was comically baffled by his complete ignorance of anything resembling a spice or seasoning. Working the earth side-by-side was a labor they loved, and they harvested their bounty with relative ease.

During the spring and summer, they'd hitch a small trailer to their van, and stuff both with their paintings and pots, traveling from show to show and fair to fair throughout the Southwest. This occupational roving gave them a financed opportunity to bask in the natural splendor of their adopted country. While doing a show in Sedona, they swam in deep pools hiding at the bottom of labyrinthine slot canyons. In Zion National Park, they restated their wedding vows while hiking up the Virgin River in The Narrows canyon. Outside of Durango, Colorado, they had a picnic under the Mesa Verde Anasazi cliff dwellings. Awestruck, they wondered what life would be like living on a ledge chiseled hundreds of feet above the valley below, and what kind of insanity drove the inhabitants to such a defensive posture.

On the road, their interracial marriage would occasionally be the focal point of taunts and epithets, but back in their hometown everybody knew them and accepted them. If the locals harbored any animosity, it had far more to do with their liberal "hippy" politics than their race. Connor and Serwa dealt with this harsh reality of racism as best as they could, communicating and discussing it openly. It wasn't easy to work through, but the honest conversations brought them closer together. So did their faith that the world would change for the better. When little Alexandra Eforiana came along five years ago, their neighbors brought gifts and hosted parties in honor of their mocha-colored daughter.

And now Connor Gallagher drove the same van and pulled the same trailer, but his dream life had turned into a nightmare the likes of which right now he didn't know how to survive. His heart sank ever lower, and even though it continued to beat, it pumped as much anguish as blood. He'd quickly sold their house and as many belongings as he could unload. If it didn't fit in the trailer and van, he figured he didn't want it or wouldn't need it.

The funeral was only two days ago, and despite the fact that most of the town attended and shared in the loss, the naturally somber affair remained lonely by the absence of their closest loved ones. Her relatives from Africa couldn't make it on short notice, neither could many of their friends scattered in various western artist colonies. Connor didn't care very much though—misery may love company, but grief prefers to be alone. That's how he felt as he absently scanned the high desert that had been his home, his dream, and that he'd now leave in an attempt to outrun his despair.

He looked at his fuel gauge and realized he needed gas before he got too far out of town, "Big Jim's Truck Stop" might be the last station for another one hundred fifty miles. Despite his desire to be alone, Connor wouldn't mind saying goodbye to the owner. James Kimball Beckstead, a gregarious bear of a man and larger-than-life local character, had always been a friend. Even though Big Jim was active in the LDS church, he frequently supported Connor and Serwa with their progressive causes. Big Jim even lobbied as much as possible to end the Mormon ban on black men holding the priesthood. "The Prophet Joseph Smith ordained a black man, Elijah Able, he was," he'd tell anybody who'd listen, "that's all I need to know."

Connor pulled up to the pumps, which were set about fifty yards from the store, and filled up the tank. He debated whether he should leave Alexandra alone in the van while he paid and talked to Big Jim or wake her up and take her. There weren't any people around, and he looked tenderly at his sleeping daughter clutching her tear-stained teddy bear. He decided not to interrupt her much needed rest, and adjusted her seat belt comfortably across her chest before he quietly shut the door.

"Mornin'," Big Jim said somberly as Connor entered. It was all he could think of to say. What do you say to a man whose wife, lover, and companion just died without any notice or warning.

"Aye, Jim, just need to pay for the gas, 'n I wanted to tell you good-bye," Connor spoke gingerly. Hesitating.

"You're leavin' then, no changin' your mind?" Big Jim asked him.

"Don' 'ave a reason to stay," he lied. Deep down, a part of him desperately wanted to remain here in this land and raise his daughter in the house he shared with Serwa—near their love, close to the life he'd known, awash in the drug of blissful memories. But right now those same memories were too painful, too raw, too close. They were daggers. For his emotional sake, he wanted to put physical distance between himself and his loss, even though he knew no matter how far he drove, he could never completely outrun his agony. It was a short-term necessity that, if continued at length, would prove psychologically destructive. He was fully aware of this but didn't know what else to do.

"Know where you're headin'?" Big Jim absently ran his fingers along the brim of his cowboy hat.

"Vegas, I figure," Connor looked lost, "leastways that's the current plan."

"What'll you do?" Big Jim was worried about him but didn't really know how to express it.

"I've a cousin lives there, Alex's godmother. We'll stay with her for a while 'til I decide what to do. Start over, I guess."

"And your studio?" Big Jim had never actually purchased any of their works—largely because by his own admission he didn't understand them—but he appreciated the time and skill that went into their creation.

Connor thought about it and only replied by shaking his head and muttering, "Don' know, I'll figure something out." The thought of their work space, filled with her laughing and paintings, had crushed him so much that he'd sold it all—throwing wheel, kiln, clay, everything. Everything of his, that is. He kept all Serwa's works and nearly everything else she touched. But he didn't tell many people he was abandoning his pottery for fear of them trying to talk him out of it. Big Jim would certainly try to change his mind.

"Did the doctors figure out why it happened?" Big Jim wondered for a second if it was appropriate to ask such a question, but he asked anyway. "I mean, she wasn't sick at all. Saw her a day or two before, she looked right as rain."

Connor rubbed his eyes—sore and red from weeping—and told his friend, "No, no clue. They said she had a blood clot in her lung that got stuck, grew and exploded. Alexandra was there and called the ambulance."

"Do they have a clue what caused it?"

"They don' know. They say it just happens sometimes." Connor looked down, as if his shoes held an answer. "No rhyme or reason. No cause they could find." He began to weep openly; his dam had burst. "I didn' even get to say goodbye, Jim. To tell her one last time that I love her."

"She knew that, Connor, she knew that." Big Jim came around the counter and placed his hand on Connor's shoulder. "Everybody knows that. You can bet that God knows too. And God will help you through this. Have faith in that. You'll need Him when you feel dark like this. I'm not one to preach," he lied, "but you need something to hold onto, and faith in God can help." Connor didn't say anything and continued to stare at the floor, tears dripping synchronously with his heartbeat.

Big Jim continued, "There's a reason for everything, even if we don't understand it. Your life is a gift, yours and that precocious daughter of yours. You have to remember, at times like these, to treasure God's gifts."

Connor wanted to believe him, to think there was something greater at work; a master plan with a reason for Serwa's death that could fill this agonizing void; a benevolent puppet master somewhere who had his best interests at heart. Big Jim embraced him; the hug felt warm and comforting.

The moment should have been soothing and calming, but it wasn't. Instead, a frightening, foreign emotion overcame the two men. Their sorrow melted into fear of its own accord. Connor began to tremble, and beads of sweat trickled down his forehead and mixed with his tears. He managed to go on, plodding through his fear. "If life's a gift, then why'd God take her away?"

"That's the pertinent question, isn't it?" Came a cool and calm voice from the angelically statuesque man who'd been standing unnoticed behind them. He had used fear to hide his presence while he listened to their conversation. Connor and Big Jim spun and faced him, held rapt by The Antichrist's penetrating eyes.

"What is? What's the question?" Big Jim muttered, his voice unaccustomed to its jittery tone.

The Antichrist spoke: "Let's get to the point, shall we? Can we truly say that life and love are precious gifts from God?" A look of sincere disappointment crept across his perfect face. "Really? Because they don't look like gifts to me. Or, properly speaking, they lack a gift's finer attributes." Big Jim wanted to protest, but The Antichrist didn't give him a chance.

"Oh sure, your lives and loves are precious—at least to you, that's presently not my point—but are they actually gifts? For example, a true gift requires nothing in return, no payment in lieu of services as it were, and once given it cannot be taken back. A gift cannot be inexplicably rescinded. Connor, pay attention to this inescapable philosophical truth: God, who is all-knowing, made a malady with the knowledge that it would kill your wife and reduce her to memories and ashes; and for added measure, God knew that it would steal your daughter's mother." He shook his head pejoratively, "You've paid a steep, steep price for your so-called gifts. It doesn't sound at all like a gift of love, Connor, it sounds like loan sharking, and it is an entirely insane thing to believe."

Big Jim looked at The Antichrist's belt buckle. His Bible study lessons on the Book of Revelation percolated under his hat, and he realized with whom he was speaking. "Don't listen to him Connor. Have faith in God, faith in the Lord!" He fell to the floor and began to pray. "I humbly ask for strength dear God, for strength not to listen to this hateful snake."

"You hear that, Connor, that groveling? Your friend is praying to the God that killed your wife!" The Antichrist's voice began to rise, but the increased volume bore the mark of urgency rather than animosity. "This man who calls himself your friend is actually telling you to pray to the source of your torment for deliverance from it! Cling to that useless and insane concept of God and you'll continue to be sorely disappointed. You may as well pray that God take your daughter, too."

Connor looked out the window and noticed two monstrous men in heavy leather jackets hovering outside the van. They stared at it with a mixture of menace and restraint. His eyes belied his fear for Alex.

"Yes. There is something unique about that daughter of yours—the way she can take an object and hide it in plain sight, make it both here and not here. I'm sure you've noticed it. My friend knocked on the window and her stuffed animal just disappeared!" He seemed quizzically whimsical in that moment. "Extraordinary! I'd actually like to see how she does it, but regrettably I haven't the time at present. That will have to wait. But for now, have no fear for your daughter, not from us. It seems to me that we're the last of your worries. We aren't the ones that killed her mother last week."

"Stop your evil!" Big Jim sputtered, cowering on his knees with his back against the wall.

The Antichrist crouched down and spoke evenly, without a hint of rancor or irritation, "Evil I may be. Good, evil, who knows? I cannot be classified by your concept of goodness. You need to read more

Nietzsche." He tilted his head, "But whatever I am, at least I make no attempt to hide it. I do not call myself love while creating hate, I do not promise life and take it away. You need to rethink—"

He didn't finish his sentence. A thunderous roar cut him short. It shook the ground and rattled the shelves, sending bags of chips and boxes of candy flying through the air. Bottles and cans burst as they crashed to the ground. Big Jim and Connor instantly, and reasonably, thought there was an earthquake.

The Antichrist knew better. In an incredibly agile movement he rose and turned to his minions outside. No sooner had he completed his 180° spin than a brilliantly flaming sword ran him through. "Raphael," he choked on his gurgling words, "your time is up."

A hulking man in faded jeans and a T-shirt withdrew the flaming weapon and pulled a pair of glowing manacles from his back pocket. "You're in no position to make that statement," he coldly replied and dangled the shackles in The Antichrist's face. Big Jim remained praying on the floor, his head down and his arms wrapped tightly around his legs.

Connor stood facing the Archangel Raphael, completely oblivious to his identity but too scared to care. The Antichrist squirmed and laughed between them, clumsily falling forward into the Archangel's midsection, "I'm in exactly the right position right now, Raphael."

Connor looked up and saw what The Antichrist saw—that the Archangel did not—a huge rotating blade about to come crashing through the window. It smashed the glass and decapitated Raphael, sending his head bouncing down the aisle with grizzly, hollow thuds. His body crumpled into a limp heap on the unconscious Antichrist. Connor watched this scene with horror, but he was unable to move; after decapitating the Archangel, War's sword embedded itself in the wall through Connor's shoulder and clavicle. He was literally nailed to the wall.

The shock of the pain prevented him from screaming but unfortunately did not render him immediately unconscious, and instead made him a captive audience to the battle outside. Even though fading, he could make out three people rushing toward War and Famine; his daughter and the van provided their only obstacles.

He heard Gabriel's rifle and watched Famine fall as his ribs exploded from his torso. Uriel unleashed a bolt of electricity that hit War square in the chest but did little more than move him back a foot or two. The Archangel Michael unloaded a machine gun with one hand and hurled lightening bolts with the other.

None of this killed War. He looked bloody and bruised and frayed, but if he was hurt he didn't show it. In a supernaturally quick movement that Connor could barely see through his dimming vision, War put his

giant arms under the VW bus and sent it spinning through his tormen-
tors, knocking them over like flyweight bowling pins. Connor screamed
for his daughter before losing consciousness.

War grabbed Famine and dragged him inside the store, setting him
on the ground next to The Antichrist. A bullet struck him from behind
and he turned and saw that Uriel, Michael, and Gabriel were racing toward the building. More annoyed than angry or afraid, he threw a ball of
fire at one of the gas pumps. The subsequent explosion could be heard
for miles, and bought him some time free from the now dismembered
and fiery Archangelic trio.

"I pray unto the father, who art in Heaven. I pray unto the Father,
who art in Heaven at the head of the one true church." Big Jim was splattered with The Antichrist's and Raphael's bone and blood, but hadn't
looked up, and continued praying. "I know this church is true, I know
this church is true ..."

War collected Raphael's severed head and tossed it into a rucksack
he pulled from the folds of his coat, and strapped it on his back. He
reached into the refrigerator case and opened a couple of beers. Big Jim's
ranting annoyed him—he was practically speaking in tongues—so with
a heavy jackbooted foot he crushed Big Jim Beckstead's head like a rotten melon. He guzzled the beers and tossed a case or two into his sack
for later. His magnificent sword came easily out of the wall, and Connor
fell limply on top of the fleshy pile that had been his friend's head. War
picked up The Antichrist in one arm and Famine in the other, and the
Three Horsemen of the Apocalypse disappeared somewhere into the
ether.

THE OTHER MONTICELLO

It was a breezy summer afternoon on the Colorado Plateau when we arrived in 1978 in Monticello, Utah. The sun wasn't setting yet, but this late in the afternoon it hung at a low angle and illuminated the wind-blown dust just enough to give the high-desert valley an otherworldly, Martian-like quality. The signs at the intersection read "Highway 191" and "Highway 666," respectively, and the bushy trees lining the four-lane roads stood quiet watch over the highways, most likely to sound an alarm should any vehicle actually have the temerity to disturb the otherwise deserted streets. A convenience store across the street may or may not have been open; I really couldn't tell.

"Good God, where is everybody?" sighed Genius. "I don't see any sign of the Horsemen, the Archangels, or Insanity. I don't see any evidence that this place is inhabited by anything other than rattlesnakes, lizards, and tumbleweeds."

"Maybe it's just that Insanity drove the people out," I commented as I looked around at streets so wide they were better suited to turning around mule trains than shepherding nonexistent automobiles. I wondered why such a small town, with a population of around 1,000 people, needed such broad thoroughfares. Turns out that was part of Brigham Young's administrative genius—what seems wide for a small sedan was just right for maneuvering horse-drawn wagons.

"Well, I cant speak tuh what Insanity's done here'n what he hasn', but I reckon I'd be more surprised if'n there was too many more people'n this."

"What do you mean?" The Muse asked Porter Rockwell.

"It's just't most'f the folks here're 'n the habit'f mindin' their own bizness. They don't have much'f uh reason fer bein' out'n 'bout. Strikes me 't more'n uh few of'm consider bein' out good fer nothin' more'n doin' the Devil's work."

"That may be true," I told him, "but I know Insanity well, and I can feel his effect in the air here, almost like I can smell it. It's nothing so pungent as garlic or as pukish as a pig farm, but more of a generally malodorous funk. He laughs about it and calls it his signature cologne."

"It's the smell of fear," The Muse put the matter much more eloquently. "People cannot understand Insanity and his manifestations in themselves or their friends and family, and as a general rule they fear what they cannot understand. In this case, they're smart to fear the unknown. If they knew what we know, the residents here would be hiding in the hills."

"Maybe that's where they are," I thought aloud.

"Can yuh tell the way yer pal went or're we jus' gonna piss 'n the wind'n hope he's thirsty 'nough tuh take uh drink?" asked Porter Rockwell.

"North," The Muse, Genius, and I responded together, our comment met by the doubtful expression of an experienced tracker.

"'N why do y'all reckon so?"

I answered, "Just a feeling we get, really, I think. I've never actually tried to figure it out. Usually there's not much of a need to give it much of a thought."

"We're connected to each other in a way that you aren't," Genius explained to Porter Rockwell. "The best way for me to put it so you can understand it, is that we operate as separate but very interconnected parts of God's mind. It's difficult to lose a thought, and that's why we really don't lose Insanity much. But when you lose something, you have to remember where it is to find it. And in these events, we interact like forgotten memories; the closer we can get to each other the more powerful the remembrance. We're not close enough to him to point him out, but close enough to remember where he is."

"That don't make uh lick'f sense," he said as he twisted the braids of his beard. "You tellin' me y'all can remember where he is even'f yuh didn' know where he wuz'r how he got there?"

"Sort of," helped The Muse, "but our ability to think isn't constrained by your concept of time. In a very real way, our future selves do remember where he is at this moment, and it's that interplay that makes this possible."

"Huh?"

"Contradiction, can you help him out a little?" Genius requested.

"It doesn't make sense and makes absolute sense at the same time, and that seems perfectly sensible to you, doesn't it?"

He stopped twisting his beard just long enough to scratch it. "Well, since you put't that way, I don' see what all the fuss's 'bout."

"Good. Now let's rent a car and get on our way," Genius added.

"Fer bein' uh genyus, yuh can be uh lil' daft't times, can't yuh?" Porter chided.

"I don't get it," Genius replied while The Muse and I chuckled at his brazenness.

"Well, fer starters, where'n the sam hell're yuh 'xpectin' tuh find uh car rental place'n this one-horse town?" He teased her, "I'd've thought uh person smart's yuh'd know this town's too small fer such uh business. There ain't more'n uh couple thousan' people! 'N what's more, there ain't uh city within mebee fifty miles that does rent cars! Yuh shoulda tol' me that 'fore we came." He looked around the crossroads like he was trying to put a puzzle together or figure out a riddle.

"Hmm," said The Muse, "I didn't think of that."

"You're a real fucker sometimes, aren't you?" Genius lamely shot back at Porter Rockwell.

"When I think it's funny mebee I've the tendency, otherways I'm genr'lly pleasant's strawberry pie. Either way, it's all wheat."

"What does 'all wheat' mean?" Genius asked him despite herself. "You've muttered that a few times."

"It means it's plumb good, that's what! If'n uh field's full'f weeds'n stuff it's no good, but if'n it's chalk full'f wheat, now that's uh darn good field! Unless'f course's livestock tramplin' through 't. That wheat just ain't wheat."

"I don't understand you at all," Genius said and looked to The Muse and me for affirmation she wouldn't find. I didn't understand half of what he said but understood all of what he meant.

"Well, let's just go somewhere that we can rent a car," The Muse said. "Hopefully it won't take us too long to drive back here. It just has the feel like we're on the right path."

I looked up and down the empty bucolic streets. There was hardly a business of any sort, and even fewer cars parked along the road or in the many driveways. I felt like I was in a backdrop for The Andy Griffith Show, and half expected to see Barney Fife chatting with his agent about a future role as a high-strung landlord on the sitcom Three's Company.

"Wait!" I shouted as I spied a solitary car parked a few blocks north on Highway 191. This car alone dared to mar the blacktop with its presence! "Let's just steal that Boss 302 Ford Mustang up the road! Look at it! It's awesome!" Although I'm not usually too much of a car junkie, I've got a weak spot for 1970s muscle cars! They looked like the type of cars that would stampede you into road kill and then make you thank them for the pleasure of the experience. Every once in a while you could possibly outrun them with a Porsche or Corvette, but when it caught up (and it always would), it'd kick your ass, eat your burrito, take all your fuel, and drink every last drop of your beer without missing so much as a single stroke of its engine's dominant authority.

"Contradiction!" yelled The Muse, clearly surprised at my idea of absconding with somebody else's automobile. "We're not going to steal a car!"

"It's not stealing; it's more of a permanent borrowing!" She may be

God's preeminent empath, but she clearly didn't have the slightest clue about muscle cars.

"Of course it's stealing; it's not our car!" she replied. "Don't give me any of your moral dissonance. It won't work on me."

She sure was cute when she tried to convince me of something, but I wasn't falling for it right now. "Okay, then it's not stealing because our need for that car to take us to Insanity is more important than the car owner's desire to have it parked in front of the house in the event that they may need it to go to the store and pick up the latest edition of Polygamy Monthly."

Porter Rockwell guffawed garrulously while The Muse was clearly not in the mood, "And none of your subjective relativism, either."

"It's hardly morally relativistic if it's true, is it?" I asked.

"Now you're just denying your moral subjectivity!" She told me what I already knew.

I was getting desperate. If I was going to have to chase Insanity around hell and breakfast and half of Utah, then at least I should be able to do so with style. I really wanted to drive that Mustang! "It's faster than going somewhere else to rent a car."

"No, it isn't," Genius spoke up. "We'll just go to another town to get a vehicle earlier in time and be back here at exactly the moment we left."

"It's more powerful," I begged. But she just said we could rent a Corvette.

"Y'all don' want niether'f 'em," Porter Rockwell broke in. "This's central Utah, for wheat's sake. We got the Arabajo mountens tuh the west, 'n the La Sal range's even bigger'n not much further!" He looked at us like we were ignorant children. Gesticulating grandly he continued: "Colorado, San Juan'n Green rivers turnin' up when yuh least 'xpec'm, too! 'N if that ain't enough, I figyur y'll be mite bit lucky'f anythin' that ain't uh mounten'r river's just uh rocky arroyo'n not uh canyon, fer the love of tarnation. Y'all need uh truck'r sumthin'."

"All right, wise ass," Genius put her hands on her hips. "Do you have any better ideas or are you just going to sit there and give us another unnecessary geography lesson using largely unintelligible and incomprehensible frontier gibberish?"

Porter feigned hurt feelings in response, "Come on now, muh friend, there's lots'f big words'n that thar insult, I'm just uh simple mounten man." He pointed to his beard with a rough finger and went on, "But I still figured't out cuz I'm just smart 'nough to be smarter'n yuh think! 'N it's shorely too bad that yer wit ain't 's keen 's yer vocabulary."

Clearly peeved but not wanting to continue the bickering, Genius decided to change the subject. "How about Blanding?" she asked. "Can we rent a car in Blanding?"

"What? Why? THE MUSTANG IS RIGHT HERE! And it's probably not even locked! We jump in and hotwire it, speed off into the sunset and nobody's any wiser. If we get busted by the cops for stealing or speeding, we can get the hell out of there and try your idea." I did my best to compromise.

"Blanding?" The Muse wondered aloud, ignoring my pleas. "What's a Blanding?"

"It's more of a where than a what, but either way we should probably figure out just where Porter Rockwell thinks he's going," Genius answered dryly as we noticed him strolling across the street without us. Sauntering, really. Or maybe more of a mosey. Okay, yes, moseying. The best way to describe the walk of a tough son-of-a-bitch with a handgun tucked into the back of his belt is most definitely "mosey." (He wore his pistol but left his duffle bag full of rifles and ammunition on the sidewalk next to us.)

"Where are you going?" she shouted at him.

We still hadn't seen anything to disabuse us of our notion that the town had been abandoned, so he was more than safe as he stopped and turned around in the middle of the road, taking his time addressing us. "That house b'hind me b'longs tuh uh friend of my friend Jubile, 'n if y'all just stay put right there fer uh minute'r two, I'll hopefully come out'f his garage havin' borrowed his fore wheel drive Innernational Scout. He owes Jubile somethin' fierce'n shouldn' ask me no questions 'bout collectin' fer'm." Mystified, we watched him approach the house, knock on the door, and enter when a bearded, biker-type answered and invited him in.

"That sounds reasonable, I suppose," Genius murmured, clearly embarrassed enough for us all as we sat down on the sidewalk. Our feet impudently taunted the otherwise unmolested road with an unappreciated podiatric invasion. More often than not, waiting for anything sucks, and in this case it sucked even more because Porter's simple action had shown just how childish we can be when faced with details that simply don't matter in the grand scheme.

"If it's so reasonable, and you're the paragon of reason, then why didn't you think of it earlier?" I chided. "What good are you, anyway?" I said as I jostled her with my elbow.

"Shut up."

If anybody or anything except the swooshing of the Spartan trees interrupted the silence during the next few minutes, I'm unaware of it. There really wasn't anything for us to do but hope that Porter Rockwell came back out with a vehicle. Even if we were inclined to leave him and go somewhere else on our own, it wouldn't have been fair to leave him to have to live a quarter century twice. Then again, it might be. He said he learned a lot from simply not dying, so maybe he'd learn twice as much by having a "do over."

Just as I began to debate the philosophical merits of that possibility, the garage door across the street slowly squeaked open, as if cajoled by a rusty and disinclined can opener. A red, old-school sports utility vehicle with broad white stripes backed out of the driveway. To be precise, it was an International Scout.

Porter Rockwell drove the beast across the street and rolled down the window "Hop in, thar's room fer all y'all. North yuh say?" he asked needlessly. Genius nodded as she tossed his gun bag on the back seat before climbing in. The Muse followed her, and I sat in the front with Porter as we drove north on Highway 191.

"Before we really get in the middle of nowhere, can we maybe stop and get something to eat? I'm starving," I said, thinking that the ominous rumbling in my stomach was getting dangerously close to registering on the Richter scale.

"We don't have time to appease your gastronomic demands," Genius replied.

"Wait! Wait! Stop, there's a sandwich shop there on the right; it'll just take a second." Maybe just to annoy Genius, Porter Rockwell pulled a U-turn and came back around to park behind the Ford Mustang sitting in front of Elmer's Authentic Navajo Sandwiches and Tacos. Irrespective of Porter's motives, I was happy for the possibility of some tasty victuals. I jumped out of the Scout. Genius sighed.

"Don't you dare touch that car!" instructed The Muse as she hopped onto the sidewalk to see me ogling the muscle car.

"Is that uh devil hangin' from the rearview mear?" Porter asked as he stood next to me, admiring the exquisite chrome and detailed paint job.

"Nah," I told him. "Well, yes, sort of. It's Sparky, the Arizona State Sun Devils mascot." He grinned as Genius spun me around and pushed me toward the sandwich shop.

A black sign with orange lettering, suction-cupped to the inside of the window, announced "open," but everything else about Elmer's screamed closed, except that the lights were on and the door was slightly ajar. Porter Rockwell confidently reached for the handle and swung it wide, "After you," he said, and mockingly genuflected.

Upon entering, I was assaulted by the less than enticing odor of moldy bread and stale cornmeal. I kicked aside dozens of unused wax-paper sandwich bags that covered the floor. Cherry fountain syrup glued paper cups in positions of permanent disarray across the counter; frozen exactly how they fell, they were papery inhabitants to the soda fountain's merciless Pompeii.

"I don't think they're open," said Genius as she looked around absently for any sign of a customer or employee.

"Insanity's been here," commented The Muse, ignoring the spat between her colleagues. She ran her fingers delicately across the clunky metal cash register as if she knew how it must have felt to the last person who touched it. She had a dazed and dreamy expression that melted into understanding nods.

"Yeah, I figured as much," Genius added needlessly and turned to leave, "but he's not here now, so let's go."

The Muse caught her by the arm and whispered, just loud enough for Porter Rockwell and me to hear her, too. "I realize that Insanity's not here, but I think somebody else is, somebody who is frightened, and who might be able help us find him."

I've never understood exactly how The Muse knows these sorts of things, but it's not in my nature to be bothered by the inexplicable. And while Genius had come to trust her friend's intuition, she frowned before quietly turning with me back toward the counter to follow The Muse's lead.

She confidently stepped up as if she might order fries and a chocolate peanut butter malt. Porter stood squarely at her side, feeling for the security of the revolver still tucked into the back of his jeans. Careful to avoid the sticky syrup, she rested her hands on the counter as she leaned over it and looked at the kitchen area for any signs of life.

"Hello!" she called out. "Hello? I know you're here, I saw you come in," she lied in a welcoming voice. Perhaps thirty seconds passed during which time nobody appeared and absolutely nothing happened. Genius wasn't impressed and shrugged in a motion that I took for a signal to leave. The Muse held up her hand, indicating for us to wait just a little longer. Annoyed, Genius again stood still.

I felt the breeze on my back as it blew through the front door, but it wasn't enough to clear the stale air either of Insanity's lingering mess or the musky odor of decaying grains. The food's smell was supported by the scent of old grease from the fryers and old grill—a grill that had been scrubbed everyday for twenty years but hadn't been clean in ten.

The pause gave me time to think about this building and the business that used to be in it before Insanity wreaked his usual havoc. Despite its derelict appearance now, people used to work here—arrived every morning hoping to be busier than the previous day. At one point years ago someone stood outside and thought, "We'll make a sandwich shop here, and maybe with enough hard work we can afford to pay our bills, raise our children and send them to college, and still have enough in the bank to comfortably retire." They dutifully made an honest living and the best livelihood they could by stuffing savory fresh bread full of seasoned beef, and spreading mayonnaise onto lightly toasted bread before adding turkey, bacon, and Swiss cheese. Precisely controlling the portions to maximize meager profits, they made sure to serve only three ounces of turkey and bacon and one slice of cheese per sandwich. They hopefully counted the hard-earned pennies from each sandwich and soda they sold.

Good friends came in with their families to share a meal and swap stories about their children and their most recent activities; they planned church functions and discussed the goings-on at City Hall. And when their children were old enough, they took their turns serving the food and sharing the burden of a family business, while their parents finally got some well-deserved rest. People hoped here, people laughed here, people struggled here, people cried about their sorrows here, and people met their first loves while learning how to properly make the family's secret sauce that was far from authentic Navajo. The walls bore silent witness to stories that revealed themselves not in the rotting wood and chipped paint, but in the hearts and memories of those who once walked here.

The discordant crunch of rustling paper shook me from my stupor. We looked at each other, trying to figure out where the noise was coming from and what was making it. As best as I could judge, it appeared to be from an open door behind the kitchen that went God-only-knows-where, but probably to a small office of sorts.

A young man timidly stepped through the doorway and into the open kitchen area. There was a cluttered aisle between him and the front counter, and we watched him as he warily watched us. He was young, early teens, probably, with the beginnings of acne that would haunt him in the coming years but that would eventually leave more internal scars than external pockmarks. Sandy hair that he had cut in the latest feathered style clung featherlessly to his head as if it hadn't been washed in some time. His blue, bloodshot eyes were keen in spite of the fact that they were red and tight from what looked like holding back tears. In fact, I felt that he may start sobbing at any moment. He dropped his head and stared at the ground in an admission of his submission to the world's weight he felt heaped upon him.

A faded brown belt with recently notched holes hung his jeans from his waist in a manner that highlighted his emaciated frame. His long-sleeved, button-up shirt somehow remained tucked into his pants, as if forcing an unwanted and unappreciated dignity on the otherwise disheveled teenager. He looked like he couldn't decide whether to befriend us or run away. I really couldn't tell which. He began to fidget with his left foot, sheepishly tapping his clubbish shoe against an old burrito carton.

"Pardon me, young man, but my friends and I were just driving through on our way to Salt Lake City," The Muse continued the ruse, which was unusual for her, "and thought we'd stop by at our favorite café for a quick bite."

"We're not open anymore," he responded, gingerly taking a couple steps toward us without looking up or making eye contact.

"I can see that. Can I ask what happened? We passed through here last spring and really enjoyed your tacos. We told all of our friends in Salt Lake about them."

His eyes remained glued to the floor while he responded flatly, his voice lacking the emotion expressed by his body. "Almost everybody left and there's nobody here to mind the shop anymore." He put his hands in his pockets and tucked his arms close to his sides, "There aren't people enough to run many other stores either, for that matter. You might as well keep on your way." He didn't really sound like he wanted us to leave, and in fact part of him exuded a desperation for communicative contact. His voice had an odd sense of the protective about it that I didn't understand, as if his staying and our leaving might shield us from whatever had beaten him and this city down. If I didn't know better, I'd say he was martyring his own feelings and needs for ours—he was doomed but would at least try to keep us from the same fate.

"Where's your family?"

A lonely tear escaped from his eye and landed on the tile with a muted splat. "I don't know where my Mother Sarah is, I haven't seen her since Ma EllaDawn died."

The Muse stammered, "I'm sorry to hear that, I, I didn't reali—"

"I haven't seen my Ma since she ran away into the desert after Ma EllaDawn killed herself. The police say she's dead. That wasn't very long after Pa took my older brother and sister away to follow the strange man who came here driving that Mustang out front." Although he practically blurted this out, I could tell by his affect that it was a rehearsed and oft-repeated explanation that he'd learned to relay only with strong emotional detachment. If he had hung his shoulders any lower, they very well may have dislocated.

The Muse looked at Genius and me knowingly, for it is one thing to suspect Insanity and another thing entirely to see his work firsthand. All of us except Porter Rockwell were thinking of the woman we met in the

Valley of Fire who'd died when she fell down a rocky embankment in the desert. Her trail had led us here, to one of her sons from her polygamous marriage arrangement. Which also meant that if we could find out where this boy's father went, we could probably find Insanity.

"What is your name, young man?"

"Lehi," he responded, finally raising his head to look us in the eyes. He considered himself old enough so that a request for his name from a complete stranger was insultingly pejorative. From the stiffening of his shoulders and the way he cocked his head, I gathered that not addressing The Muse as "Ma'am" in his response to this particular question amounted to an act of open rebellion. I don't pretend to be as intuitive as The Muse, but I could tell that his emotions were quickly tipping, that he was growing tired of our presence. Although he didn't tell us to leave, we had worn out our welcome. His painful emotions that had only moments before wrapped themselves in misery now adorned themselves with defensive barbs. Take all the usual teenage angst and douse it with real, unabashed, and uncontrollable tragedy and you begin to get the picture.

"Do you know where your father went with this strange man, Lehi?"

"Why? Are you here to get money he owes you, too? Because we don't have any," he replied, his tone icy cold. "You don't have to put on some lie about traveling through and stopping for lunch if you're only bill collectors. Have a look around, the cash register's empty! Take the ice cream machine and sandwich station, if you're that desperate to make us even poorer. You think I'm just going to write you a check for the money he owes you? Like I'm going to pull a fat wad of hundreds from my pocket? I wouldn't give it to you even if I did have it!"

The Muse realized she had touched a raw nerve and wanted to avoid doing so again. Time for a different approach. "Did Elmer leave with your father? This is Elmer's shop, right? Where's Elmer?"

Lehi's eyes were a thousand flying daggers. "Elmer is my father," he told her through gritted teeth. "Thanks for sticking around long enough to jab me with that unfortunate reality."

His despondent melancholy had morphed into an angry and complete hatred directed squarely at us. His emotions were misdirected. Hidden far below the surface in a place he dared not visit, he hated his father, not us. When The Muse spoke with him across the kitchen, Lehi saw her as absolutely beautiful and extraordinarily pleasant in every manner and gesture, but he nevertheless found her repulsive. Because of what he'd gone through, he felt he didn't deserve beauty in his life and was angry that she was denying him his guilt, even if he didn't realize it or lacked the emotional vocabulary to express it.

Aside from the enormous grief over the loss of his mothers, the sorrow and mixed emotions he bore stemmed in part from the suffering he thought he delivered to the one person by whom he so longed to be loved, even though he hated. It made perfect sense that he'd randomly lash out and refuse to place the anger and hate where it properly belonged: with his father who bore responsibility for his mothers' fate and also abandoned him, instigating his living nightmare.

People and friends who had known Lehi their whole lives wouldn't recognize this brash behavior and would likely attribute it to teenage bratty selfishness. They'd say he'd become a jerk and didn't care about other people's feelings or anything else, for that matter. And while his emotions manifested themselves in precisely this manner, his behavioral changes stemmed from a much greater injury than general teenagerdom. Everything he knew had been reprehensibly stolen from him: his mother, father, older brothers and sisters, his social network and friends. How should people expect him to bear these wounds? He spent such an incredible amount of energy and time trying to maintain control of these uncontrollable emotions that he scarcely had time to consider other people.

Later on I asked The Muse what would happen to him. She told me that he may someday recover from his tragedies to a life of "relative normalcy, but it's going to take a great deal of introspection and strength of will. He can't deal with either his hurt or anger until he realizes which is which and where they should properly be directed. I feel for him."

And at this moment in the sandwich shop, I felt for him, too. It's a terrible thing to be betrayed by one you love and to still love them, and even more so when you're little more than a child and that person is your father. It's practically impossible to put these conflicting and swirling emotions in perspective, and to ask a child to do so is, well, insanity. I also could empathize because we weren't here to help him, and he knew it.

While we were temporarily taken aback by the tone of Lehi's response, he followed up, "It's obvious that you and everybody else are far more concerned with my father's whereabouts than with my family or if we have enough to eat or money to pay the power bill, or if they're shutting off our water! We didn't do anything. He did! So, since you want Elmer so badly, why don't you just go follow that crazy man, too! Half this town has! Why not people from Salt Lake now? The whole world and a crate of Postum can go with them for all I care!"

"Lehi, I just—" The Muse tried to speak but he cut her off.

"I'm surprised you haven't seen it on the news. Everybody else has! It's the biggest headline everyday! They're in Moab. Canyonlands National Park, actually. Why don't you get out of here and leave me alone?"

We looked at each other dumbfounded. This was proving even worse than we expected. "Does the Scout have a radio?" I leaned over and asked Porter in a cautious whisper.

"Yup," he whispered in return. We could just zap ourselves there, but we had no idea what we'd be facing. Remembering what Insanity did to Jesus, we knew that we'd better approach with caution.

"Let's go," Genius said. Porter and I turned with her to go through the door, and we heard The Muse address Lehi as we left.

The near-hypnotized boy quietly listened to her attentively. "Lehi, with every sleepless night comes the hope of the dawn. It is this hope that a new day's sun will herald a better, more promising day that makes the darkest of nights bearable. And the dawn always comes, Lehi, always. But in order to see the dawn for what it is, you must also feel the darkness. For the new day to bring an end to the sleepless nights, you must first embrace the night for what it brings. The night is dark, and you must own it. The night is bereft of joy, and so you shall be. It is painful, and so you shall be in pain. You fear it, and so you shall be afraid. When it tells you to cry for your losses, so you shall. This is the only path that leads through the darkness to a truly different and better world. Any other way is not through, but around. There is no shortcut, only charlatans who will take you on a distorted path that will lead you right back where you are and don't want to be.

"Do not fight the hurt that pains you. Do not fight the sorrow that weighs so heavily upon your heart. Do not fight the anger. As frightening as it may seem to you, you must invite these feelings in. You must confront them honestly and most importantly, vulnerably. And for a time you may even need to completely prostrate yourself to their caprices. These feelings are not unlike an illness, and you must both succumb to and bear the terrible and agonizing heat of the fever before you can begin to recover.

"All this has been cast upon you unjustly, but cast upon you it has been. And now that this is the undeniable case, you must experience these emotions to the fullest, lest they consume you. You must swim in the cold, deep, dark waters that you most fear. If you do not, you risk ruin to yourself and those about whom you care. To deny these feelings and emotions is to deny yourself, to negate your own humanity. Be human, Lehi. Cry a little because you're frustrated, but cry more because the pain hurts.

"And anger is a gift, Lehi. Be angry, for it is often a sign that something is wrong that you should try to right. Anger can serve as a powerful tool with which you can and indeed should protect yourself against those who would mistreat you. It is your body's way of informing you that you have been treated unfairly, and it is further a call to put an end to such actions. But do not confuse anger with hate. Hate is anger corrupted. It results from denying that you're angry, that your heart is broken so badly that you hardly sleep, and that you are in constant anguish. It is the drug that lures you with promised numbness via emotional redirection, but always drops you off exactly where it picked you up. It denies that the road must go through the night and instead will lead you far from that necessary path and into a wilderness of acerbic despair.

"Hate cannot ignore sorrow and hurt and suffering and anguish, so it twists them into something unrecognizable, even to you. At some point, you won't even be able to make the connection between the object of your hate and the underlying reason for it. Even now, you may have trouble seeing that your hatred of my beauty stems not from anything at all that I've done to you, but rather from your contorted anger toward your father.

"Lehi, it is okay that you hurt. It is right that you are angry. Give yourself permission to admit this to yourself. Embrace these feelings to move through them. It will not be easy, and may take years and leave lasting scars. Over time the wounds can heal, even if some days are worse than the day before.

"Don't listen to those who persist in telling you to deny your feelings. Some of these people may in fact have your best interests at heart, but they lack the proper tools to effectuate your interests and are usually too busy with their own problems to notice this. It is all right, Lehi. You are going to be okay. Not today, and probably not tomorrow, but do not doubt the coming of the dawn, for it always comes."

Lehi stood transfixed, neither dejected nor defensively bitter. Rather, he gazed upon The Muse in quiet, pensive longing while great rivers of salty tears poured from his puffy, bloodshot eyes. The Muse walked into the kitchen toward him, her arms open wide. He rushed to her and fell into her comforting arms. Great pent-up waves of angst came spewing forth in spasmodic heaves and mournful sighs and wailing sobs. And Lehi, son of Elmer and Sarah, began the healing process by letting go in the warming embrace of a total stranger.

On the Road Again

OR

No News Would Have Been Good News

We had been driving northward toward Moab, Utah, for at least thirty minutes before anybody interrupted the silence with conversation that we knew was incapable of properly describing our feelings, even though each one of us could have spoken volumes. We had seen a boy's life torn from underneath him like a cheap rug by a careless but clever magician. No, Elmer wasn't the conjurer; that was vintage and pure Insanity deftly guiding the strings, hidden safely from view by Lehi's mental curtain that struggled between blaming his father for the insanity and Insanity for his father. None of us could put the image of the heartbroken boy behind us, but we wouldn't talk about it for some time. Years would pass before we discussed it in detail, in fact.

"Turn the radio on if you don't mind, Porter," Genius broke our hushed reflection, "there might be some news about Insanity and what he's up to."

He had to switch on the overhead light to see as he turned the volume knob on the radio. Although the speakers blared rock music rather than the desired news, he didn't change the station, at least not right away. Instead, Porter, The Muse, and I listened to a Spanish guitar playing repeating chords behind a gruff, yet soft voice. A bass guitar added timely whole notes. Somehow the song just seemed to fit with the somber mood in the Scout. Except Genius was having none of it, and instead stared vacantly out the window at God-only-knows-what.

Why do waves come crashing, splashing on the shore? For all their ceaseless thrashing, they're crashing evermore.

Ceaselessly they're holding then folding toward the ground. Ever grows the woe and moaning of their mournful sound.

"Isn't there a news channel or something you can pick up?" Genius asked, ignoring or failing to see the irony of the lyrics. She's too smart to be completely ignorant of their meaning, but myopic enough to fail to internalize this fact. Genius is as Genius does—subtle intuition isn't her strong point. It takes all her effort to muster up half the emotion of a depressed Vulcan. Spock would be proud. "It really would help us if we could get some insight into what we're facing in Canyonlands. Who knows what Insanity's done by now. Try the AM frequency."

Porter Rockwell answered in his usual mountainy drawl that scorched Genius's erudite baked potato, "It's uh long drive, couple'f hours, leastways. Won't do yuh no harm tuh listen tuh the song fer uh bit. From all I've seen'f yuh, strikes me yuh could use yerself uh good lesson'n patience."

"Porter, I'm not in the mood, just change—"

"Ah calm yerself justa couple minutes 'til the hour changes tuh ten. Y'all'll git better news then anyway, they're always recappin' the day's top stories't the tops'f the hours."

Genius pretended to let it go for the time being and sat back against the stiff, vinyl bench seat. And by "let it go," I mean she sighed loudly and tapped her feet annoyingly against the rhythm.

Maybe they're begotten and forgotten by their maker because they're wonton rotten remnants of the maker.

Doomed for all eternity, serenity has fled. Success an ambiguity, insanity rules our head.

Could it be, in the waves, caves of all long gone, there is a grave, save the soul? A hope that lingers on.

I looked out on the lonely, two-lane highway while the chorus repeated. If I hadn't seen the beauty of this country during the day and my description was guided only by my impression of it at night, I'd call it desolate. But having seen it colorfully ablaze in the sun's glory, I think isolated is a better word choice than desolate. I was pretty sure that we'd scarcely seen even one building since we left Monticello, and even fewer cars. The ubiquitous darkness swallowed our headlights before they made any significant dent into the desert's darkness, and the sparkling stars that watched from above laughed at the headlamps' inability to defeat the Earth's measly shadow. I knew there were mountains and canyons and rivers and mesas and trees and all manner and form of weathered sandstone formations in the distance. At least I thought I did, but I couldn't see them.

I considered asking Genius to epistemically prove that anything existed in the void between us and the stars—the ravines and mesas and canyons—whether we could really be certain that anything exists beyond our sensation of it. Then I looked at the tantrum she was having and thought better of it. She often explained things in the most didactic of ways, and in her current pique she'd make it worse by sprinkling her answer with heavy pedantism. As is my bent, I simply ignored that I wanted to ask the question in the first place.

The night was so dark that the only way I could ascertain faint topographic outlines was to look out the side window long enough for my eyes to readjust from the struggling glare of the headlights. From all appearances, we might as well have been driving on a treadmill in an empty, remote corner of space that direct light had not yet reached. Even the moon had seen fit to stay away from this night's dense opacity. Sometimes she knows best.

The song faded out completely and Porter Rockwell fiddled with the dial to find a news station. Genius stopped her whiny fidgeting and paid attention to the crackly voices that managed to ride the airwaves so far from their towers.

"You watch, Jim, you bet all your money on what I'm saying—take it straight to the bank and don't stop for directions! The New York Yankees and Los Angeles Dodgers will play in the World Series and the Bronx Bombers will come away with another world championship."

"Hold it right there, I don't think you know what you're talking about, Al. I really believe that the Red Sox'll catch up to them, if—"

Porter let a smile escape the side of his mouth that let me know he's a Yankees fan, then abruptly switched stations.

"Stay tuned for the late hour on The Brick, 'cause we're gonna play The Who's new album, *Who Are You*, in its entirety, commercial free and uncut, right here on Stomp the Brick KFQ—"

"That's uh good album," Porter said as he continued down the dial. "They shore's hell ain't The Doors—who is—but those crazy limeys kick some serious ass."

"And now it's time to really boogie down, to get down! I said let's get down, lower than Nixon's self-esteem! Let's do it to it 'cause there's nothing to it with Stayin' Alive, the Bee—"

"Fuck disco," Porter exclaimed as he cut short the annoying refrain. "It wuz bad 'nough first time 'round. I ain't gonna listen tuh that shit twice. Ain't got no wheat't all. That's all the FM chann'ls out here, mebee thars somthin' on the AM."

"Just what were you thinking when you came up with disco?" I asked The Muse.

"Hey, I just invented it," she laughed, "If I remember correctly, you and Insanity had to do some serious overtime to get people to actually listen to it!"

"Hmm, yeah, I guess you're right, we've done better work. I try to forget about it but The Devil reminds me all the time." I told her, "There's no chance he'll let that go anytime soon."

"No way, it's one of his few golden goose eggs where he actually doesn't get blamed for the calamity."

"Disco! Fer the love of wheat that shit shorely sucks! I blame the whole lot'f yuh, cuz ain't no way human kind's got that kind'f evil innem! It's 'n aural atom bomb!"

"Aural?" Genius asked. "I'd have thought that word outside both your vocabulary and your ability to pronounce it correctly!"

"Oh, I'm chalk full'f surprises, if yuh just gimmee half uh chance," he observed, gamely smiling. "'N fact, I'll just go 'head'n oralize uh lil' somthin' fer yer aural benefit right now: 'Fuck yer obtuse erudition!'" He winked at her through the rearview mirror. "How 'bout that?" He didn't wait for a response, but went on, "At least I know well 'nough not tuh 'quate the way uh person talks with what they know."

I laughed while The Muse restrained herself enough so that only a small giggle managed to escape her lips. Genius fumed. Not that she hated Porter, but rather she hated being one-upped, and often confused the messenger with the message.

She stewed and was about to issue what she no doubt thought a witty rejoinder when Porter interjected, "Here's the news fer which y'all so've been hankerin.'"

"It's ten o'clock in Central Utah. Good evening and welcome to your High Desert News on AM 1350. Local news in a moment, but first some world headlines. In what has become a regular occurrence for the current Administration, President Carter again today implored the leaders of Israel and Egypt to come together and resolve their respective differences ..."

"Those two 'rascible sides ever git thar shit'n uh coherent 'nough pile tuh quit lobbin' bombs't each other?" Porter asked.

"It's not so simple actually. Last time Insanity was free, he got Ramses the Great and King Solomon the Wise to use the Middle East in a reality chess match that takes about six thousand earth years to complete," I offered in my best deadpan. "They're pretty intense about their game, and I figure it won't get sorted out until about 4242, by my calculations. It's beyond ordinary human control to stem the violent tide. Tragic, really."

"Yore shittin' me! Yore tellin' me't they've been fightin' 'n gotta keep doin' so fer two thousan' more years cuz some old dead kings're playin' uh celestial board game?"

"Yeah, like I said, it's terribly sad. But what am I supposed to do about it?"

"That's not the real reason they're at each other's throats and you know it, Contradiction," Genius opined. "Porter, he's just yanking your chain."

"Well," I told her, "my explanation makes just as much sense as the real reason, doesn't it?" Really, it did, and she was well aware of that fact. In truth, I rather think my historical patriarchs using Jews and Arabs as hapless, unwilling players in a chess match far more plausible than the actual truth. Heck, when Genius first told me why they'd really been killing each other for so long, I thought it was so outrageous that I asked her in complete seriousness if she'd drank Bob Marley's bong water again!

Genius thought about my comment for a second and began, "I guess so; I mean, it is farfetched. If I wasn't there I never would have believed it. Honestly, who could really have predicted that millennia of bloodshed and internecine slaughter would be based upon the simple and undeniably ridiculous fact that the—"

"Governor Matheson ordered more troops to Moab today—"

"Cut it," said The Muse, "here's our story." Porter would have to wait for Genius's definitive history of the indisputably singular cause of Arab and Jewish conflict.

"... to replace the high number of troops who have inexplicably gone AWOL or outright joined the charismatic cult leader, who, I might add, has done a smashing job of frustrating local officials in their attempts to deal with the escalating situation. Colonel Bryce Young of the Utah National Guard is here with me tonight to answer some of our questions. Colonel, what accounts for your apparent inability to keep order within the ranks called out to forcibly extricate the rapidly expanding cult-colony from the northern section of Canyonlands National Park?"

"Thanks for having me here tonight, and let me begin by saying that there is some information that I am not at liberty to divulge at this point in time. And I cannot comment on your question. Suffice it to say that the truth is that I don't have an answer for this insubordination, plain and simple. Every time our troops get close to the leader at his compound in Island in the Sky, they start speaking in tongues, shouting gibberish, as it were, and pulling out their hair or putting down their guns and taking up sides with the enemy. I'll tell you this though, we'll get this taken care of. But like I said, I cannot directly comment on that."

"All right then, next question. We have reports that cult snipers atop the cliffs killed more than twenty soldiers approaching on the White Rim Trail below. One survivor described the bloodbath as 'shooting fish in a barrel.' Is that how you'd describe it, Colonel?"

"No comment, except that the witness's outrageous description is remarkably accurate. Besides that, I'm not at liberty to divulge any information I may or may not have about our troop movements that may or may not have taken place."

"And what of the rumors that some soldiers, as soon as they got close to the stronghold, began shooting themselves and/or each other?"

"This is an extremely troublesome and inexplicable development about which I've no comment at this time except that I can neither confirm nor deny that the situation about which you asked me occurred or did not occur."

"But you just confirmed it."

"Then I deny that I confirmed it. And I have no comment on my original confirmation and/or my subsequent denial thereof."

"Okay, I guess. Then can you confirm that the entire northern region of the park extending dozens of miles west from the Green River, east to the Colorado River, has been cordoned off, even to the military?"

"That hardly seems realistic, does it? But I cannot comment on that at this time."

"There are also stories of soldiers in the first wave who scaled the thousand-foot walls at the base of the mesa/peninsula, then promptly jumped to their deaths upon meeting the leader."

"I can neither confirm nor deny those horrific deaths."

"Hmm ... okay ... and do you have any hard numbers on the amount of people that are presently up there?"

"We're guessing that there are at least five hundred."

"Is there a reason you haven't gone in there yet with overwhelming military force?"

"I'm not at liberty to discuss strategy at this time, but we're considering a massive air strike."

"Can you confirm that there are women and children who will be at risk from such a plan of attack?"

"I can confirm that I can't deny that it's possible any actions we may or may not be currently contemplating, on which I'm not commenting, might in fact put innocent citizens at risk. But I cannot discuss that at this present juncture."

"How do they have power and food and ammunition, considering that they're stranded on an isolated desert mesa?"

"Well, we're not exactly sure. Suffice it to say that they've obviously been planning this long in advance, decades probably! They have generators, as well as hordes of food and ammunition near the ancient Anasazi storehouses at Aztec Butte. But anyone with a whiff of a brain can see that a successful undertaking of this magnitude couldn't have been thrown together willy-nilly over a few months by some insane and haphazard amateur. No, this was the work of pure genius, and we're clearly up against a master of planning and deception."

"Hey, Genius, you've been busy!" I laughed. "I didn't know you were helping Insanity out, too, playing both sides—"

"Shut up and keep listening," she instructed while chuckling.

"... Have you tried to take out their provisions and ammunition dump with an isolated strike?"

"I cannot discuss strategy regarding what we may or may not do, or what actions we've contemplated, but I can say at this time that we have most assuredly considered it."

"Then since you can't discuss what you will deny you admitted, is there a particular reason that you haven't yet destroyed their supplies that you will, of course, refuse to comment on?"

"No, I'll not respond to that. But I will say that our best intelligence photos show that the old Anasazi storehouse has a sign in front that reads Elmer's Authentic Navajo Sandwiches and that there is a balding, middle aged man, along with young teenage boys and girls, preparing sandwiches on top of and inside the building around the clock."

"So they're using human shields?"

"With spatulas. Yes. But I can neither confirm nor deny that."

"Well, thanks for coming on the program tonight, Colonel Young."

"You're welcome."

"After the break, we'll have an expert in mass migration psychoanalytics who will discuss the strange phenomena of people leaving Monticello and Blanding, Utah, to regions further north—"

I turned the radio off, figuring that we'd gotten about all the information that we'd need.

"How long until we're in Moab?" Genius asked.

"Mebee few hours, I reckon," Porter replied. "From there we'll take the White Rim trail northwest'f Moab'n use the dark's cuver'n our way tuh Island'n the Sky—no headlamps. I reckon'f we can git thar well 'nough 'fore sunrise we might could ditch the Scout'n walk up the Shafer Trail, nice'n quiet like, 'n sneak up 'n 'em. They got no reason tuh blow it up when they don' know we're thar."

"But in any event, the White Rim road will take us below the redoubt, right?" Genius requested of the Mountain Man.

"Yup, I don' figure I can git yuh no closer. If'n we 'proach from the north, he'll blast's tuh bits, 'r leastways I'd have tuh shoot lots'f 'nnocent people 'fore we made't thru."

"He'll probably take off when we get that close, anyway," The Muse cut in. "I don't think he wants a confrontation with us; he's got to know that he can't win. At least that'll put us on his trail without him having a small army for protection. We'll get him."

I handed Porter a picture of Insanity, taken from our days together with Winston Churchill, and told him blankly, "Shoot him on sight."

"'N what'f I go plumb insane 'fore I have uh chance?"

"Actually, Porter," The Muse told him politely but firmly, "the truth is that you're already considered crazy. The Archangel Michael told us that you were so completely nuts that there's nothing Insanity can do to you."

"Hmmm, I reckon that might be true," he replied without any trace of hurt feelings as he scratched his beard.

The Muse told me later that Porter wasn't at all crazy and in fact he had full control of his rather formidable mental faculties. But since she didn't really know how he'd react to Insanity, she hoped that the firmness of his belief in his invincibility would protect him. As history would have it, she was largely correct. Mostly.

The End's Beginning

It was about five in the morning, and for the last hour or so my head had been bouncing around the Scout's interior like a restless buoy. We were on the White Rim trail heading south toward Island in the Sky. Having completely failed to get accustomed to the jarring and bumping of the vehicle, I understood why it was called a trail and not a road. No pavement, lots of rocks, and many deep gullies and other some-shit that makes trucks go bounce. Of course, the fact that Porter couldn't see twenty feet ahead of us probably didn't help the experience either.

When we first came upon the trail off the main road outside of Moab, it was blocked by an inept but large and well-armed military contingent. The Muse, Genius, and I were prepared for Porter to blast his way through. But we were happily surprised when he simply drove a couple miles north of the roadblock and took a four-wheel drive detour. "Didn' I tell yuh that y'all needed uh four-wheel-drive?" he said.

Luckily, we hadn't seen anybody since the soldiers at the main highway. Apparently the news was correct that the entire area had been evacuated, even of military personnel.

The first morning light appeared like a mirage over the La Sal Mountains to the east—nothing that you would call sunshine, but certainly a trumpet proclaiming its arrival. The sunrise is a great moment of solar anticipation.

"Are we going to make it to the Shafer Trail before sunrise, Porter?" Genius asked.

"I don' think so," he replied without worry. "Took us uh lil' longer'n I'd hoped tuh take the long way 'round the army. So I guess we can't ditch the truck'n sneak up the Shafer Trail by cuver'f night. Plan B?"

"Plan B it is," I said. "Get as close as we can below the stronghold, try somehow to get Insanity's attention at the ledge, then shoot him. If he flees by zapping himself to God-knows when and where, we follow."

"Why don' yuh just zip yerselfs right up tuh him'n take'm by force?"

Genius responded for the three of us. "That would be good, to be sure. But first, we don't know exactly where he is so there's no way of knowing if we could get close enough to grab him. And second, Insanity's an odd duck, but not entirely daft. As soon as we popped up, he'd have us shot, and we'd be right back where we started. We'd made that mistake the first time he got loose."

"It could always be worse," I added, thinking about what Insanity had done to Jesus.

"So," Genius continued, "hopefully we can get a view of him from a distance when he thinks he's safe—and you can put a bullet through his head."

"Won't yer friend know yore gittin' close?"

"He might, you never can tell what he's going to do about what he knows. Or what he knows at all, for that matter. Either way, I can tell he's near and hasn't left yet," Genius told him.

"He probably feels us coming," The Muse muttered.

"Hopefully, he's busy with a sandwich or something," I added.

"I cannot believe you were right about that," Genius snapped. "Who would have thought he'd hide himself up on a deserted mountaintop and establish a colony dedicated to making his lunch."

"Me, actually, I thought it," I bragged. "Glad you finally acknowledge it." I know Insanity well. It's my job to project the ability to deny what you know and to relativize morals.

We took a westward turn, and by now the daylight had broken enough that I could make out the timeless and impregnable cliffs a few miles ahead. The first direct rays of sunlight illuminated the distant peaks.

"Porter," The Muse asked, "see that little recess in the cliff ahead? Is that a trail I see heading up the rock?"

"Yup, Shafer Trail. Bunch'f years ago, some ol' herders blasted't 'nto the rocks, 'n park service keeps't up."

I began to see more of the surroundings and was impressed by the numerous rock formations that looked positively ghoulish in the half-light. Slender, rocky brown poles supported massive white rocks on their tops, playing a trick on gravity I couldn't explain. It seemed almost like thousand-foot thumbtacks had been dropped randomly around the edges of the mesa. Perhaps the Titans used this area as a corkboard. I made a mental note to ask Cronus about it next time I visited Tartarus.

The horizon looked entirely imposing and unforgiving, so alien that it may as well have been Mars. Cliffs to the right, jagged bluffs straight ahead, and precipitous chasms dropping into the Colorado River on my left. The latter were noticeably marked by an eerie white rim all along its narrow ledge, as if to serve as a warning not to approach too close. For my money, if you can't see the mile-wide canyon, you probably won't see the five-foot-wide limestone strip, either.

When we had finally driven to within a mile from where the Shafer Trail clawed its way to the top of the mesa, I noticed an unnatural dot of light shining toward us from atop the coppery escarpment. "Did you see that light shining on top of the ridge ahead?" I asked.

"Yup, I saw it," Porter replied first. "My guess's that yer friend's checkin' tuh see who's comin'."

Genius, who clearly hadn't seen the light atop the ridge from the backseat, perked up, "That could be bad if-"

But Genius was interrupted by a series of blasts that exploded the Shafer Trail off the side of the cliffs. I was struck with the image of a dynamite razor sheering unwanted human activity from an austere geologic formation. Another question for Cronus.

"Can one'f y'all drive?" Porter asked us all but looked only at me.

"Yeah, why?" I acknowledged with a word as well as a nod, confused as to why he'd want me to take the wheel.

He got out of the truck, took his bag of weapons out of the back, walked over to my door, and lit a cigarette. "Cuz I figure that'n just uh few minutes thar's gonna be uh heap'f shootin', 'n I don' reckon yuh know how tuh operate all this stuff," he gave me my answer as he removed something that looked like a homemade, shoulder-mounted missile launcher.

"Well, you're right that I don't have any idea what to do with one of those, but it looks like fun," I stammered as I scooted over and took the wheel. "Where to?"

"Come on now, thar's only one road'n we ain't goin' backwards! Hit the pedal son, thar's uh fight 'head singin' my name!"

"Get as close as you can, right next to the mesa's face," Genius commanded. "We'll all be able to tell if Insanity leaves, and we can take off after him. Porter knows what to do if he decides to peek his head over the ledge."

What could I do? It seemed that there really weren't too many good choices. I looked quickly at Genius and The Muse, then stomped on the gas, heading straight toward the cloud of raining debris. Island in the Sky jutted out from the cliffs on my right and extended a mile or so to my left, the road trailing surreptitiously underneath—a left turn in a right angle from hell. Porter told us that the ledge below the mesa's most southern point was wide enough that we might be able to get out of range of the expected fire from above.

"So you want us to go straight into firing range, take a hard left at the cliff, and drive directly below them for a mile and hope we can get out of range?" I asked. I was struck with the image of a small ship sailing across the Atlantic to Florida, coming under heavy fire and turning south just before the shore and hoping to find shelter in the Keys.

"Yup, that sounds 'bout right. Don' git scared on me now! Hit it, son!"

I momentarily took my eyes off the road and looked up to see a growing line of people amassing along the overarching bluff. "I hate it when people shoot at me."

"Bah! Git ready!" Porter shouted as bullets rained down and covered the road with angry earthen jets.

"Slow down uh bit'n steady the wheel, will yuh!" Porter yelled as he crawled halfway out the window, seating himself precariously half way in and out of the truck. "This ain't 'xactly easy, yuh know. Genius, gimme the launcher with the missile'n it."

She handed it over as the truck jolted and jumped from a rock that I decided to run over instead of around.

"Shit! Ain't no good. Just stop the damn truck fer uh secon'," he screamed as he flopped out before I could come to a complete stop. I could hear shells hitting the ground in front of us, even though we were still slightly out of range. Porter hefted the launcher atop his shoulder, took aim and fired.

I watched the smoky trail of the shell for the second or two before it crashed with an "oomph" at the feet of our attackers along the rim's edge. At that same instant, dozens of people exploded into the air like a horrific human firework.

Porter rushed back into the cab and threw the launcher on Genius's lap, "That should lessen the fire'n make'em think twice 'bout standing on the ledge!" He looked at me and smiled like the crazy man he was. "Hit the gas, son!"

I was about to floor it, to forge ahead into the battle. Adrenaline pumped a strange mixture of excitement and fear through my veins! Of course, half the people shooting down at me from the stronghold weren't there anymore. That helped allay the fear. That and the fact that I can usually just ignore that I'm scared or frightened.

But despite my frenzied desire, I didn't drive into the melee, not at first anyway. An unexpected distant explosion sent shockwaves through the air and took us all by grim surprise.

"What the fuck did you just do?" Genius screamed at Porter.

"I din' do nothin'," he shouted. "Leastways nothin' that'd cause that kind'f noise."

"I think it came from the northwest," I said as I surveyed the sky in that direction. And sure enough, a large, smoky plume rose a few miles north on top of the mesa. "You see that?" I asked.

"Yeah, I see it," said Genius.

"What do you figure it is?" asked The Muse.

"Mebee the army finely had 'nough'n broke through the northern barricade."

"Look, the people are scattering," I told them as I pointed to the running throngs atop the cliffs. "They don't seem interested in us anymore."

"They're not scattering," The Muse said in a reflective whisper. "They're fleeing. South along the ridge, the only direction they can flee an assault from the north. And they've blown up the Shafer Trail, which could have served as an escape route."

Droves of people ran along the ledge toward the southern cliffs. Where they hoped to go, I had no idea, but they seemed a little too much like lemmings at this point for my liking. More booming detonations pounded our ears from the north.

"Drive," Porter barked. I floored it southward along the base of Island in the Sky toward its narrow southern promontory. People still scampered along the top as we came to a widening of the ledge on which we'd been driving. What before had been a narrow strip of land no more than a few hundred yards wide now stretched broadly for almost a half mile, high above the deep river canyons that fell to our left.

"Stop!" Porter yelled, and we screeched to a dusty halt precisely below the southernmost tip of the mesa. "The people aren't runnin' tuh nothin', but away from somethin'. Problem's that they ain't got nowhere tuh go." He pointed up at the jagged ledge where Island in the Sky ended, "That's the only place they got. If your boy's with'em, I'll take'em out. He still up thar?" he asked.

"Yeah, he hasn't gone anywhere yet," I said.

"But he's confused," said The Muse.

"How can you tell that?" I asked her.

"I just can. Something's not at all right up there," she said, as we listened to the continued explosions that were becoming more frequent and alarmingly less muted by distance. To complicate matters, a low, humming sound I thought was far-off helicopters had joined in the explosive cacophony.

"Can you see the choppers?" Genius asked as she searched the sky. By now the sun had risen completely over the La Sal Mountains to the east, and she shielded her eyes when she faced that direction.

"Nah, don' see 'em. Thar probably flyin' low through the canyons, tuh 'void bein' seen directly." He lit another cigarette and offered me one. I refused. I only smoke cigars. "Ain't no point presenten'n easy target, I reckon'. Y'all shore yuh don' wanna zap yerselves up thar'n see what yer boy's up to?"

"I don't think it will work," Genius said.

"I don't know that it will do any good," I added.

"I just don't want to," whispered The Muse, as she nodded her head toward the cliff, her face contorted with disgusted horror. "They're jumping."

We jerked our heads up, terrified at the sight of people plunging from the thousand-foot cliffs. Most didn't even stop to consider their fate before they leapt, and those that did only hesitated for a second, if that long. The Muse flinched and turned away. Porter, Genius, and I watched with morbid fascination as more than a few hapless victims splat on the rocks below. From this distance, they impacted with a muffled whump that sounded like balloons popping inside an insulated cardboard box.

"Yer boy's doin' quite uh number'n all those followers'f his. I'd say he's plumb good't what he does, I'll giv'em that."

"He's not doing this. Making them leap to their deaths, I mean," The Muse told Porter with a twinge. "I don't understand exactly why, but this is different somehow." The way she said this made my skin chafe and crawl, and my heart skipped a beat. We watched Insanity's unwitting legions dive to their deaths, and hoped he'd show his face at the ledge. Porter had his long-range sniper rifle at the ready, should the opportunity for its use present itself.

"Do you hear how close those helicopters are? They're so loud!" Genius commented on the growing whir. "I can't believe we can't see them."

I thought about that while I watched a large group stop on the edge and assemble around one man on the precipice. Genius, The Muse, and I knew who it was, even though we couldn't directly see him. The cult had stopped their tragic plummets to shield Insanity. They huddled tightly around him, literally and figuratively at death's edge.

"I don't think the copters are in the canyons below," Genius added. "I think they're on top of the mesa chasing them."

"You think they're herding them?" I asked her. "Why doesn't Insanity leave?" My skin itched and I began to sweat, and I could see that the others were also physically disturbed.

"Does bein' this close tuh yer friend always make yuh feel so anxious?" Porter asked, "I feel like I'm crawlin' out'f my skin." He said this more as a comment than a complaint. His body may have known fear but his mind didn't recognize it.

"Not usually," said The Muse. "Not to us, at any rate."

"I'm telling you, those choppers are almost on top of us," Genius yelled, as the noise had grown exponentially in the last minute.

"By my ears, thar here, I reckon," deadpanned Porter Rockwell, "right ... 'bout ... now!"

"Shit!" I shouted as the assembled mass exploded off the cliff, their bodies bursting as something shot them mercilessly off the mesa. A final flurry cast every last person to their painful demise. Absolutely everybody, that is, except Insanity, who now stood alone atop the ledge. He had his back to us, facing what he must have decided presented the more immediate and graver danger.

"How in Christ's name did the chopper's machine guns miss Insanity?" Genius screamed, "And why hasn't he zapped himself out of this?"

"I don't think he can move," said The Muse, "it's like he's scared stiff. And he doesn't get scared."

"I don' figyur those're helicopters we're hearin'," said Porter. "They sound more like motorcycles, if'n y'all ask me. Harley Davidsons, I reckon." I ignored this comment and asked him if he had the shot.

Yeah, gimme uh secon'," he replied.

"Shoot that fucker!" I yelled to be heard over the droning choppers.

Orrin Porter Rockwell had ice in his veins. He had faced down innumerable cold-blooded killers and locked eyes with dozens of criminally dangerous mortal enemies. And so I didn't understand why he had beads of sweat dripping from his forehead or why his body anxiously agitated from within. But his trigger finger was calm and cool as he fired his shot.

Porter never missed in his life, and he had no reason to believe he would now. The crack of his rifle split the dry air, and Insanity doubled over. The shot went straight through his back and heart, and he stumbled backward toward the cliff and was ready to flop off the edge.

But he didn't. He should have, but he didn't. In fact, he'd never touch the dusty desert ground below that claimed all of his acolytes. Not this time. And just as surprising, neither would he collapse in a lifeless heap on the precipice above.

One of these two things should have happened, had to have happened, in fact. Yet, they didn't. Don't get me wrong, it wasn't as if some trick of physics kept him in a suspended state between standing erect and flopping into a heap. Nothing that complicated. No strange scientific gimmicks. No bodily purgatory. Instead, as had happened so often lately, what happened next defied all expectation. Luckily, however, what my mind lacked in understanding my mouth made up for in action.

"Fire! Fire!" I shouted. "God damn it, Porter Rockwell, fire!"

THIS IS THE END

Porter Rockwell's first shot echoed with accurate destruction. As Insanity was about to collapse from the bullet Porter put through his heart, a massive arm protruding from a hulking giant on a motorcycle swept him up. And then dove off the cliff. That's when I yelled at Porter to shoot them. But just as he got the next shot off, the riders (one dead and one unfortunately not) disappeared into the ether between the here and now, and the there and then, and left only a careening motorcycle in their wake and a bewildered projectile.

"Damn it!" shouted Genius. "Now they've gone and complet—"

Another crack from Porter's rifle ended my ability to hear her, and my eyes were ripped from the first falling chopper by two more motorcycles speeding off the cliff. Porter didn't give them time to disappear to God-only-knows where, and he didn't miss this time, either.

Before he could zap himself away, The Antichrist's head erupted into a bloody geyser that almost snapped his neck off his body. This gruesome spectacle was immediately followed by the report of Porter's next shot that appeared to spear War through the chest. To this day I have no idea how he hit those two flying targets as they flew off a cliff nearly one thousand feet above us. But as surprised as I was by his accuracy, the speed with which he took his next action was positively heroic. While The Antichrist and War plummeted, Porter grabbed a grenade launcher, gauged the trajectory, and fired low along the horizon where the Two Horsemen weren't, but where his best guess told him they'd be in a couple seconds.

"You missed!" yelled Genius, half astonished at his shot and half gloating.

"Nah, I got one'f 'em," he responded. And he was right, for The Antichrist's thud as he hit terra firma was immediately followed by Porter's trailing grenade. *BOOM!* He wouldn't be going anywhere for a few hours, I hoped.

We all turned quickly, hoping to see War's dead body hit the ground like The Antichrist's, but it didn't. At the point of impact, where there should have been a maimed body and mangled motorcycle, a dense and angry mushroom cloud spouted high into the sky. It was a nuclear Old Faithful that was far from old. It was faithful to be sure, but regrettably to the wrong master.

"What'n the sam-hell does that mean?" Porter asked dumbly for all of us. Which of course meant that none of us had an answer.

"I have no clue. But let's get the cuffs we have for Insanity and put them on what's left of The Antichrist before he comes to," Genius started shouting instructions.

"I don't think he's going anywhere for a while. Besides," I told her as I made out War's massive figure striding toward us through the smoke a quarter of a mile away, "I'm not so sure it's going to be that easy to get The Antichrist out of here. Should we leave?" I asked. "This won't end well."

"Porter, kill that man now!" Genius shouted as she stood in my face, jabbing my chest painfully with her finger. "Listen, we've got The Antichrist dead and in our grasp, and I'm not about to tell Michael and Uriel that we let him get away without a fight." The Muse tossed me a gun from Porter's bag. "Get ready!"

"You're right," I yelped, ignoring my fear. "Bastard's got it coming!"

Porter picked up his launcher and a missile, loading the latter onto the former before hefting the heavy contraption onto his shoulder. He quickly let loose his volley, and as soon as the projectile left the barrel, War jumped high in the air, landing closer to us and easily one hundred yards from where the missile crashed into the desert floor.

"Shit!" Porter shouted as he picked up his rifle and fired a few shots. "That thar's one hell of uh nimble fellah!"

"Fuckkkkkkkkk!" I said as I emptied the magazine of my Uzi, the recoil robbing my aim of anything resembling aim.

"Aahhhhgggggggg!" Genius screamed while she fired her .45 magnum at War's chest.

"Now might be uh good time tuh go 'n get yer friends, don' yah think?" Porter whispered as we watched War nimbly contort his mountainous frame, dodging every bullet without incurring a scratch. It was too easy.

"Yeah," The Muse shouted excitedly, "I'll go and see if—"

War put a well-aimed shot through her throat that fiercely ended her train of thought. Or any other thought she may have had, for that matter. Genius flew back into a heap immediately after. I closed my eyes in anticipation. But I didn't get hit. Not that War wasn't shooting at me, but rather that I had jumped behind Porter, and War's bullets bounced right off him. Although admittedly they did push him back a few feet.

Porter bent down to pick up an extra ammo clip just as I was about to zap out of there, and for a split second I was exposed, which was a split second too long. That was all the time War needed. I didn't hear the shot, but I felt a terrible searing pain in the side of my head as I fell. What was left of my vision flashed white lightning, and I slumped to the ground, conscious, if barely. He'd hit me, but only with a grazing shot to my skull, and he hadn't killed me. Unfortunately, however, he'd left me too dazed to realize that I could get out of there. On the other hand, I did remain somewhat alert enough to see the extraordinary battle between the Apocalyptic Horseman and Orrin Porter Rockwell.

Both seasoned combatants promptly realized that their various guns weren't going to get the job done, so Porter simply stood his ground while War confidently strode toward his prey. At ten meters, I saw blood streaming from the shoulder of War's black duster where Porter's shot had sliced through him. He had hit his target but missed the mark by a few inches.

At ten feet, War reached behind his head into his coat and pulled out the same two-handed, double-edged, serrated broadsword with which he'd skewered Leviticus. With a maniacal gleam in his eyes, he held it forth for Porter to see, twisting it in the light; he wanted him to know he was going to run him through with it, wanted him to feel the fear of the blade before it gutted him, wanted to torture him with fear, and on top of that with the fear of that fear.

Porter would have none of it. "Wow! By the looks'f it yuh gots yerself uh real nice piece of metal thar. Plenty sharp, too! But I say, I figyur by the wild look'n yer eyes'n the fact that yore just standin' there not doin' nothin', that yore uh might bit confused 'bout what yuh should do with it." War didn't reply and looked at him with cold menace.

"So here's what yuh do, uh lil' advice from me tuh you, cuz I'm that kind'f guy. Yuh come'n at me 'n see if yuh can pierce me with't. Take yer best shot, don' be shy now. But'n fairness, I gotta tell yuh 'n 'dvance, 't won't work. 'N fact, most likely I'll end up takin' that sword out'f yer hands'n shovin' 't so far up yer ass it'll fork yer tongue." He said this in dead seriousness but with a sardonic grin. "Do you like the taste?"

At this insult, War jumped at him with astounding speed, and despite his most agile attempt, Porter didn't have time to completely dodge the ferocious battery. It didn't matter though, as the sword didn't break his skin and the strike only succeeded in as much as it knocked him a few feet to the side. War looked at his prey with savage vitriol! He'd delivered upon him his most beastly attack, the same that had nearly flayed Leviticus, and it hadn't even left so much as a mark on this impetuous mountainy ruffian.

Porter took advantage of War's hesitation and snatched the sword from his strong grasp, breaking it in two over his thigh. Cracking his knuckles, he scolded, "Is that all yuh got? I ain't even worked up uh sweat!" Porter grunted and hit War with a brutal right cross that sent him tumbling to within a few feet of the ledge.

War took the punch better than I'd have expected, and shot back up, engaged Porter ferocious thundering blow for thundering blow. It was like the greatest of heavyweight fights, and there was no referee to stop it. If there had been, she might have thrown in the towel for War, as he was beginning to take the brunt of the beating and could no longer hold his ground. Porter sensed this and doubled his attack to put him away, brutally crushing War's jaw with an overhand right. War staggered back and then retreated a few feet by jumping away from Porter, safely putting some distance between him and his seemingly invincible tormentor. He looked thoroughly puzzled but stoic at the same time. He didn't know what he was facing, but he also didn't fear it, he just couldn't figure it out. The Horseman was buying himself time and had no intention of retreating and abandoning his malevolent master. Like a great tactician he was trying to find Porter's weaknesses.

Despite my painful gash, my head had mostly cleared, and I probably could have zapped myself out of there, but as Porter was clearly winning, I saw no need to rush off and get help. In fact, I even stood up to watch War take his well-deserved ass-kicking.

Porter Rockwell didn't want to ease his assault and flung himself forward to dispatch War for good. But the resourceful minion wasn't done yet and struck Porter with a lightning bolt to the chest that stopped him in his tracks. While it didn't appear to do any skeletal damage, it was so powerfully electric that it unknotted his braids and stood all his hair on end, even his beard.

"Ah, I ain't never felt nothin' like that b'fore. Kinda electrifyin' 'f I do say so." He laughed and looked at the hair that was still sticking up on his arms.

And War laughed, too. Nothing like Porter's cocky guffaw, but instead a guttural snigger that began almost inaudibly, then got stronger and louder, more confident. Bellicosely so. Far more abruptly than it had begun, he stopped his menacing chortle and positively smiled, nodding his head slightly, as if he'd just discovered a secret whose knowledge he'd long since desired. And then he spoke in icy coldness, in the same low grumble of his laugh, the only words I'd heard him speak.

"Samson."

"Not really, but if't makes yuh feel 'ny better tuh think that the hairy biblical one beat yuh, so be 't."

War nodded, smiling maliciously as he lit a cigarette and took an exaggerated drag, ignoring the pain radiating from his shattered jaw. He nonchalantly bent down and picked up the handled half of his frightful sword.

"Won' do yuh no good no how," Porter laughed. "Yuh learn as well's yuh speak, I take it!"

War exhaled through his nose and raised his empty hand with his palm facing upwards. In it, he produced a small, floating fireball; he gently blew on it and it began to spin. For a moment his eyes followed the spinning orb, then he looked up intently. Taking another drag from the cigarette hanging from his mouth, he blew the smoke at the fireball with a whoosh that sent it flying at Porter. He didn't have time to avoid the blazing projectile that momentarily lit him up like a human candlestick.

Although I had no doubt that his flesh survived the fire well enough, I could tell by the nauseating smell that his hair and beard weren't so lucky. It was Porter's turn to be exposed and vulnerable, bald as a babe with his clothes melting painfully to his blistering skin.

And now, Orrin Porter Rockwell, the great and notorious Danite Chieftain, fierce, loyal, and fearless mountain man with Herculean strength who had lived nearly two hundred years, stood silently naked in front of this Horseman of the Apocalypse who would now deal him his death. He had lived long enough to regret the wrongs he committed and long enough also to seek redemption from the one person least likely to forgive him—himself. And at this, his dying moment, he was resolute, unafraid, and unapologetic.

"Don' take all day," he said, right before War viciously heaved what was left of his sword through Porter's chest. His torso exploded and he flew over the cliff into the Colorado River below. But I didn't stop to see him actually land, because no sooner had this happened than War grabbed me by my throat and began to squeeze slowly. I could tell by his grunting that he was enjoying my suffering.

As the light slowly faded and I succumbed to the frightening and painful darkness of strangulation, I heard a faint crash and a thud. The crash was the blow that hit War, and the thud was the sound I made as he dropped me.

Light burned its way back into my brain as Jesus helped me to my feet. Through my hazy vision, I could see Deuteronomy and War rabidly exchanging white-hot lightning bolts, profligate pyrotechnics, and indecipherable epithets.

"Are you all right?" Jesus asked me.

"Yeah, I think so," I coughed. "My head hurts like crazy though. I hope Deuteronomy decapitates that fucker."

"He's trying, but I think he'll be lucky if he can simply hold him off long enough for us to gather up The Antichrist, The Muse, and Genius and get out of here."

A droning whir caught our attention, and approaching military helicopters appeared on the horizon. I thought I could hear fighter jets, too.

"Pick up those cuffs and let's get them on The Antichrist," Jesus yelled over the battle and approaching military clamor. I scooped them up and we ran to The Antichrist, but War saw our surreptitious movements on the periphery and cut us off with a fireball that sent us hurling to the ground.

"I hate that guy," I shouted. Once again the pungent odor of singed hair had its way with my gag reflex; this time it was from my own arms.

"You don't know the half of it," spat the unexpected voice of the Archangel Michael, as he helped Jesus and me to our feet. "That damned beast is nearly impossible to kill!" Uriel stood next to him, and they both looked like they'd been through hell. Their wings were scorched in some places and torn in others, and their clothes were stained with more blood than their bodies could carry at any one time.

"Commander Mike!" I yelped. "Uriel! Where are Gabriel and Raphael?"

"Hopefully, Gabriel's trailing Famine, and we're pretty sure Raphael's head is in that sack on War's back, I'm not sure where his body is," he yelled as he ran with Uriel to join the fight. "Get The Antichrist in those shackles, and if anything happens to us, take him to The GateKeeper, he'll know what to do."

Jesus and I ran to the wreck of a beautiful motorcycle and an even more beautiful face. I tapped The Antichrist's mangled legs with my foot to make sure he was in fact currently dead. Jesus stood and stared, lost in his thoughts, as he considered his diabolical and obscenely evil twin.

"Put them on him," he tossed me the cuffs. "I can't touch him." I looked at him in surprise.

"It's that matter/antimatter Christ/Antichrist thing. We can't touch. In fact, I'm not even sure we're supposed to meet."

"Well, he's not awake so half your problem is a nonstarter," I told him as I clicked the restraints shut. "You know, how do these shackles keep Insanity and him from zapping themselves places?" I asked The Christ, having never actually considered it before.

"Truthfully? I have no idea," he replied. "Genius explained the physics of it once, but I tuned her out."

I turned around to watch the battle at the same time that a helicopter decided to make a secular entrance, raining bullets on the participants from two mounted machine guns. Uriel was unmoved by their fiery display and cut it short with a vaporizing lightning bolt. A fighter jet came zooming above the copter's smoky debris and dropped a heavy bomb on the cataclysmic melee, putting a cease to the action. When the smoke cleared, Deuteronomy, Uriel, and Michael stood covered in bloody soot, furious as they realized War had slipped away.

"Damn it!" yelled Michael, wiping a stream of blood from his eyes and forcing his hip back into its socket. It made a sickening kerplok sound. "I hate them!"

"Do you know where he went?" I asked Mike as they approached, limping gingerly.

"Yeah, well, a general idea," he responded as he surveyed the wreckage of motorcycles, helicopters, Insanity's followers, and The Antichrist.

"They're in Europe," Uriel finished his thought. "We'll know more about the specifics of when and where as we get close."

"I'm pretty sure he and Famine had a prearranged meeting place," Michael continued. "The problem is that they're enough ahead of us that we're going to be a step behind; it's been this way for a while." He spit out more blood. "Damn it, damn it!"

"Michael, you need to go help Gabriel," Uriel interrupted, "he's probably pissing himself right now, even if he hasn't caught up to them yet. I'll take The Antichrist back to Elephant Rock and meet up with you. The GateKeeper will have him back inside before he even regains consciousness." She looked down at the bloody heap and addressed me with newfound respect, "Did you do this? Impressive."

"I wish. Porter Rockwell did."

"Nice work," Michael added. "I've been trying to do this for weeks! I told you he's good."

"He almost had War, too. You should have seen it, broke his jaw nearly off his face, he hit him so hard. But then War burned his hair off so he was vulnerable." I remembered the stench and had to choke back some vomit. "That was the end of that. And Porter, for that matter."

"Yeah," Uriel said, "War's good. We keep finding out the hard way. He doesn't say much, but packs a wallop." She turned to Michael, "Get going! Don't worry, I'll be there soon." The Archangel Michael disappeared to continue the good fight against War and Famine.

Uriel sighed heavily, "I don't know what those two are capable of without their dear leader," she said, kicking The Antichrist hard in the head. "As much as I hate to say it, I don't know if their disorganized chaos is any better than organized." She picked up his limp body. "See you later. Jesus, Deuteronomy, if you want to join, you know where to find us?"

"Yeah," Jesus replied, "but while you're going after War and Famine, Deuteronomy and I are going to try to work on undoing the damage they've done."

She shrugged her shoulders, "All right, adios!" With that, Uriel and The Antichrist vaporized to Elephant Rock.

"Contradiction, you want to come with us?" Jesus asked me, "We could use your help."

I told them that I might join them later, but I wanted to wait for The Muse and Genius to come to, and then I'd like to relax at Foresters and Lager Heads for a while. This whole experience had really been taxing. I was beat. "Deuteronomy, are you all right? I mean, I really am sorry about your brother, and I'm concerned about you, too."

"Thanks, I'll be okay," he said with more wistfulness than sadness.

"Let's go," said Jesus as they shook my hand and left.

"Where is Porter," a voice from behind me caught me by surprise. The Muse slowly sat up, maimed and groggy. "Are you all right?" She touched my head wound as she looked around. "What happened with War? Is Genius okay?" she asked as she poked her limp body with a pointy stick.

"Quit poking me! I'm all right, I think," Genius yelled as she took a deep breath and slapped the stick out of The Muse's hand. "Yeah, I'm okay, I guess, but I'm more than a little pissed off. Where is The Antichrist? Where are War and Porter?"

"Look," I said, thinking that a good and thorough explanation would take more breath than I cared to spend at the moment. "The short of it is that Porter's gone and Uriel took The Antichrist back to the Valley of Fire."

They both looked at me with disbelief.

"How long were we out?" The Muse asked.

"Uriel was here? Was she with Michael?" Genius demanded.

"Your head doesn't look so good," The Muse unnecessarily informed me.

"It's a good thing you don't have a mirror," I told her. "Don't worry, I'll give you all the details. But believe me, it's going to take some time, and right now I'm totally exhausted. Let's go to Oregon to get some good beer and take it back to the bar and I'll tell you all about it. As a matter of fact, let's get some sandwiches, too. I'm starving."

Epilogue

"So tell me," Deuteronomy enthusiastically asked his good friend Jesus, "what are we doing here, again? Who's up next on the list?" He adjusted himself to get comfortable on the bus stop bench, and inhaled the cool, December Alabama air.

Jesus reached into the pocket of his white, short-sleeved, buttoned-down shirt and handed Deuteronomy a list. Taking a drink of the Southern sweetened tea he loved, he told his friend, "Someone's going to come to this stop and do something miraculous. It won't seem like it at first, and in fact she may even shrug it off at times. But make no mistake, it will take great strength and personal conviction. You'll like her. We'll just stay with her a few moments, however; she's quite accomplished on her own and doesn't need much help."

"I know, I know," Deuteronomy replied happily, "just that additional little something to help them see things through the darkest of times. That extra indignation that keeps the fire lit in the rain," he said as he used a worn pencil to cross Rosa Parks—Alabama, off the list.

He looked at it one last time before folding it up and handing it to Jesus. Gandhi—India ...

* * *

Meanwhile, on another day, half a world away, two colossal men sat calmly in a shallow trench amid the wretched sounds of war along the French River Somme. They didn't speak much. In fact, they hardly ever spoke. It was such a chaotic environment that nobody who served with them would ever remember they had met them. Most of them died anyway. But the prisoner these two behemoths kept with them at all times would occasionally chance to speak.

"Explain to me just what we're doing here again?" the shackled captive demanded of his unfeeling wardens. "And you two have to know that your absurd belt buckles clash with the rest of your Prussian military attire, don't—"

War interrupted Insanity with a vicious slap across his face. Famine let slip a small cackle as War took a crumpled piece of paper from his tattered jacket and stuffed it violently in Insanity's hand.

"Find him," War groaned, barely audible over the sound of the machine guns cutting down the latest British infantry wave.

Insanity had been through this with them on many occasions in many locations, and no matter how mercilessly they beat him, whatever remained of him was defiant and indignant. "How the hell am I supposed to find this guy in this interminable maze of trenches? He's probably dead anyway! Look, there are bodies everywhere—you love this stuff, it's your work, you find him!" and he threw the wadded paper back at War.

War punched him hard in the gut. "Find him," he grumbled again.

"Ugh, you're an asshole! I don't even have any idea where to start!" He looked at War and Famine, who remained quite unmoved by his assurances that his help was useless. "Fine, I'll just shout it out! Maybe that will work. Will that make you feel better? Better enough to stop pummeling me?" He took a deep breath and screamed, hoping more to piss off his captors than to find their objective. "Who the fuck is Hitler?"

*   *   *

"And four makes five," Wovoka smiled and dealt the cards to the relaxed players sitting around a stone table below Elephant Rock. Coyote lapped her beer from its stein that had been ergonomically designed for her long, canid snout.

"This is a great beer," she said as she used her long tongue to lick the chocolate-colored foam from her jowls. "Where did God get it again?"

"Oregon,"The GateKeeper finished what was left of his first pint. "God's favorite brewery is the Deschutes Brewery in Bend, Oregon. This is their Black Butte Porter."

"It's pretty country up there," Wovoka mentioned wistfully.

"I've been all over the West, I shorely have." Porter Rockwell picked up his cards with one hand and a beer with the other. "But I don' reckon I've ever actually set foot nor hide'n Oregon, leastways not since it's been uh state. I've half uh mind tuh make uh trip tuh see it. Y'all wanna go?" He set his beer down and twisted his beard's braids, separating them from his long gray locks that had reappeared.

"Sure," Wovoka answered, "we can ski if we go in the winter."

"I can't go," The GateKeeper muttered.

"And I can't ski!" Coyote looked up from her beer just long enough to put in her foamy two cents worth. "But you can carry me on your back in one of those baby-carrier backpacks! It will be awesome! Imagine the slaphappy faces of the people as they try to figure out why a coyote in a parka is cruising down the hill on the back of a yeti cowboy!"

"Well, Coyote," Wovoka said, "you can come along for the ride then." He picked up his cards as she nodded absently. "Now listen, Porter, I suppose you know the rules of poker, but lest Coyote try to convince you otherwise, there are only four aces in the deck."

THE PLAYERS

CONTRADICTION
ALIAS: COGNITIVE DISSONANCE.
Fresh from Neville Chamberlain's *Denial of the Obvious* and Immanuel Kant's *The Joy of Moral Ambiguities*, Contradiction lends his skills as the story's Narrator. "I always wanted to get into narrating! It's been a joy to tell myself that I don't care about things that I do care about!"

GOD
God portrays God as an omniscient, omnipresent, and omnipotent Supreme Being whose stubborn and seemingly philosophically inconsistent detached deism precludes any frank admission of these qualities.

THE MUSE
"I'm just happy to finally have a role without a hackneyed, self-important, and exceptionally tedious invocation! I haven't had this much fun since I inspired surrealism!"

GENIUS
"After The Christian Right's surprisingly effective assault on rationality, it's been absolutely fantastic to reprise my role as the embodiment of God's intellect! To tell the bitter truth, I never thought I'd work again after my part in Creationism and the Deep South."

INSANITY
"It's a great role, really. One part socially pathological and the other part pathologically social! Plus, I got paid in sandwiches! How can you top that?"

ARCHANGEL GABRIEL
ALIASES: GABRIELUS, CHERUB.
Widely acclaimed for his role in The Nativity as the audacious Angel who kept a straight face while telling a young betrothed virgin that she'd been knocked up by God, Gabriel brings an inflated sense of austere credibility to all his outlandish and tedious pronouncements.

LEVITICUS
ALIAS: GOD'S WRATH (BOOK III OF THE OLD TESTAMENT

PERSONIFIED).
Best known for his stellar work naming an Old Testament book after himself, Leviticus spends his spare time publicly berating animals that don't chew their cud (11:3-8), making sure women are worth forty percent less than men (27:3), keeping handicapped people from approaching church altars (21:16-23), and angrily hating pretty much everything that isn't his little brother Deuteronomy.
Likes: hating things. Dislikes: things he hates.

DEUTERONOMY
ALIAS: GOD'S WRATH (BOOK V OF THE OLD TESTAMENT PERSONIFIED).
Deuteronomy's literary foray outdid his older brother's with thirty percent more misogyny (20:13-14 in war, kill all the conquered men—women take unto yourself), new ridiculous dietary prohibitions (14), doubly cruel genocidal aggrandizement, and plainly pagan sacrifice instructions (12:27). The "Brothers Wrath" have a running contest to see who can put the most people to death via prolix dogma.

WOVOKA
A Northern Paiute Shaman born around 1856 and raised in rugged northwestern Nevada, Wovoka unexpectedly came out of a well-deserved retirement to appear in this novel. Although he's happy history hasn't completely forgotten him, he's more than a little disconcerted that a fair portion of his ancestral lands have been overtaken by something called a "Wal-Mart."

THE DEVIL
ALIASES: LUCIFER, SATAN.
A petulant ass with a penchant for spicy cigars, played by a petulant ass with a penchant for spicy cigars.

JESUS
ALIAS: GOD'S LOVE.
"It's a fabulous opportunity," says Jesus about reprising his part as God's Love. "It really allows me to explore my human side, but without the usual anti-Semitism and excess bloodletting."

JUDAS
Christ's most notorious disciple would like the civil authorities to note that Jesus is the person listed directly above him in the credits and that he's blowing him a literary kiss. Judas expects his payment in euros, as

shekels don't seem to have much value now.

COYOTE
ALIASES: THE GREAT MISCREANT, THE TRICKSTER.
This is Coyote's first appearance in a novel since she received the coveted award for "Mythological creature most likely to dispense invaluably sage advice while pissing on your leg."

THE GATEKEEPER
ALIASES: OMNIBENEVOLENCE, THE CRIMSON SERAPH, THE SERAPH.
One of only two Seraphim, six-winged Angels of the Highest Order, The GateKeeper is God's goodness in its purest form. "The best part of this role is its absolute moral clarity and lack of morally ambiguous character development."

EVIL
ALIASES: OMNIMALEVOLENCE, DEPRAVED SERAPH, FOURTH HORSEMAN, DEATH.
The GateKeeper's opposite is also a Seraphim Angel of the Highest Order. He is God's Evil in its purest form. "The best part of this role is its absolute moral clarity and lack of morally ambiguous character development."

ARCHANGEL URIEL
ALIASES: FIRE OF GOD, LIGHT OF GOD.
Uriel comes to us after her performance in the second book of Esdras, where she adroitly explained some stuff to Ezra by not explaining it. This keeper of cosmic mysteries and ruler of the divine order asks that we ignore her role in Milton's *Paradise Lost*, where she unwittingly led Satan toward the Earth. "Not my best work."

ARCHANGEL MICHAEL
ALIAS: FIELD COMMANDER.
When first asked to reprise his role as the Commander of God's armies, Michael responded, "Oh hell yeah! I've been bored to tears with stale roles like hiding Moses's tomb from Satan and protecting Eve's bones. I still have my celestial armor! I keep it locked up in the Book of Revelation!"

ORRIN PORTER ROCKWELL
ALIAS: BRIGHAM'S DESTROYING ANGEL.

Old Porter Rockwell is thrilled to play the role he was born to play—himself. This outlaw, guide, mountain man, law man and confidant and bodyguard of Brigham Young and Joseph Smith comes to us of his own free will because God told him to.

THE ANTICHRIST

After his award-winning, twenty-year run as the lead in Saddam You, The Antichrist happily jumped back into his role as the diabolical leader of the Horsemen of the Apocalypse from the Book of Revelation. "My work is a constantly evolving challenge. I have to be able to be whoever people abhor most at any given moment. It's moved way beyond simply opposing Christ."

WAR

We thank War for taking time from his busy schedule to reprise his role as the most violent Horseman of the Apocalypse. Look for him and his slaughter on his never-ending worldwide tour; he's always playing somewhere and doesn't anticipate running out of work anytime soon. "It's a growth industry."

FAMINE

"It's been right cool to get back into biblical work," Famine says of his role as the apocalyptic henchman who robs the world of nourishment. "I mean, the whole Irish potato thing got stale, and it's not even a challenge anymore to starve poor people, you know? It bored me." Thanks to genetic engineering and thoughtless globalization, you'll see him in the forthcoming starvation epic, *Corn, Salmon, and Rice*.

EXTRAS

ELMER
ALIASES: SANDWICH GUY, THE FAT MAN.
Elmer lives in Monticello, Utah, and has a bad comb-over and big belly. He calls sandwiches tacos and calls polygamy the directive of the Lord. He's a respected civic leader, loves his wives, and adores his children.

LEHI
Lehi is a teenage boy from Monticello, Utah, who is thankful for this challenging role, but tired of having to explain his name to ignorant gentiles. Following the lead of innumerable adolescents, he blames his parents for this worst of travesties. (Lehi was a Mormon Prophet

whose son Nephi was urged by God, around 500 B.C., to sail from the Middle East, across the Atlantic Ocean, to found the Nephite civilization in Central America. Mormons believe that after the resurrection, Jesus took a prolonged working holiday in the New World to teach the Nephites Christianity.)

PETER
Peter guards the gates of Heaven and operates a bar—and laughs at the dead people and drunks who frequently cannot differentiate between the two establishments.

EDNA
One of Elmer's three wives and Lehi's three mothers. Surviving matriarch of a destroyed family.

CONNOR GALLAGHER
An Irish potter known as much for his jovial brogue as his pottery. Whether or not you can understand him, he'll ramble endlessly about his wife Serwa and daughter Alex.

ALEXANDRA EFORIANA AKOSUA
This precocious little girl is the daughter of Serwa and Connor. She will not tell you where she hides her teddy bear, so don't bother asking.

SERWA AKOSUA
An expatriate painter from Ghana.

JAMES KIMBALL "BIG JIM" BECKSTEAD
A gregarious, larger-than-life westerner with a trademark larger-than-Texas cowboy hat.

DETROIT HOMELESS MAN
I'd like to thank Sir Richard Attenborough for appearing as the Detroit Homeless Man. But Richard Attenborough doesn't appear in this book as a homeless man or any other character, so thanking him for work he didn't do would just be weird.

STONER #1
Every good story needs a stoner.

STONER #2
Two stoners are twice as good, three are just overkill.

About the Author

Brett Cottrell was born and bred in Las Vegas, Nevada. His writings blend religious and political satire with whimsical, action-packed absurdity. He's been a bartender, drummer in a rock and roll band, legislative intern, and attorney. He studied political theory at Boise State University and graduated from the George Washington University Law School. Cottrell lives in Washington, DC, with his wife and their opinionated dog, Tico.

Also Available from Rosarium ...

Jennifer's Journal: The Life of a Suburban Girl, Vol. 1
Jennifer Cruté
978-0-9903191-6-0

"Jennifer's extraordinary odyssey is at once hilarious, sly, witty, provocative, and, at times, heartbreaking. I absolutely adore this book."

—Barbara Brandon-Croft, *Where I'm Coming From*

By turns funny, poignant, melancholic, and life-affirming, Jennifer's Journal: The Life of a SubUrban Girl is a graphic memoir that chronicles the life of a quirky, petite, freckled-faced African American illustrator and artist. The journal depicts Jennifer's struggles with work, depression, sex and sexuality, and religion while poking fun at the stereotypes she encounters along the way.

Stories for Chip: A Tribute to Samuel R. Delany
Edited by Nisi Shawl and Bill Campbell
Introduction by Kim Stanley Robinson

978-0-9903191-7-7

Featuring the writings of Christopher Brown, Chesya Burke, Roz Clarke, Kathryn Cramer, Vincent Czyz, Junot Díaz, Geetanjali Dighe, Thomas M. Disch, L. Timmel Duchamp, Hal Duncan, Fábio Fernandes, Jewelle Gomez, Eileen Gunn, Nick Harkaway, Ernest Hogan, Nalo Hopkinson, Walidah Imarisha, Alex Jennings, Tenea D. Johnson, Ellen Kushner, Claude Lalumière, Isiah Lavender III, devorah major, Haralambi Markov, Anil Menon, Carmelo Rafala, Kit Reed, Benjamin Rosenbaum, Geoff Ryman, Alex Smith, Michael Swanwick, Sheree Renée Thomas, and Kai Ashante Wilson

www.rosariumpublishing.com

Coming Soon ...

"*DayBlack* is a new kind of comics reading experience."
—Geeks of Doom

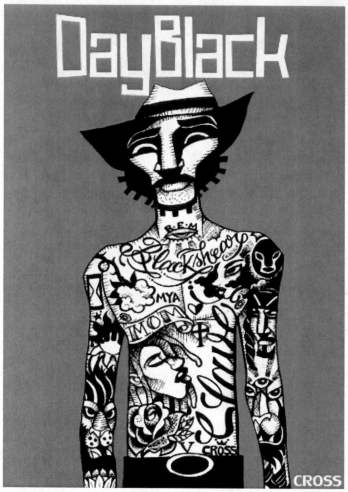

DayBlack, Vol. 1
by Keef Cross
978-0990319122

Beneath the polluted clouds of DayBlack, Georgia, exists a murderer. After hundreds of years of killing to survive, he no longer wants to simply exist . . . he wants to live. DayBlack is the story of Merce, a former slave who was bitten by a vampire in the cotton fields. Four hundred years later, he works as a tattoo artist in the small town of Day-Black. The town has a sky so dense with pollution that the sun is nowhere to be seen, allowing Merce to move about freely, night or day. Even darker than the clouds are the dreams he's been having that are causing him to fall asleep at the most awkward times (even while he's tattooing someone). As he struggles to decipher his dreams, someone from his past returns with plans for him—plans that will threaten his new way of life and turn him back into the cold-hearted killer he once was.